THE
WINKER

ANDREW MARTIN

corsair

CORSAIR

First published in Great Britain in 2019 by Corsair
This paperback edition published in 2020

1 3 5 7 9 10 8 6 4 2

A CIP catalogue record for this book
is available from the British Library.

ISBN 978-1-4721-5397-5

Printed and bound in Great Britain by
Clays Ltd, Elcograf S.p.A.

Papers used by Corsair are from well-managed forests
and other responsible sources.

Corsair
An imprint of
Little, Brown Book Group
Carmelite House
50 Victoria Embankment
London EC4Y 0DZ

An Hachette UK Company
www.hachette.co.uk

www.littlebrown.co.uk

THE
WINKER

A Friday afternoon in late June, 1976.
London

When we music industry journalists play the game of 'Which star kept you waiting longest?' the name of Lee Jones does tend to come up. So when I am summoned to the artfully dark lobby of his hotel for 3 p.m., I do not expect to be shown into the actual Presence until at least four. But no matter, I am well prepared, with a full packet of Slim Kings and the latest Ed McBain in my handbag. I have barely ignited my first cigarette, however, when a rather vampiric flunkey looms out of those expensive shadows.

'Abigail?' he says. 'You can go right up. Lee's in room 513.'

'Is he alone?' I crassly blurt.

'Afraid not, love,' the flunkey replies, apparently genuinely apologetic.

Ascending in the lift, I speculate on the extent to which Lee will not be alone. My best guess is that there might be two or three personal assistants in room 513 – the door of which is opened by a mysterious hand – but it gradually becomes evident, as I step inside, that this is a suite rather than a room, and that at least six discrete – and very *discreet* – individuals are bustling about in service of their master. Nobody seems to mind my presence, even as I begin taking notes.

By accident or design, the vibe of 513 is very much that of the last two Picture Show album sleeves: Deco filtered through a pop prism. The severity of the parquet floor and chestnut leather armchairs is offset by more emollient offerings, in the form of white shag rugs and animal-print throws. It is an exceptionally hot afternoon, but heavy white curtains baffle the sunlight. A telephone enthroned on a yellow chaise longue is – and has been – ringing, seemingly to prove the importance of the flunkeys' mission, because none of them is answering it.

The focus of their labour is not Lee Jones himself who – as I overhear from reverential whispers – is currently 'bathing' (as opposed to 'having a bath', which is what the rest of us do). Rather, the flunkeys are preparing the clothes he will be inhabiting this Saturday evening. The principal garment is an outrageously green suit, and I am permitted to watch as it is carried out of the dressing room and laid on one side of the huge double bed. Another flunkey bears the shirt – white with black buttons – which is delicately placed on top, the wings of its collar aspiring to the incredible width of the jacket lapels. The suggestion is of an extreme hipster – a small one – who has been flattened by a steam roller. The eyes of the wearer are then denoted by a pair of unearthly green sunglasses which are carefully propped on the pillow. Finally our hero's shoes are brought out by a functionary who is buffing them with a blurred brush. The polish is either magical or simply neutral, because these shoes have two colours: white with tan spats, 1920s style. They are placed at the foot of the bed, and – the ensemble complete – the footwear flunkey nods his head in genuflection before retreating.

Suddenly, the man foreordained to inhabit this ensemble is alongside me, in white towelling bathrobe (as opposed to a dressing gown), and it seems the blurting mood is still upon me, for I respond to his shy, questioning smile with, 'You've gone blonde!'

'I can see the horror in your eyes,' he says, in his precise, ever so *slightly* camp way, 'but I assure you it's temporary.'

'You mean?'

'Only a rinse, dear,' he clarifies.

But there never was any horror, of course, Lee Jones being such a very perfect little unit. It is a curious fact that many big music stars are extremely small, and it is said that Lee's 'good mate' Marc Bolan (five foot seven) calls him 'titch'.

He picks a silver box off the bedside table and offers me a cigarette. I decline, and Lee himself mutters that he is trying to give up, which is a shame, since the clothes awaiting him seem to demand a cigarette in a holder.

'The suit,' I say, pointing at the bed, 'it's a Tommy Nutter, right?'

Lee frowns somewhat, before relenting with a smile: 'The maker of the suit is, shall we say, *sub judice?*'

(One of the flunkeys will later confide: 'It's an Edward Sexton, but that's off the record, love. You're allowed to say the shoes are Anello & Davide.')

'Come over to the window,' Lee says. He pulls back the heavy, expensive curtain, and I am somehow shocked at the sunniness of London.

'What are we looking at?' I ask.

'East Marylebone, shall we say?' (He knows we mustn't disclose the precise location of the hotel, or he will be besieged by worshippers of both sexes.) 'But what we're really seeing is the start of summer.'

As I look down, his meaning is obvious. Summer is latent in the exuberant redness of the red buses, the way people leap – almost bounding – on and off them, the joyous greetings on street

3

corners, the bustle of the café terrace opposite. Even the Wimpy Bar on the corner looks festive.

'They say it's going to be a hot one,' Lee says.

I risk a satirical note: 'You're going to be needing a lot of sunglasses!'

Much to my relief, he smiles. 'Look at those nice ladies on the traffic island. Watch how they walk.'

They are tottering across the road in their slung-back platforms.

'I don't understand how they manage it,' Lee continues, 'in those elevator shoes. Somebody should take a slow-mo film of it to find out – like those photos the Victorians took of horses running. Sorry. The things I come out with!'

Pre-eminent among the things Lee Jones has 'come out with' are the brilliant songs he wrote for his group, Picture Show, show-cased to best effect on the classic album, *The Picture Show*, which was *the* soundtrack of '71 with its admixture of summery pop with sinister undertow. The follow-up has been long awaited, and the rumour was that it would be out this year. But it seems pop music in 1976 will not be dominated by that latest work of Lee Jones, but rather by talk of his retirement. Or something like it, because it appears that Lee does have a new project 'of a somewhat different kind' in preparation. He calls it a programme, but it is certainly nothing as everyday as a TV programme. He has agreed to discuss it 'in general terms' (whatever that means). Meanwhile I find myself identifying strongly with the eponymous character in Lee's biggest smash, 'Perplexity Jane'.

> Her questions come – they are too many
> Answers? 'fraid she won't get any
> I'm only a man, not so deep
> But there are secrets I must keep

He is still looking down on the busy street.

'Are you really retiring, Lee?'

The phone is ringing again. He turns slowly towards me, and I am favoured with one of his trademark . . .

The phone did ring, causing the journalist – who was called Abigail – to disappear. That was something she would tend to do, being entirely imaginary. In the same moment, the grandeur of the room diminished somewhat; but not completely. 'Glam meets Deco' about covered it. It was a two-room flat, but a big one. The kitchen was bit less high-end than the main room (and a bit more Conran Shop), but Lee hardly ever used the kitchen. The fridge contained some milk; also some Cokes for his cognac and Cokes. On the breakfast bar was a packet of Alpen and a jar of Spangles ('Old English' type), Lee's favourite sweets which he liked to decant into the jar, and which he sucked in lieu of killing himself with cigarettes. (You probably *could* kill yourself with Old English Spangles, but it would be a very long-term project indeed.)

On the bed lay the suit and the sunglasses, ready for occupation. Abigail had not mentioned two items lying alongside. First, a soft silk cap à la Robert Redford in *The Great Gatsby*. It was a stylish item but the important thing was that it could be carried in his pocket, and when he put it on, it would obscure the magnificence of his hair. There was also something Lee called 'the folder', which was neither a garment nor an item of stationery. It was made of seasoned oak and tempered steel. Lee avoided the obvious word for this article, it being rather brutal and unartistic. He had replaced other words he didn't care for with 'partner', 'the programme', 'bringing into the programme' and of course 'trademark'.

The light in the room was now inflected with the decadent,

dark gold tone of Friday evening ... and the phone really was ringing. Lee watched it doing so. This would be Geoff, wanting to go for a drink, which would turn into maudlin reminiscence about their Picture Show days. Geoff never seemed to realise that one album, two singles and no hits (dear, imaginary Abi tended to over-estimate their success) did not amount to the kind of achievement Lee cared to recall.

Rather than picking up the phone, Lee picked the phone *up* – still ringing – and put it on the bed. He liked things better when they were on the bed. He put the sunglasses on – they were Vuarnets – and scrutinised himself in the long mirror. Looking good.

He let the bathrobe fall, and then he looked even better. He lay down on the bed next to the phone, contemplating it as though it were a lover he might or might not take an interest in. Eventually, he picked up the receiver, and he could hear Geoff's voice even before he put the thing to his ear.

'Lee? It's Geoff. What are you up to?'

'I'm *extremely* busy.'

'I was wondering if you wanted to come up to Dingwalls? See Nils Lofgren? I'm doing a review for *Sounds*. I've got two comps.'

A review for *Sounds* – that'd be good for about five quid maximum.

'Like I said, Geoffrey, I'm *busy*.'

Geoff was speaking again, but Lee wasn't listening. He was thinking about Geoff's old lady, a small very determined person called Pam, whom he didn't love and who loved Lee, much as Geoff himself did. Amusingly, Pam was into do-it-yourself but she *didn't* do it herself: Geoff did it. So he was forever unpacking flat-pack furniture at her behest, blocking up fireplaces, or building car ports for his rusty Hillman Imp.

Geoff was a now a full-time journalist. Even while Picture Show was extant, he'd done shifts on newspapers. He was a sub-editor, which was the journalistic equivalent of what he'd done as a musician: playing bass. A bassist, like a sub-editor, was a backroom functionary. Geoff's principal meal ticket was some dowdy little organ that was produced in Fleet Street, only for the entire run to be put on northbound trains then dumped on the doormats of wheezing Scottish grannies. The *Sunday Recorder* it was called – something like that.

Geoff was saying, 'You say you're busy, man, but with what? I thought you were a gentleman of leisure these days.'

'If you must know, I'm trying on sunglasses.'

'Well, that's not going to take all night, even for you.'

Lee sighed.

'You had on quite a cool pair last Christmas in the French pub,' said Geoff, trying to claw his way back into favour.

After five years away, Lee had returned to London last Christmas.

'Pam thought they were cool anyway,' Geoff was saying. 'She told me that only you could get away with wearing sunglasses at five o'clock on Christmas Eve.'

'There was a very low sun.'

'Yeah? She thought they were Vuarnets, a French classic; said you were on a kind of Alain Delon trip, with your hair dyed black, and that gangster Crombie with the velvet lapels.'

'Did she? Well, you can tell Pam that I never try to look like anyone but myself.'

'Listen, I could pop round and see you on my way to the gig. Bring a bottle of wine?'

Lee pictured Geoff spilling cigarette ash on his grubby loon pants, and – more importantly – on Lee's new sofa. 'I don't think so.'

'I'm very curious about this new place of yours,' Geoff was saying. 'What's it like?'

Geoff was fascinated by Lee's money, which annoyed Lee because there wasn't as much of it as Geoff thought.

'Small,' said Lee. 'But then there's only one of me.'

'That's the understatement of the year. I'll call you in a few days, OK?'

'Fine, but I can't guarantee to be free.'

Geoff was still protesting as Lee put down the phone. It was as if they were a pair of squabbling fifteen-year-olds instead of being dangerously close to forty. Even by Geoff's standards, it had been a tiresome call. For one thing, Lee was now going to have to replace the Vuarnets. He stood, and walked to the window, carrying the phone. He liked carrying the phone even when he wasn't speaking into it. He would flip the cord in a negligent way he'd learnt from films, like a laid-back cowboy with a lasso.

He looked down at all the milling men and women, animated by sunshine and thoughts of the weekend, such modest blessings. But if any one of them looked up now, they'd be in for a *real* treat, given what he was – or was not – wearing. Lee was almost certain that every single one of those people down below had failed to notice the release of *The Picture Show* five years ago. They had just carried on with their lives as normal. But they would not be carrying on as normal after tonight, because he would be amongst them in a way he couldn't help thinking rather god-like. Put it like this: he had solved the problem of not being able to be everywhere at once, and it was for their own good, because the thing would bring them realisation: insight into their fellow humans. He would bring them realisation through the programme, and the programme would be starting tonight.

Later the same day.

Paris

At 7 p.m. Bertrand, the keeper of the newspaper kiosk off Boulevard Saint-Michel, reached down behind his counter for two copies of *The Times*. Handing them over to Charles, he said 'Times two!' He'd said that six days a week (*The Times* not appearing on Sundays) for twenty-five years. Otherwise he and Charles Underhill conversed in French.

Bertrand had never asked why Charles collected his paper in the evening rather than the morning, when the news would be fresher. But perhaps he'd worked out the answer for himself, which was that Charles wanted to avoid the world, and news that appeared disturbing at seven in the morning might have ceased to be so by seven at night. Charles had the same theory about letters, and he carried in his pocket one of the morning's arrivals, to be opened shortly.

He walked around the corner, to the Tabac au Bon Vin. Mme Bonnet poured his *petite Muscadet* as soon as she saw him, but first Charles collected his four cigarettes from her husband at the tobacco counter. M. Bonnet − like Bertrand at the kiosk − was humorous, so he held out two cigarettes in each hand, pointing them towards Charles like a gunslinger of the Old West holding two pistols. It had taken Charles ten years to interpret the gesture, but it didn't matter because he'd always laughed anyway.

As he collected the cigarettes − Gauloises − Charles saw himself being stared at by a young man at the bar. Yes, this must all seem very stilted and peculiar, Charles thought, as he moved into position to drink his wine. Now that it was coming up to the twenty-fifth anniversary, he had been rather reviewing his Parisian life, and it seemed stilted and peculiar even to *him*. In Britain, for instance, the newspaper and the cigarettes would be sold in the same shop. But Charles believed the formalities imposed on him by the French might just have saved both his sanity (insofar as he *was* sane) and his life.

The kid was semi-attractive in an agitating way: good figure, and good black hair worn long. Bad skin though. He looked uncomfortable in cowboy boots and heavy denims that would surely become untenable as summer progressed. He was smoking English cigarettes: fancy, pretentious ones in a red packet. The really irritating thing was that he was making notes with a biro in a little bent notebook, while frequently glancing at Charles. His wine glass was empty, so perhaps he'd be leaving soon. But he was now raising a finger to summon Mme Bonnet. *'Un autre,'* he said. He was English all right, and his accent was appalling. Another sidelong glance at Charles was now being followed by another note. This was invasion of privacy, and the youth's eyes – dark blue, clashing with his skin – had an X-ray quality. It was the eyes the women would like (if they liked anything about him) but Charles had had enough of them, so he drained his glass.

Crossing the road to the Jardin du Luxembourg, he regretted having left the Bonnets so quickly, and without explaining that he wouldn't be in next week. But the Jardin was having its soothing effect. Lingering sunlight; the French, poised and posed along the avenues of chestnut trees, with patrolling gendarmes on hand to ensure everything fell into line aesthetically. Charles took his usual place on one of the grey steel chairs near the pond. He liked to pick one aligned to the central fountain.

The chair was slightly tilted back in a way that encouraged contemplative smoking. Two of the four cigarettes in his shirt pocket were for him, two were for Syl. He lit the first of his. The second he would smoke in the flat along with Syl, who smoked both of hers there – in the living room in winter, on the balcony in summer. Blowing smoke, he was thinking of the Riviera. Tomorrow, as always in June, he would be making his excursion to Nice. Paris was safe, and Nice was perhaps not, but the holiday did him good, as even Syl – who begrudged being left behind – acknowledged. When the cigarette was finished, and not before, he took the letter from his shirt pocket. He had not been able to read the smudged postmark and still could not make it out, except that it was from the place he had fled a quarter of a century ago: Grande Bretagne.

He ripped open the envelope and stared at the postcard within. Looking up from it, he surveyed the Jardin and the sauntering French. He looked again at the postcard. Here in his hand was almost exactly what he didn't want to see.

It was a little black and white card, marked in the top left *Oxford, The River*, and showing a boat full of university rowers. The image was faded – impossible to tell whether it was a blurred aerial photograph or an etching. The rowers – an 'eight' – looked small from the high vantage point, and very vulnerable. Their oars were like the legs of those delicate insects that live a tenuous life on the surface of the water, until swallowed by some monster from below. There was no message on the back, and the implications were making his heart beat faster, like a car engine that surprisingly fired up after twenty-five years in storage. It must be from Patrick Price.

... Dr Patrick Price, the loud-but-unfathomable American postgraduate student – mathematician and musician – who had lived below him in college. A dozen or so people might have guessed what Charles had done in 1951. But if anyone knew for sure it was Pat Price, and he was one of the few people from Oxford days who knew where Charles lived.

11

Ten years into his exile, Charles had bumped into Price on the Rue de Rivoli. It had been a dark rainy afternoon, and they'd been crossing the road in opposite directions. Price had a meek young man in tow; Charles was with Syl. 'This is my mother,' Charles had said, and Price had kissed Syl's hand when they reached the pavement. He was wearing the fawn mac he had always sported in college, while booming away in the dinner queue. ('Charles,' he would shout, 'I want to buy some drugs! Can I see you later?' It was his idea of satire, and a bit too close to home, since Charles did have access to a supply of Benzedrine inhalers, any one of which would keep you awake all night, if you sucked the cotton wadding inside.)

Price was fatter, Charles had thought, so that he now resembled a badly wrapped parcel. He introduced the boy: Charles didn't catch the name. 'He's an organist,' Price had said, 'but then aren't we all?' Syl had laughed at that. She liked the larger-than-life type of homosexuals because they were somehow safe: a known quantity. Charles had surmised that Price probably wasn't fucking the boy – not his type. It was said he was into rough stuff and would take the late train from Oxford to London to find it. Price was a good part-time musician, and he and the boy would no doubt be playing some concert in Paris. Charles didn't stick around long enough to be invited. But he'd let slip his postal address.

It hadn't seemed to matter though. There had only been one letter from Price in the fifteen years since, excluding the card in Charles's hand. It had come a couple of years after that rainswept encounter. Price would be in Paris again. Might they have lunch? Charles had written back immediately, lying his way out of it. He squinted again at the postmark. Yes, he thought he could make out *Oxford*. Pat Price still lived there as far as he knew, an eternal student or quasi-don.

It was now quite impossible to concentrate on *The Times*. A walk might help, so Charles took the long route back to the flat, winding through the sixth arrondissement with the sun fusing into a golden ball over Montparnasse. This was *l'heure agréable* on the crowded café terraces. For those drinkers and diners life was – he assumed – full of potentiality. Charles had had no potentiality but he did have his annual holiday in Nice, which suddenly seemed a safer haven than Paris.

On Place de l'Odéon, he dropped the card into a bin. It was necessary to get this day over with and be on the train to Nice. No postcard could find him there. He cut along the diagonal of Rue Monsieur-le-Prince, aborting the long route.

About the same time.

London

Soho seemed slow to Lee – slower than in the Sixties, but then he'd been pepped up a lot of the time back then, very familiar with the blue triangle of the purple heart. Hence the B side of 'Perplexity Jane', namely 'The Blue Triangle'. Broaching Wardour Street in his green suit, coming to the heart of Soho, Lee pretended that Abigail was alongside him. She would be scampering to keep up, notebook in hand.

Abigail said, 'You made your debut here, I think? In 1961? At the famous 2i's coffee bar?'

'Correct on all counts, and I was performing as Young Lee Jones, because I *was* young at the time.'

'How old exactly?'

'In sixty-one? Twenty-two. I remember, on the afternoon of the

13

gig, seeing the bill going up outside: "To-Nite: Young Lee Jones", with *tonight* spelt t-o-n-i-t-e, and that was the really exciting thing: to think I'd fallen among people who'd take that kind of liberty with the English language.'

'And you were playing the famous twelve-string?'

'Right again – the old Tanglewood. Satin tobacco sunburst finish. I wrote "Perplexity Jane" on that.'

'And Major Ronnie Henderson came to see you, and signed you up to his stable?'

'Yes. His stable – which was like that very dirty one in Greek mythology. It was a bit of a mixed blessing being signed up by Major Ronnie. The Stones and the Beatles were about to get up and running, but Major Ronnie – or *Colonel* Ronnie, as he referred to himself after a particularly good lunch – was still thinking in terms of Tommy Steele. He thought a young singer should be a sort of cheeky chappie. Artful Dodger kind of thing.'

'Hence the old trademark. I mean, you'd be doing that in all the photos.'

'Yes, I was pretty constantly trademarking back then. But all those photos are lost. At least, I hope they are.'

'Your hair would change a lot.'

'My hair's always changed a lot. It's very versatile, my hair. I don't see why anybody would want the same style every day, any more than they'd wear the same shirt every day. But mainly I had a quiff – a black one. Think a young Cliff Richard only more menacing.'

'You were a rocker, in that case?'

'No, because I was playing an acoustic, and I would wear cardigans. With toggles! This was on the advice of Major Ronnie who, as I've intimated, was basically from the music-hall era. He'd been in the Guards, so naturally he was . . . well, need I say

14

more? He dragged me away to a dank basement off Shaftesbury Avenue, where he set about grooming me for stardom. A doomed project, I fear.'

'What went on in that basement?'

'Put it like this: Ronnie had a recording studio in there, a photographic studio, and a very unmade double bed.'

'Ronnie's dead now isn't he?'

'To say the least.'

'What was the music like?'

'Pop-folk – a bit Seekers. By the way, Abi, don't let anybody tell you The Seekers aren't cool. Brilliant chord changes. They were a big influence on my writing. At the time, I had a really nice little thing called "Window Shopping". It was concerned with all the frustrations of the world, one of which was Ronnie Henderson. Naturally, he didn't like it. Called it droopy. Hated minor chords, did Ronnie. I mean, he didn't know what a minor chord *was* but he hated them. He didn't much like middle eights either, and there was a really nice middle eight in "Window Shopping". Kind of mood swing. It went upbeat at that point, albeit briefly.'

'It was never released, was it? Because I think I know all your back catalogue, even the rarities.'

'No, Abi, it never was, and now it never will be.'

'Because you've given up music.'

'That's about the size of it.'

'You know, I find that hard to believe, for an artist so . . . '

Young Abigail had been lagging behind, what with having to get down all her hero's *bons mots*, and now she was gone. Everything Lee had said (or thought) had been true. In their 'conversation' they had encompassed the first false start of his music career.

15

As he closed in on his target, Lee was thinking of how Soho had been different then. There'd been plenty of normal shops as well as the pubs and clubs. Now it was all lurid reds and yellows, and the hot sky sagging down over Wardour Street was itself red, because it was that kind of summer's evening. He walked on, past Books 'n' Mags . . . Mags 'n' Books . . . Bed Show . . . Striptease . . . until he came to the shop he wanted. It had no name, unless you counted the word DUREX written in white on a big red board over the door. The façade appeared to be made of a series of propped red and yellow boards, like a house of cards. Alongside the usual products aimed at the lonely gentleman was a slightly unexpected tonsorial theme: HAIRPIECES AND WIGS, ALL HAIR DYES AND RINSES; also SUNGLASSES – AMERICAN AND CONTINENTAL.

He'd thought of this place immediately on learning that Pam was able to name the brand of sunglasses in which he'd intended stepping out this evening. The proprietor was sitting at his little counter and reading the *London Evening Chronicle*, with the radio playing. Bloody 'Chirpy Chirpy Cheep Cheep'. Lee would have hated its cloying refrain ('Where's your mama gone?') anyway, but it had also been the big success in the year of Lee's big failure; and its release in '71 had coincided with the death of his own mama in the big house in Devon, which had left him exposed to the full force of his father, until he too had kindly died, leaving all his money to Lee – betokening lack of imagination rather than paternal love.

The bloke – who was about as beautiful as the average sex shop proprietor – was giving Lee the once-over, but then nobody did anything less with Lee. He went into the one dusty corner that was free of porn and picked up a pair of sunglasses – Ray-ban knock offs. He read the amusing price: 60p. He put them on but there was no mirror, so he turned to the proprietor.

16

'What do you reckon?' he said, lifting the glasses up.

'Look all right,' the bloke said, grudgingly. But the moment Lee handed over the money he said, 'What *else* do you think I'm going to say? That you look a right dick?'

Lee smiled and put the sunglasses back on. 'I *know* I don't look like a right dick. *You*, my friend, I'm not so sure about.'

He stepped out of the shop, and back into the dirty red sunshine. A cab was coming along; he hailed it by waving the sunglasses.

'Where to?' said the cabbie, and that indeed was the question.

Lee didn't actually know where he was going. It was a very important decision for him and others, but he didn't know. Then again, only he would be making this decision, so why not savour the moment?

'Head sort of west,' he said.

'Chelsea?'

'Yeah.'

Why not? He hadn't really been to Chelsea since coming back to London. He realised he hadn't yet checked his look in a mirror, so he shuffled across the back seat to see himself in the driver's rear-view. The white quiff was holding up nicely: good job he wasn't even slightly receding. The greenness of his eyes was also extraordinary. The driver was watching him in the rear-view – and smiling. A queer cabbie: now that was a turn-up! Nice-looking chap too, with his five o'clock shadow and leather jacket. Touch of the Al Pacinos. He seemed to be sucking a sweet ... Yes, and he was now bringing it to the front of his mouth, and kind of baring his teeth, letting Lee see that it was a Polo mint, exhibiting the circularity of it. Well, each to his own. Lee grinned.

Trademark?

Definitely not, in view of what was coming.

On the King's Road, the driver said something Lee didn't catch. He leant forward, asking him to repeat it.

'See the little punks.'

'Oh,' said Lee. 'Yeah. It's their scene now.'

And they were welcome to it. Apparently, the punks didn't give a fuck about anything. Unfortunately that extended to their music, but they interested him. Their look – essentially drainpipes and leather jackets – wasn't new, but then design was re-design, as he had very often told young Abigail. Also, they had a Situation going on, in their own primitive way.

They were passing the Chelsea Kitchen. Suitable venue? No, because the tables were in booths; no sightlines. Now came the Pheasantry night club, where he'd watched others living the life he ought to have lived. He'd seen Jagger in there once, and he'd given Lee a direct look from the other side of the red rope. It had been a look of pure jealousy, because Lee was by far the better looking man. Now they were passing The Rag Machine. What a name! No wonder the punks smelt blood. He remembered it as Tara Browne's place. Or had it been in South Ken back then? God, he was getting old. Coming up on the left the Chelsea Potter, which he'd once been chucked out of because of a shout-up match with Bob Barton the drummer, who wouldn't play the little fills Lee's songs required but just slammed away like he was in Deep Purple. Thoughts of Barton always triggered memories of their big interview, in the *Melody Maker*. Barton, drunk, boasting of the diversity of his musical tastes. Stockhausen had come into it, for heaven's sake! Nonetheless that was the interview they had reprinted on the album sleeve.

This jaunt down memory lane wasn't working out too well. Whether the places reminded him of his first disillusionment in the early Sixties, the years of hustling that followed or the short flight of Picture Show . . . it was equally bad either way.

In spite of this being cocktail hour on a warm Friday evening, there weren't enough *people* on the Road; and the ones who were there looked tired and badly dressed, staggering on their stack heels, reeling from the traffic noise and fumes. At this rate, he'd have to close the taxi window. He kept seeing those big Rovers, one of which his old man had driven, which resembled wardrobes laid on their sides, or giant moving coffins. Now they were coming up to World's End. All the real action had been down here, and this was where the punks were brewing up their rebellion. He looked for Hung on You and Mr Freedom: both gone. He'd sort of known that. He couldn't remember in which of the two he'd paid three guineas for a velvet appliqué suit. A tonic, to cheer him up, since things were already on the slide at that point.

Proper Fulham now. But there were no real venues here. Leaning forward with a nice smile in spite of everything, Lee asked the driver to turn around. So here came the King's Road again, but this time he didn't look.

He got out of the cab on Sloane Square. He put on the green jacket, so that he was once again a man in a green suit. He walked into Colbert and had two glasses of white wine, which did something to improve his mood. Colbert was a pretend French brasserie, and always had been: an old reliable compared to those fleeting King's Road joints. As he stood at the zinc bar, he was getting a lot of looks, but Colbert was too formal.

Stepping out, he put on the cheap sunglasses, and he knew he was smiling even though he hadn't consciously smiled. All he required now was a small collection of women (or men).

Lee stood beneath the blazing neon of the Royal Court sign. What with the circulating buses – people standing on the platform, trying to catch a breath of air – and the many open-topped cars, the traffic was like a merry-go-round. It hypnotised him for a while. Then he headed east, thinking of Belgravia. Lovely word, and an interesting place of rather aristocratic sleaze – Lord Lucan territory! But he didn't get that far, because when he passed Eton Terrace, he heard 'Happy Birthday' being sung by some women. It was coming from that little boozer called The Antelope, so he went inside: a cosy wooden world full of trapped sun, and slowly unwinding fag smoke – and there was a table-full of women wearing paper hats. The singing carried on. They were consistently a semitone flat. They were about a dozen in number; quite a healthy collection of middle-class girls in floaty skirts – that sort of gypsy vibe – and he was looking at all of them.

Then he looked at one of them.

About the same time.

Paris

'You positively bounded up those stairs,' said Syl. 'You're demob happy.'

Charles put the newspaper and the cigarettes on the velvet cloth of the table. From her chair, Syl regarded them sceptically. She had perhaps expected some bonus present from her son, by way of apology for his impending trip: a Maigret novel from a book box on Quai Voltaire perhaps. (She read crime novels constantly, and if she was in a bad mood, she would laboriously recount the plots, defying Charles to tell her to shut up.) But Charles didn't feel very guilty. She was no longer up to accompanying him to Nice; her young French friend/personal slave, Jasmine, could look after her rather better than Charles could, and it was accepted on both sides that he needed an annual escape.

At punctuation points like this he would see the flat as others would see it: draped green and red velvet, stacked books, floating dust; two zig-zagging Chinese screens annoyingly blocking the way to the bedrooms. Paper, kindling and coal in the fireplace, ready for the slightest drop in temperature. The flat was in part a storeroom for Syl's purchases at the Vanves flea market – one of the few remaining places that inspired her to actually walk. Currently she was 'into' portable writing bureaux of the early nineteenth century. Charles recalled that they were due a visit from her slightly criminal friend Gustave, the antique dealer. He would arrive with his little, very French van (it had those peculiar vents in the side) and there would be a clearout of the flat, and a little pile of cash left on the velvet table cloth. But sometimes Syl *bought* from Charles, and on one occasion Charles had made a purchase.

It was a year after his arrival in Paris. He had accompanied Syl to Gustave's dusty warehouse in Belleville. They had come to a series of sinister black metal cabinets – tall and thin, and vented like the van. Smiling, Gustave had asked Charles how he would like to *'acheter de la sécurité'*. He had then unlocked one of the cabinets to reveal half a dozen shelves within – a handgun on each shelf. The guns were black, like the cabinet, and they looked modern to Charles, but they all dated from the War. Gustave said that, because of the War, and the occupation, *'La France est inondée des armes.'* The implication was that, since gun ownership was so common, Charles might as well join the club. Gustave had recommended a small pistol – that he described as an 'M.A.B. Model C' – because it was 'nice to hold'. He had shown Charles how to remove and insert the magazine, which contained five rounds. It would come with a spare magazine, and Charles could always return for more ammo if required ... which was presumably a joke on Gustave's part. He knew that Charles lived under a shadow and he could not have been envisaging him using more than one of those rounds – and that on himself.

Syl said, 'Have you had your first smoke, Cal?'

The affectionate 'Cal', so he was off the hook as far as the present was concerned.

'I had it in the park. I'll take the second one on the balcony. Are you coming?'

She frowned. 'Where are you going to be staying again?'

'I haven't decided yet.'

'Extraordinary.'

But she knew his preferences. He would find a little *pension* near the station, where English people were unlikely to be encountered.

Ten minutes later, he had got her out on the balcony, and they were smoking with the *pichet* of white wine and the plate of salted almonds between them. The *pichet* was one of Syl's antiques, and its size – small – ensured that Charles would not have more than two glasses. The balcony overlooked the Jardin du Luxembourg, the lonely, northerly part of it that they never entered when they were actually *in* the Jardin. Syl lit her cigarette. 'Don't walk up Colline du Château in the heat of the day.'

'As if I would.'

'Avoid the tourists' rosé, especially in quantity because it'll give you a terrible headache. Wear a hat at all times.'

'Not indoors, surely?'

'In the places you go, it hardly matters.'

'Of course, I *will* be frequenting the gay bars,' he said.

This was a joke, although he *had* once had one of his little adventures when they were together in Nice. It had begun with his ordering an entire bottle of rosé when they were supposed to be having their aperitif. Over their dinner he'd drunk all of it, then excused himself to go off on the prowl. Syl had probably guessed the dénouement: a grope on the stony beach.

'You'll notice I'm keeping silence,' she said, and she began munching some nuts. After a while, she said, 'I do wish I was coming with you.'

'So do I.'

'Rubbish.' She smiled at him in her manipulative way. She pointed at the wine, inviting him to pour her some more. 'I loved the antique places at the harbour, and what's that stationery shop called?'

Papetière Rontani, at 5 Rue Alexandre Rontani. *Articles de Bureaux*. They both loved that shop on a hot afternoon, with its wooden cabinets, and a smell of paper and glue.

'What was in that letter you had?' she said. (It was perhaps the thought of stationery that had prompted her to ask the question just then.)

'Nothing to worry about.'

She sipped her wine. 'I don't believe you.'

'It was from Pat Price. Remember him? He's coming to Paris again, wants to meet up. It's going to be no trouble at all to put him off.'

Not believing him, she pouted, which she ought not to do, because of the powdery lines around her mouth. It was a shame, because she'd been having one of her beautiful moments immediately beforehand.

He said, 'Of course, I'll bring you some glacé fruits from Maison Auer.'

'Please don't bother,' she said (which meant he must do it). 'I will probably be feeling very fat when you come back. You know how Jasmine is always cooking.' Jasmine insisted she eat an evening meal. Left to themselves, she and Charles only had nuts – sometimes a lot of nuts – instead of dinner.

She lifted up her glass, then put it down again. 'Twenty-five years this summer,' she said, and she smiled – one of her 'brave' ones – at Charles. 'Do you want my spare cigarette, Cal? I know you do.'

She was right about that, of course.

Later the same night.

London

At two o'clock on Saturday morning, Lee was in the 100 Club on Oxford Street. He sat at a sticky Formica-topped table, on which stood half a dozen plastic pint glasses, but they were nothing to do with Lee: he was sipping a cognac and Coke. It had not been possible to go home. He had thought of going to Maunkberry's or Tramp. He wasn't a member of either but he'd always been able to blag his way in. Then again, there was a danger of being recognised in those music industry places. The 100 was OK territory because it was not really part of the pop scene. It was just a big red noisy hangar with pictures of jazzers around the walls. They were all young men, but they looked like one's father. On the weekends, the jazz gave way to R'n'B, so four villainous-looking blokes were chugging through a number that might have been called something like 'Back In The Night'.

As he watched about fifty dancers dancing, Lee himself was 'back in the night'.

The programme had begun. About half an hour after he'd trademarked the girl, the birthday party had broken up. She'd lingered with her friends on the far side of the bar, but with many glances in Lee's direction. Whether he'd then come up to her, or

she'd come up to him, was difficult to say. Anyhow, they had converged. He could tell by her print dress that she was a conservative
sort of girl, so he said, 'Sorry about that. A bit crass . . . '

'What?'

'The . . . you know. Eye contact.'

'The wink?'

'You put it with a rather brutal frankness,' he said, laughing,
'but I suppose that's what it was. It was just a way of saying hello.
A nod would have done just as well.'

'I think a wink . . . sorry, that rhymes. I think it's fine if you
can get away with it. You did it very fast. I nearly didn't notice.'

'Did your friends notice?'

'No, but I told them. I said, "That man's just winked at me."
My dad used to wink at me when I was a little girl. He did it very
quickly, like you. I liked it.'

'And what did it mean, when he did that?'

'It meant . . . everyone's stupid in this world except the two of
us. What did your wink mean?'

It seemed she was quite a bit bolder than her dress.

'It didn't quite mean *that*,' he said. 'I wouldn't want to exempt
myself from the stupidity of the world. I'm probably part of it.
But I think it meant . . . well, let's wait and see what it meant,
shall we?'

'I like your ensemble.'

Ensemble. It would turn out she worked in publishing. He had
noticed several paperback books in her big denim bag: a profes-
sional quantity.

Lee said, 'I was a bit worried about the colour.'

'I think the green is somehow really brought alive by the black
buttons on your shirt.' Clearly, she was undressing him mentally.

'You should see my white jump suit.'

'You're kidding.'

He smiled an ambiguous smile – a good one.

'Now,' she said, going red, 'that can't be your natural hair colour.'

'Of course not. I'd be a freak of nature if it was!'

'What *is* your natural colour?'

'Would you believe I've forgotten?'

'No.'

'You're quite right. It's sort of mousy, I'm afraid.'

'And what do you do? For a living.'

'Can I buy you a drink?'

It was another two hours before he could get her out of the pub, and she was quite drunk by then. She had kept flitting between Lee and her birthday party colleagues. She had apparently wanted to introduce Lee to them, but he had remained on his side of the bar, justifying this with self-deprecatory stuff like, 'Oh, I'd only bore them,' and it seemed to him that she wasn't *overwhelmingly* keen on presenting him. She possibly did think he was a freak of nature, albeit a beautiful one, and this was all just as well, because he didn't want to be too describable by them.

It was about ten o'clock when they were out together in Sloane Square, the merry-go-round of traffic still turning, the air still hot and now dark greenish in colour, so that the girl – her name was Victoria – looked on with something approaching contempt as he stopped in the Square and put on his cheap sunglasses.

'Do you have a problem with your eyes? You're not famous are you?'

As far as she was concerned, he was a former actor turned property developer, restoring an old house in Devon while inter-mittently visiting London on business. But she *was* into music, and it had occurred to him that she might be amongst the very few Londoners who had bought *The Picture Show*. Unlikely though, because she was a fan of those university student acts: folkies like John Martyn, and Fairport Convention, who, naturally, she referred to as 'Fairport', as if they were all her friends. Whenever Lee looked at a picture of Fairport Convention, he just couldn't see the point of it, or them. It was like being invited to admire a bus queue: an apparently arbitrary mixture of men and women, ranging from ugly to moderately good-looking, and none of them with the remotest particle of a dress sense.

As they hit the start of the King's Road (she lived 'down that way') he knew he was losing his hold over her. She had disengaged his arm and was tending to walk a little way ahead. Once, she said, 'Do keep up,' like a mother talking to a child, but she didn't really want him to keep up, and he was becoming angry, because this was so often how it went between him and the ladies: the stunning effect of his beauty would wear off with amazing speed, just as the beauty itself would eventually wear off, and by the way, who was he kidding about his hair? Never mind the bloody economic recession, what about that fault line running diagonally back from his forehead. In ten years' time he'd be a little bald man, trying to compensate by wearing smoking jackets and double-breasted silk waistcoats, and playing the Lord of the Manor before a clutch of sniggering villagers. He'd be his dad.

They were passing some of the punks. Lee's suit was arousing comment – 'For *fuck*'s sake,' observed one youth, a spotty cockatoo in a leather jacket.

'I find them interesting, don't you?' said Victoria, from three yards in front of Lee. 'We're doing a book about them.'

'You know about the Situation?' he called ahead.

'What situation?'

'Guy Debord. The world-famous French philosopher. We're all trapped in the Spectacle, but we can disrupt it by –'

'Well, you're certainly trapped in *your* spectacles. Really, do take them off, it's absurd.'

'– the mass entertainments and distractions of society,' he continued. 'Like Fairport Convention for example. Like Abba. The Situationist disrupts the Spectacle by creating a Situation.'

'Are you sure it's not the other way round?'

'Yes. Of course, the punks only make a Spectacle of *themselves*. And have you heard the music? It's unbelievably ...'

But she was running away from him now, as fast as her moderately high platform soles would take her. Then she leapt, landing neatly on the platform of a number 11 bus. She waved back at him, laughing, 'Sorry, William, love!' (That's what he'd called himself.) 'Thanks for a lovely evening!' She was standing next to the female conductor, who also smiled – so this was feminism. It would have been undignified to give chase.

He had drifted sadly into the nearest boozer – the Chelsea Potter, where he'd sat, practically motionless, over a single whisky (they had no cognac) for about an hour. The Potter was a pub in a single room, somewhat like a church hall. There were plenty of women in there, and plenty of men, but he wasn't going to attempt a second trademarking in one evening. Very few ordinary people could appreciate the amount of moral courage the programme required.

Something on the bar had begun to bother him: two gently glowing plastic Ds. To the average punter they signified Double Diamond beer, but to Lee they suggested Dave Dunbar, head of A&R at Insignia Records, who'd called him in about his first solo demo soon after he'd come back to London. He'd played it as they both sat there: but Dunbar would be talking, and then actually making phone calls, as the tape played. He'd sadistically offered a glimmer of hope: 'I'm hearing one number one after another here,' he'd said, in between calls. He'd be in touch. But all that had happened was that the cassette – minus its case – had been returned three months later (which was three months *ago*) wrapped in an unsigned compliments slip. It was on that day that Lee had stowed the Tanglewood in the broom cupboard of the flat, and he'd hardly looked at it since, let alone played it.

Lee had come out of the pub at ten thirty.

It had seemed that the taxi drivers were deliberately ignoring him. The street was nearly empty as he walked past the Chelsea Kitchen and looked left: a curved white side street he'd never noticed before. It was lopsided: a pretty terrace of small white houses on one side, the backs of bigger houses on the other. There was one person in the street and it was the girl he'd trademarked: Victoria. She stood alone on the pavement, so she either hadn't gone home or she'd gone home and come out again. She might have been in a pub, because there were pubs around the corner, or she might have been telephoning, since there was a gently glowing phone booth at the far end of the little street. She seemed frozen to the spot as he approached. Only her eyes were moving, as she verified that all the windows on either side were dark or curtained, which was amazingly fortuitous, given the relative earliness of the hour. This street had let her down badly. She was removing her elevator shoes as he approached her with the folder unfolded in his hand. She had been preparing to run away for the second time.

*

In the 100 Club, the band was packing up. A DJ had taken over, and he was showing unexpectedly good taste. He'd just played a nice reggae song that Lee didn't know, and now he was playing 'The Bottle' by Gil Scott Heron, which was one of Lee's favourite dancing numbers. He was feeling the music for the first time in years. His heart was telling him he was alive in a way he hadn't known since the early days of Picture Show. He could feel the beats, count them as if they were musical. Whatever happened now – and anything at all might happen – he had affected the world. The future was bright. (If probably short!) Lee finished his cognac and Coke and stood up. This was what the unaccompanied women sitting on tables by the dance floor had been waiting for – not to mention the accompanied ones.

There had been some difficulty in bringing the girl Victoria into the programme (which was to be expected with the first one) and the right-hand sleeve of his Edward Sexton jacket was so badly stained he'd thought of chucking it, but it was just too good a bit of schmutter. So he'd carried it out of Chelsea over his shoulder with the sleeve turned inside out. In the gents of the French House pub, which Lee had called into on his way back from Chelsea, he had soaked his hair, and combed it right back, keeping it down with a few smears of soap. Then he'd put the Robert Redford cap on. So it was a very Thirties look he'd got now.

The jacket was hanging on the back of his seat. He could see it from the dance floor. It was unlikely to attract attention by virtue of the reversed sleeve, and 100 Club males – Neanderthals, mainly – were not likely to notice the beauty of the cut.

Lee was a good dancer, and the almighty groove of 'The Bottle' offered the chance to try some moves he'd seen on *Soul Train*. A number of women started dancing near him, but he would keep smiling and turning away from them. What was the male equivalent of being a prick teaser? He dreaded to think!

When he sat down again, most of the women who'd been near

him on the floor sat down too, watching for his next move ... which was just to go up to the bar, and order another drink. He turned around to look at the ladies. He was supposed to be keeping a low profile, but he couldn't resist. He'd kept the cap on, but he took it off now to let them see his hair. It was completely different from what it had been at the start of the evening, after all. He was quite capable of noting the admiration while conducting an imaginary conversation with Abigail ...

'A kind of vortex forms around you when you dance, Lee.'

'Yes, well, some of those moves involve quite wildly flailing arms.'

'But it's more like you're giving a sort of master class.'

'Well, it's ninety-nine per cent perspiration – as you can see. But I do try to give value for money, as you might say. I take dancing pretty seriously. Practise a lot on my own.'

'You seem very "up" tonight?'

But then she was gone, banished by the force of another great track: 'I Hear You Knocking' by Dave Edmunds – and the women were wanting him to dance. One in particular was maintaining pretty constant eye contact. Her outfit was pretty cool, kind of micro-sportswear: sneakers, stripy socks, hot pants, and silk track top (or silk-*effect*; it was probably polyester). She was blonde, and small like him – a bit Goldie Hawn. She was with a friend who was similar but less so: like an earlier prototype of what her friend had become.

Trademark?

Now here was the beauty of the programme, because he was exercising power whether he did or not, and in this case he would not. He turned back towards the bar.

But then the girl was alongside him.

'We think you're a rock star. My friend and me.' On cue the

friend appeared, on the far side of the girl, keeping her distance but eavesdropping.

'What makes you say that?' he asked, and he was extremely curious on the point. If she associated him with Picture Show, that meant she probably knew his name. In which case she was safe – and he wasn't.

'My friend thinks she's seen you on TV.'

But he'd never been on TV, and she wasn't doing herself any favours by reminding him of the fact. He looked towards the friend, who gave him a sceptical half smile. She was the more intelligent of the two.

Lee said, 'I can honestly tell you I am not a rock star.'

'Prove it,' said Goldie, who was clearly drunk.

'It's notoriously difficult to prove a negative. Do I *look* like a pop star?'

'Yes,' they said in unison, Goldie excited, the other matter-of-fact.

'Do you think I'd be here on my own if I were a pop star?'

'My friend reckons your band broke up,' said Goldie.

Lee was frowning. They might be on the right track after all. Goldie was offering him a cigarette: a Virginia Slim. Everything about her was touchingly feminine.

Lee said, 'But you can't remember the name of this band?'

They meekly shook their heads. 'Tell you what,' he said, 'if I showed you my wallet, that'd prove it.'

'Why?' said Goldie.

'Because there's naff all in it. From memory, a quid note and a couple of stamps. Excuse me, ladies, I'm off to the loo.'

As he set off in that direction, he heard Goldie say, 'A couple of stamps! He's a wind-up merchant, he is.'

So Lee turned round, and said to Goldie, 'Actually, I think it's

just one stamp. Second class!' And it was then that he did it –
trademark – and she laughed.

So it was going to be two in one night after all, he thought,
standing at the urinal. Off to a flying start! It had been such a
gift, and the two had presented the ideal audience. That is to say
there *were* two of them: one to receive the trademark (to be the
'partner', as he liked to think of it), the other to witness. He began
wondering how long it was going to take before people worked
out the rules of the programme. That was up to the newspapers
and TV; and up to him to make sure the trademark was always
followed through in the correct way.

He pulled up his fly and swivelled to the mirror. His hair had
started going a bit bouffant again, a bit Mr Whippy. So he took
out his comb, and applied water. As he did so, the smoochers
started – 'Your Song' by Elton John, which he could take or leave,
but this DJ would have some good stuff up his sleeve, and so it
turned out because 'Let's Stay Together' by Al Green came on as
he approached Goldie again.

Her real name, it turned out, was May. She was quite apologetic
about that. 'It's such a short name,' she said, with her head on his
chest. (Because her name wasn't the only short thing about her.)
'People always ask you to repeat it. They think you've started
saying something else, then given up. Like Maybelline, say.'

He nearly tried to console her by telling her his own short
name, but in the end he went with 'Alec', thinking of a Scottish
saxophonist he'd once booked for a session. (It had been that dead
time just after Christmas; a cheap studio, not properly heated, and
Alec's hands had gone numb. At least that was how he explained
his poor playing.)

Now it was 'Let's Get It On' by Marvin Gaye, and little May
was even closer than before. She was cute: it was very rare for Lee

33

to find a girl smaller than himself. Her friend was dancing with a big bloke in a rugby shirt on the opposite side.

When the lights came up, May did not let go of Lee but only sighed. Looking over her head, he noted the battered condition of the dear old 100 Club. It was all black and red plastic – Old English Spangle colours – and they seemed to want to make a design feature of beer crates. May was sleepily holding on to him as her friend came up to say a perfunctory goodbye. She was going off with Rugby Shirt.

The great thing about the weather was that it required no coats, so no need to queue for the cloakroom, and they were straight out into hot, desolate Oxford Street. Lee had one arm around little May. With the other hand, he held the green jacket carefully over his shoulder. Once he'd verified that there were no taxis in sight, he said, 'Let's get a taxi. But where to?'

'Your place is bound to be better than mine,' she said, in her touching way. 'You and your second-class stamp! I don't think you are a rock star, but you might be an actor or a male model.'

'I live north,' he said. 'It'll be easier to get a cab on Tottenham Court Road. We'll cut the corner by going down Hanway Street. Do you know it?'

They were in that glum alley five minutes later. There were two bars, both shut, but a red smoulder came from inside the one he used to frequent: Bradley's Spanish bar, a scruffy spot where Spaniards opposed to General Franco drank with young Londoners who hadn't the foggiest notion who General Franco was. Lee believed they still had a jukebox full of Fifties classics, but it only accepted old money. Even as she walked, little May was nearly falling over with the effects of booze and fatigue. After a quick adjustment – and he did say 'Excuse me,' a gentleman to the end – he had the folder unfolded in his hand. Then little May fell over for a different reason.

Walking home through Fitzrovia he kept looking up at the full moon. It was a beautiful thing but dead; a sightless eye that could never close; a ridiculous and useless thing. But that was not his problem. Lee was very happy as he walked through the lonely streets with the beautiful jacket over his shoulder, because there'd been no trouble at all about bringing little May into the programme, and he knew he would soon be famous.

The following Friday evening.
Nice, France

It was 7.15 on the Promenade des Anglais, so Charles lit a cigarette.

He'd had a good week in Nice, and in a minute, he would call Syl and tell her about it, using the pay phone located twenty yards from the blue steel chair on which he sat. He was living on borrowed time, not having called her until now, the evening of his last full day in Nice. He had put off calling because he didn't want to learn that another postcard had been sent. But in the course of the week, this had seemed less and less likely, and Syl would have told him by now if one had arrived. She could always call his little hotel, because of course he had sent *her* a postcard on the day – the hour, indeed – of his arrival, telling her the phone number.

The card of last week *must* have been sent by Pat Price, but it probably wasn't as sinister as it looked. There was a limited palette of Oxford postcards: they showed the High Street, the Radcliffe Camera in sunshine, All Souls by moonlight . . . and quite a few must show a river scene. There were two rivers in Oxford, after all. Having selected his card, Price had simply forgotten to write a message – an easy mistake to make if you were dispatching the card in an envelope, especially if you were a shambolic eccentric like Pat Price.

Charles might have been inhabiting a postcard at this very moment – a hand-tinted production at that. The sea before him was first white (the frilly waves), then turquoise, then – further out – very dark blue: ultramarine, he supposed. The plane flying above it was white and light blue (exactly the same blue as the telephone receiver that waited in the glass booth to his left). Most of the cars crawling along the Promenade behind him were white or very red. The leaves of the palm trees along the Prom were as vividly green as if they had been plastic, which they might very well be for all Charles knew. On the terrace of the Canne à Sucre, next to the Palais de la Méditerraneé, they had new chairs this year, and these were orange. Charles couldn't remember what colour they had been last season, so the orange must be a success. The Palais itself, that Deco sun temple, was still shuttered and closed, as it had been for – what – twenty years? It must be spooky inside – hot shadows and pigeons flying through the crumbling casino. The façade was plastered with posters, many to do with jazz concerts. But jazz was a subject Charles avoided.

His habitual seat was a little way west of the Palais, which he calculated to be the centre of the Prom. Being in the middle of the Prom Charles was at the fulcrum of the city, and with his cigarette halfway down there was equilibrium: he sat in shirtsleeves, but with his best cotton sweater over his shoulders. Waves were coming in, although not the tide, because this was the Med; some people still frolicked in the sea, but it was happy hour in the Canne à Sucre. The evening was poised, and so was he. Charles was in control. He had been in control for twenty-five years, with only the occasional lapse. Only by having the occasional lapse could Charles appreciate the benefits of being in control the rest of the time.

He extinguished his cigarette by leaning over and rubbing it slowly on the warm tarmac. In the phone booth, he realised he need hardly have bothered, since the booth reeked of fags. He put in his fifty centimes – which ought to be enough. There was no chance of Syl being out, of course. She would be reading a thriller, with the book propped against the flower vase, and the phone – a heavy black thing that looked like a miniature mausoleum – a foot away on the slightly ruched velvet tablecloth. He heard it ring twice. Syl picked up.

'You're calling me on your last day,' she said. 'I hardly know why you're bothering.'

'I tried yesterday, but there was a problem with the line,' Charles lied.

'Nonsense,' she said. 'How's the weather been?'

He told her, in the course of itemising his days, which he knew would be required. Much of his holiday had been conducted in memoriam of Syl, as though she were already dead. For example, on the Tuesday – the one day of rain – Charles had toured the antique shops of the harbour. Then he had made a pilgrimage to the Papeterie Rontani, where he had bought her a new address book, although most of the addresses she would transfer into it were more than twenty-five years old. On the Wednesday he had gone to Villefranche-sur-Mer, which Syl had loved for its furniture shops. Charles had paddled in the sea. Yesterday, he had taken the train again, this time for Monaco, and Syl's critique of the place had been running through his head as he strolled around the harbour: 'So flashy, yet suburban at the same time.' He pictured her saying that, sitting on a café terrace, touchingly oblivious to the absurdity of her tennis visor. What was her other pet phrase for Monaco? *All glitter and no sparkle.*

Back in Nice yesterday evening, he had taken his first glass of wine in the bar of the Negresco, at a cost of ten francs. But he withheld from her the outrageous price: she would have said he was suburban for worrying about it. Syl – Charles had worked out – was glad that her son usually behaved in a controlled way, but she also scorned him for it. She liked the raffish types in the Negresco. She considered them to be *mondaine*, a word whose meaning Charles could never quite apprehend. It perhaps meant 'at ease with the world', but you had to be in the world to be at ease with it, and Charles was not in the world.

Syl was now giving her own news, which concerned her slave, Jasmine. Her husband had fallen over on Rue Monsieur-le-Prince. He'd cracked his head, but he was going to be all right. 'Probably drunk,' Syl added. She seemed on good form. Maybe there was enough life left in her to come south next year? She was getting into her stride about the drinking habits of Jasmine's husband. He let her ramble on.

There had been one irritation in Charles's week: yesterday evening, on his way to the Negresco, he had spotted the annoying British boy from the Tabac au Bon Vin. He must have been just passing through Paris on his way south. He had been on the Prom, inspecting a fancy vintage car – Charles knew nothing about cars – exhibited outside the Forum Cinema. He still wore the heavy denim outfit, even though Nice was ten degrees hotter than Paris had been last week – and he had clearly recognised Charles from before. Obviously, the boy was horribly observant. Then, when Charles had come out of the Negresco, his bad mood – caused by the price of the wine – had been compounded by seeing the boy again, still on the Prom and smoking furtively, watching people and taking notes. Charles had considered going over and telling him to desist from his pen portraiture; to point out that in Nice – or anywhere – people were entitled to go unobserved. He had wanted to penalise the boy in some way.

Syl was saying, 'Of course, her mother was a great drinker as well –'

Then the line went dead.

Sometimes the operator would come on when that happened, always sounding very cross, as though it was the caller's fault. But not this time, so Charles put the phone down. As a precaution against just this eventuality he'd given her the number at the start of their conversation, so Syl would call back in a minute. Through the dirty glass of the booth, he could see a young man, coming out of the sea with great grace, which was not easy on that stony beach. He wore those tight, long-legged trunks: Bermuda shorts they were called, and if the name was at all accurate, it made Charles want to go to Bermuda. The young man was now pushing back his black hair, as though for the particular benefit of Charles, who found himself – ludicrously – doing the same in response. The phone rang.

'I forgot to mention,' she said, 'you've had another letter.'

'Open it,' he said, and he could feel his heart working, like the clock of his life starting up again, demanding action. Syl made a sound with paper, but he suspected she'd already opened it. (And she hadn't 'forgotten to mention'; she'd been saving it up, to punish him for his late call.)

'It's a postcard,' she said. 'No message. It's blank.'

'What's the postmark?'

'Oxford.'

'The picture?'

'A college.'

'Which college?'

'I don't know. There are trees and the river in the foreground, then fields. Then the college. It's sort of in the distance. What does this mean, Cal? You're scared, I know.'

She said that with relish, he thought. On the horizon to the far left, a cruise ship was heading out to sea. He wanted to be on it; or on the roof of the crumbling Palais, in which case he would leap off. 'I'm not scared, Syl. It's probably just Pat Price messing about. That was a kind of game when I was in college. People would send blank postcards.'

'Rubbish.'

'Look, Syl, I have to go now.'

'Why?'

'We'll talk about it when I get back.'

The line went dead again, but this time it was because she'd hung up. He quit the booth, then crossed the Promenade des Anglais, not waiting for the 'walk' light. He almost ran to the *tabac* and tourist trinket shop that was immediately west of the derelict Palais. He bought twenty Gauloises. He crossed back in front of the Palais and sat down on the terrace of the Canne à Sucre.

'Hello, my friend,' said the grizzled waiter, who might have been Tunisian, liked to speak English, and knew Charles from previous years.

'Rosé please,' said Charles. 'A bottle.'

About an hour later.

Nice

Howard could not speak French, but he had worked out that a *cave* meant a cellar or basement; that some of the basements in Nice were underground wine bars – and whether by accident or design, most of those places did look like caves in the English sense. He believed that the one he was in was called – or known to the

English as – the Old Town Cave. It was subterranean, although there was a single window, semi-circular and corresponding to the pavement – so that you saw a bright display of people's feet going past, which was like a reproof, an indication of what you ought to be doing: walking *past* the bar.

But some of those pedestrians would be entering the bar a moment later and Howard kept glancing up, hoping to see one particular pair of shoes. There was nothing special about them. In fact, they were so ordinary – plain black plimsolls – that only a very beautiful person would have worn them.

The girl was quite piratical: very dark, with big hooped earrings, and the back of her hair tied up in an arrangement both simple and complicated. Aside from the black pumps, she wore a black long-sleeved T-shirt with a chic rolled neck and a pair of multi-coloured pyjama-like trousers. Unfortunately, she was perpetually accompanied by a thin French cunt who appeared to be called Fabien, because other French people would come up and say '*Ça va, Fabien?*' and so on, even though this solicitousness was all one-way traffic: Fabien never seemed to ask anybody else how *they* were doing. He would mutter to the girl while looking into the distance or staring rudely at third parties; and he made hardly any response when the girl would suddenly explode into life, having her *own* say. She never seemed to get anywhere, because Fabien would just shake his head or shrug while looking elsewhere. But she didn't seem to mind, and she would sympathetically lay her hand on his knee when she'd finished, as though Fabien was ill, and could not be expected to show normal politeness.

Fabien always had a jumble of accessories on the table before him: cigarettes, lighter, an expensive camera, and sometimes a small cassette recorder. He wore a big chain round his neck, together with a card on a ribbon, some sort of pass or permit, no doubt guaranteeing him access to all the most exclusive places in Nice, and once the girl had worn the same card round her neck, which was depressing. Fabien was at least ten years older than the girl, and therefore also than Howard, who had her down as early twenties, like himself; and Fabien's hair was dyed black, whereas Howard's hair was real black. Even so, the girl had never once looked his way.

Howard's glass was nearly empty. He looked with resentment at his notebook, which had his slow, un-abbreviatable name – Howard Miller – written on the front, as though it were a school exercise book. The book was full of nonsense, thoughts written down for the sake of writing. Because Howard *was* a writer after all.

Looking up, he saw feet on the stone steps leading into the Cave. Not the black pumps; these were scuffed espadrilles, but they belonged to a person of interest. Howard had his people of interest just like any detective, or like the detective he had once created: Marsh. This man now emerging into the Cave was a controlled English homosexual of about fifty, and if he made it into Howard's next book, he would do so under the name of Christopher. Howard had clocked Christopher both in Paris and here in Nice, which was interesting in a novelistic way.

He was passing Howard's low table, approaching the dusty bar, which was rammed into the far end of the Cave amid a tangle of fairy lights, and presided over by a youngish bloke called Eric, because it was possible to be a youngish bloke called Eric in France. So far, Christopher had not looked at Howard. He had entered the bar self-consciously, with head down. Probably this was his first visit to the Cave. Certainly, Howard had never seen him here before.

Howard wondered if Christopher would recognise him. He was

42

amazed by how uncurious most people were, but this man was intelligent. He was also posh, with sad blue eyes that matched the colour of his linen trousers and shirt. He might be some ex-government minister forced to resign after a scandal. He wore a bit of red ribbon tied around his thin wrist, and this, to Howard's mind, was a memento of the bad thing that made his eyes sad. Christopher was currently negotiating with Eric about a drink, being very polite. Now he was receiving a glass of wine – rosé – and sitting on a stool at the bar. He was side-on to Howard, and looking down at his wine, apparently worried. Slowly he lifted his head.

Christopher spotted Howard and looked away. Then he looked back, so now it was Howard who looked away. When Howard risked another glance, Christopher was still looking at him. Howard, going red, looked down at his empty glass. He looked up again, and Christopher was still staring at him. *Does he fancy me?* Howard wondered. Was that really possible? Howard never knew how attractive he was to women, let alone men. Christopher was climbing down from his stool. Surely he couldn't be coming over?

'Hello,' he said, standing over Howard. He was tall, as well as upper class. 'We seem to be on the same circuit. I've seen you on the Prom, scribbling away, and now here you are, scribbling again.'

He hadn't mentioned the Paris scribbling.

'Oh,' said Howard, well aware that he was now crimson. 'I'm a writer.'

'Yes,' said Christopher, smiling, 'you certainly are.'

Upper class, tall and sarcastic.

'I'm working on a book,' said Howard.

'As a writer, you would be. Can I buy you a drink?'

'Oh,' said Howard. It was the second time he'd done that. 'Thanks. A beer please.'

'What kind?'

'Doesn't matter. Any. A *pression.*' Better to get out of the way immediately that he had no French accent. He offered his hand. 'Howard Miller,' he said.

They shook, and Howard was braced for Christopher's real name, but he just said, 'What sort of things do you write?'

'Fiction. Well, I've written one novel, and I'm working on another.'

'The first one was published, I assume?'

'Yes, but you've probably never heard of it. It was called *Marsh.*' No flicker from the man, just the patronising smile. 'That was the name of the main character,' said Howard, hating himself for elaborating. 'He's a policeman. It was a thriller, supposedly. A literary thriller.'

'Well reviewed?'

'Pretty good. Except for one.'

'You must be very young. I suppose you were at Oxford or Cambridge?'

'Why do you suppose that?' said Howard, relieved that he was finally standing up for himself. 'I didn't apply to Oxbridge. I went to York.' But then he said two wrong things in succession: 'It worked out pretty well. I got a decent first.'

'Naturally,' said Christopher.

Howard said, 'I don't think I caught your name.'

'I'll get you that beer.'

Howard nodded meekly. He had been completely outmanoeuvred. Then he heard footsteps and voices on the stone steps, and in came the French cunt, with the beautiful girl following behind. Howard prepared to be ignored. He was always ignored by people he wanted to notice him, and vice versa. But it was as though some potion that had made him invisible for the past few

44

days had suddenly worn off, because she was looking directly at him. Christopher was returning with the drinks, and the girl was obviously noting that Howard had company for once as she took her seat alongside Fabien.

'Cheers,' said Christopher.

'Yes,' said Howard, raising his glass. (He was never any good at 'cheers', even when feeling relaxed.)

'Do you do any journalism?' asked Christopher, who smelt of cigarettes and wine; he was slightly pissed.

'Some book reviewing,' said Howard. 'A couple of things for the *Times Literary Supplement*, and once for the *Yorkshire Post*.' (Why did he always over-elaborate?)

On the other side of the bar, Eric was bringing drinks to Fabien and the girl. It seemed they were entitled to waiter service but instead of thanking Eric, Fabien was fiddling with his camera. He lifted it to his right eye. The big lens was pointing towards Howard, who hated being photographed. But Howard, powerless as ever, now had his picture taken – and with a great clattering flash ... Or maybe it was Christopher whose picture had been taken? Christopher seemed to think so, and he didn't like it.

'Excuse me,' he said to Howard, rising to his feet.

Was he going to hit Fabien? Howard hoped so, but Christopher merely began addressing Fabien in French while Fabien muttered and looked the other way. The girl had folded her arms. She was looking down, perhaps smiling secretly. Now Fabien opened the back of the camera, and began angrily pulling out the film, exposing and so ruining it. He sat back and lit a cigarette, looking at Christopher with disgust, as if to say, 'Happy now?'

The girl flashed a glance to Howard. She smiled. He hadn't the slightest idea of what to do in response. (What would have assisted him in handling the situation, he thought, would be to

45

have had sexual intercourse with somebody on some previous occasion.)

Christopher returned, as if nothing had happened. 'So you've never done any investigative journalism?'

'Nope,' said Howard. 'Why did he take your picture?'

'We were both in it, but he said it was really of you. He said you had an interesting face, which is true.'

'Do you live in London?'

Howard took a long drink. Christopher was definitely gay, but this did not seem to be about Christopher fancying Howard. He had come over for some other reason. 'I don't want to be rude,' said Howard, 'but you're asking me a lot of questions, yet you won't even tell me your name.'

'I *am* being quite impertinent,' said Christopher. 'And, yes, evasive, but it might be to your advantage if you bear with me.'

'In what way?'

'Financially. I'd like you to find somebody for me.'

Howard looked at Christopher's face, seeking some acknowledgement that this was a detective story parody.

'Somebody in London?' he said. The eyes of the girl were on him again. (Maybe he really did have an interesting face?)

'More likely Oxford.'

So that explained his earlier question about universities.

Howard said, 'Why do you want this person found?'

'I'd like to postpone my answer to that, if you don't mind. I can offer you two hundred pounds in cash for a couple of days' research in Oxford.'

Almost half the advance for his novel.

'Two hundred and *fifty*,' amended Christopher, who evidently thought Howard's silence had been a bargaining tactic. 'Can you let me have your phone number?'

Howard looked at the girl. She seemed to be encouraging him with her smile. And the flat did have a phone. So far, he'd had nothing to do with it, but he'd written the number on a scrap of paper in his wallet. He now transcribed this on to the back page of his notebook, which he tore out and gave to Christopher, who said, 'Can I take it you accept my offer?'

Howard realised that in spite of the man's upper-class accent and plausible manner, he must be a lunatic. 'No,' he said, 'you can't. I have a book to write.'

'But may I call you to discuss it?'

Howard sighed; but, hearing himself sigh, he thought he was being pompous. 'Call me if you like, yes.'

'I'll be in touch,' said Christopher, and he quit the bar.

The girl was now standing, with her hands in her trouser pockets in a superbly casual way. She walked over to Howard, who felt very small at his low table. Fabien remained in his seat, speaking to some guy in shorts and tie-dye shirt who'd come to pay court.

'Mind if I join you?' the girl said.

Even though this promised to be the highlight of his entire life, Howard's 'All right' came out grudging. It was only when she did sit down that he realised she had asked the question in perfect English.

'Emma,' she said.

'Howard,' said Howard, who then blurted, 'You're English,' because he was quite shocked. Normally a person like this would be French.

'So are you, and so was that man who was talking to you. We get everywhere, don't we?'

She was raising her arm, summoning Eric for waiter service. The black pumps, pyjama trousers, hair ribbon: to have all this just six inches away . . .

'He was obviously coming on to you,' she said, indicating the staircase, meaning Christopher.

That was flattering. Surely it implied Howard was *worth* coming on to? The drinks arrived.

Emma said, 'You're a writer? Correct? Because, I mean . . . you're always writing.'

He told her about his book, the good reviews (and the one bad one), the contract for the second.

'And you're on holiday in Nice?' she said.

'Not exactly,' he said. 'I'm here to write my second novel.'

'Cool,' said Emma, and if Howard really had been cool, he'd have left it at that, and asked her something about herself. But he realised this too late, having already begun to explain the following.

His editor had offered four hundred and fifty pounds for a second novel, the same as he'd offered for the first. Howard had said to his agent that he thought advances were supposed to go up. 'That depends on sales, my boy,' he'd said. It was not encouraging that he called Howard 'my boy' and Howard did sometimes wonder whose side he was on. Howard had accepted the offer, and then his agent had phoned him with news of a great 'supplementary'. Howard's editor was offering him free use of his holiday flat in central Nice for the writing of the novel. Howard had said to his agent, 'I think this is because he's had a stab of conscience about the low offer.'

'God,' his agent had said, 'and I thought *I* was cynical.'

Probably his editor had been motivated by kindness: Howard had a floor to sleep on in London, but his main base was still the family farmhouse in Yorkshire, and it was difficult to avoid being dragged out of the farmhouse, and into the work of the farm. Howard's dad would keep saying, 'What are you actually doing?' as Howard bashed away on the giant Imperial typewriter in the cold, stone room that was called the back parlour, and the answer, 'I'm writing a novel, Dad,' never did seem satisfactory.

Even so, he had been minded to refuse the offer of the flat. He would come out a net loser, because of the cost of getting to Nice. But his agent had advised that a refusal would be undiplomatic. So Howard had bought a new typewriter, a Remington portable, and booked the trains. He'd crossed the Channel on the hover-craft, which didn't so much hover as bash its way across the sea with – even on a sunny day – the impression of a violent rainstorm hitting the windows. Howard had thrown up on the Remington, which fortunately had been in its case. He'd been balancing it on his knee, being scared of having it stolen.

He'd spent a day – and the equivalent of a tenner – in Paris on his way to Nice. Then there'd been the shock of the heat; and of seeing the books his editor kept in the flat. 'Not one but two Leon Urises,' he said to Emma, but she didn't seem to share his indignation.

He should drop the subject of the flat.

'Going back to that man,' Howard said, indicating the stairs and meaning Christopher. 'He wanted me to find somebody.'

'OK, who?'

'He didn't say. It was like a Borges story or something.'

'Or a Robbe-Grillet film,' she said, 'where nothing is explained.'

'Robbe-Grillet?' said Howard, attempting – and failing – to copy her pronunciation. 'I don't know his stuff.' He offered Emma a Black Cat, which she accepted without a word, which was great – as though they'd known each other for years.

'Well,' she said, blowing smoke, 'he was nominated for an Oscar, and he won the Golden Lion.'

'Really?' said Howard, carefully striking a match, because this *could* go wrong with a fiddly French match.

'But he's not very good,' she said, and she laughed.

She probably knew more about films than fiction but this was highly promising. Howard indicated Fabien, who seemed quite autonomous (he'd gone over to Tie-dye's table). 'Who's your friend?'

'That's Fabien. He's a film director, and he would like you to be in his film. He thinks you have an interesting face. He thinks you look extremely English.'

Howard didn't want to look even slightly English; he presumed nobody did.

'So he was taking *my* picture?"

'He wanted to show it to the producer.'

'I can't act.'

'You don't have to act. But it would be useful if you could drive.'

'I *can* drive, yes.'

'That's excellent. You've passed the audition! Your lines will just be a couple of sentences, which you'll say in English because you'll be playing an English character. He's called "The Englishman With The Car". Are you into cars?'

Howard said, 'Look,' and he slid from the Black Cat packet the picture card that came free inside: it read *Vintage Cars, Series of 50*, and showed a 1930 Alfa Romeo. Six cylinder, overhead camshaft.

'Is this why you smoke Black Cats?'

'Partly,' said Howard, going red, because clearly this was not a very mature reason for choosing a brand of smokes. 'I learnt to drive when I was a kid. My old man's a farmer, and he had a lot of old bangers lying around the place. He'd done stock car racing when he was my age. If I was in this film . . . would I get paid?'

'Of course – and you *are* going to be in it. The pay won't be much, but you will have a very interesting experience. Fabien's a brilliant director.'

'When are you shooting? Because I might have to do something else first . . .' (He pictured himself in Oxford, peering in through windows, accosting strangers, *looking for somebody*. Surely that would never come to pass?)

'We would need you in about a week's time.'

So he might have time for a quick trip to Oxford.

'What's the car? I mean what model?'

'I don't know,' she said, and she didn't seem to mind that she didn't know. She touched Howard lightly on the knee, creating the effect of an electric shock. 'I will now pitch our film to you,' she said, and she went into one of her speeches. He was so transfixed by the perfection of all her gestures, and the charming formality of her speech, that its content meant nothing to him at first. But it gradually appeared that she was speaking of three young middle-class French people who'd come to the south of France on holiday. They'd rented a remote villa on the coast, not near any form of public transport. Being French, they were all beautiful and bored. The man was in a relationship with one of the women. The other woman was jealous. The man then began flirting with the other woman, and started a relationship with her, but possibly only to annoy the first woman.

'So you see, they have reached a state of miserable torpor,' Emma was saying. 'Something has to happen.'

'Yes,' said Howard, 'it does. Who wrote this, by the way?'

'Fabien.'

Good – he could be rude about it. 'So far,' he said, 'it sounds like every French film ever made.'

'There is an element of pastiche. One day, they all go for a walk in the countryside, and this is when they meet The Englishman With The Car.' (She pointed at Howard.) 'And don't have a haircut, by the way. The car is broken down, and he offers to sell it to them for a cheap price. They buy it on the spot.'

'How?'

'The Frenchman gives the Englishman a cheque. But he's buying it on behalf of all of them.'

'So he's carrying a cheque book on a walk in the country?'

'Correct. So they get the car repaired, then they all go off and have individual adventures in it. The man meets someone who gives him a really good business opportunity. One of the women meets another man, and the other woman meets another woman.'

'She's gay, then?'

'So it seems. A bit, anyway. One day they all need the car to bring these matters to a culmination. The man needs to go to a crucial business meeting, the women need to go and meet their lovers. So they all have a terrific fight about who should have the car. The man eventually drives off in it, and he has an accident.'

'He gets killed, I hope?'

'It's only a minor injury, but the car is a complete write-off. So then they're all back at the villa, playing their emotional games again. And that's the end.'

Howard said, 'What's your involvement in this?'

'Associate producer.' She adjusted the back of her hair with lightning speed. 'Also, I play one of the two women.'

Fabien was looking over from the bar, preparing to reclaim Emma.

Howard said, 'Why does the man with the car have to be English?'

'Because it's an English *car*. I'm going to send you the script. We have an English language version for investors. Your lines will be highlighted in a special colour. I'll drop it off at your place if you give me the address.'

He wrote down the address of the flat, and he was brave enough – after a slight hiatus – to add the phone number. Fabien glowered over, but surely he couldn't be jealous? Emma was acting on his behalf, and presumably with his authorisation. She was now standing. Howard's time with her was up, and he'd better quit the bar rather than sitting around looking lovelorn. He nodded to Fabien, and the great auteur gave a slow unsmiling nod in return. Howard climbed the stairs into the softly hot, bustling night, with the feeling that he might have gained a lot of good material for his stalled second novel. But he had the feeling that he might have to live through the material first.

Very early Saturday morning in Nice; Oxford, spring 1951

Charles's hotel, near the railway station, was Nice backstage, and his third-floor room was level with a mesh of heavy wires. Occasionally a train buzzed along beneath them – or more often, at this time of night, a single engine released from a train. The train wires were grey, and beyond them was a grey freeway. The railway lights put an orange haze into the the night sky. At four o'clock, Charles had been woken by a nightmare in which he had returned to the flat, to find Syl inexplicably absent. As at 221b Baker Street, the newly delivered post was pinned to the chimney breast with a dagger, and all of it was in the form of blank post-cards from Pat Price.

Charles looked down into the empty railway canyon. If an engine came along and he jumped in front of it, he would be far more certainly dead than those people who jumped in front of the Metro trains in Paris.

But now he was ceasing to be in Nice, picturing instead Oxford scenes: the bucolic backdrop to academia. The cattle in the rain on Christ Church Meadow, as seen from a leaded window on a stalled winter's afternoon. They tended to be taken away as the chapel bells were ringing for Evensong. Anyhow, they were never there at night. Then he saw his second-year room: elegant fireplace and wood panelling offset by empty bottles of brown ale, overflowing ashtrays, broken digestive biscuits, record sleeves scattered around the gramophone. He saw himself, moping on the window seat at three in the afternoon, smoking a Woodbine and planning the night's debauchery.

It was hard to be debauched in 1951, whereas decadence and bohemianism would be available off the peg in a little over ten years' time. It had required real will power: the drinking of an entire crate of brown ale in a single evening; the tearing of holes in one's jumpers, experiments with facial hair and Brylcreem; obtaining by mail order revivalist (New Orleans) jazz records, and playing them at all hours, in his own college rooms and those of others. And if the other chap had had the decency, at 2 a.m., to muzzle the trumpet of the gramophone with a handkerchief, Charles would be the one to take it out. The music was a weapon; he didn't really like it, whereas the homosexuality came naturally and was exciting, partly because illegal. Even now, looking back, he could think of few scenarios more stimulating than the early evening walk from his colleges to the public lavatory in St Clement's – although it was rivalled by the memory of certain rooms he had occupied during his National Service with Second Army Signals: weak sunlight falling on trestle tables, metal trays overflowing with correspondence called 'traffic', maps on the walls and the clattering of the teleprinter. Charles would be eyeing the locations clerk – or whomever – and in a surprising number of cases, the clerk would be eyeing him back.

54

To annoy his dying father, he had arranged for his National Service to be as dowdy as possible, resisting any suggestions of the commission his public school background ought to have dictated. Second Army Signals, Rear Headquarters, had been a moveable feast: West Farnham, High Wycombe, Tunbridge Wells – Sunday-ish places that he associated with fogs and fucking.

A loud train brought the railway line below back into view. An electric flash lit up the graffiti on the black stone wall above: *Contre les Crimes Racistes.*

*

Charles saw before him a river in a different dawn, with a loud, cold wind blowing through the trees on this side of it. He was walking towards the trees with a man or boy called Neil at his side. The idea had been to get some fresh air, whereas a better idea would have been to say goodbye for ever to Neil after the failed experiment of the early hours. No two undergraduates at Oxford could avoid each other entirely, but you could perfectly easily *ignore* somebody. If anybody ever stood with a clipboard on the High Street, totting up the number of neurotic young people cutting each other dead . . . it would probably run into the hundreds every day, and most would be doing it for the reason Charles ought to have been doing it: they had gone to bed with the wrong person.

Neil was a state school product, a physics student from the Midlands who'd been 'forced' at school, like rhubarb, and exempted from National Service on health grounds. To the Army, he was probably weedy and hollow-chested, whereas to Charles he was lithe and long-lashed, and the fascinating thing was that

55

he seemed to know it. He wore his hair long, for example, and an element of his seeming shyness was coquetry. Throughout the Hilary and Trinity terms of Charles's second year (which was Neil's first) Charles had been receiving looks from him – in the porter's lodge, the dinner queue, or those college sherry parties, open to all comers, which Charles might attend out of anthropological interest, on his way to a more exclusive gathering – until finally the 'traffic' had become overwhelming.

The culmination had come in the dark and blustery first week of the first term of the following year – Michaelmas Term. On the Friday of that week, a friend of Charles, who lived in a big Victorian house off the High Street that formed an annexe of the College (and it was baldly called The Annexe), held a party. The Annexe housed those intrepid spirits who shunned the cloistered protection of the college itself. By rights, Charles ought to have lived in The Annexe, but he had done well in the room ballot and so lived in the medieval heart of the college, occupying a bowed and buckled set in Library Quad.

By rights Neil ought *not* to have lived in The Annexe, and he ought not to have been at that party: he wasn't part of Charles's rowdy set; didn't care for jazz and heavy drinking. He had probably come to complain about the noise, then become entranced after two or three unaccustomed drinks. Charles had watched him carefully as he handled the approaches from the various college queers. Dancers kept blocking his view – they were having a 'stomp' – so Charles had to keep shifting his position, creeping over armchairs and sofas that had been shifted to the edges of the room. He enjoyed watching Neil smoke the cigarette that someone had given him. All his gestures were meant to say, 'I've done this hundreds of times before,' but actually conveyed the opposite. Then the dancing had devolved to a party game: the one where everybody sits in a circle, with somebody designated 'the murderer' in inverted commas. Secret lots were drawn to determine who was 'the murderer' and Charles wasn't surprised that he drew the short straw, and surely everyone else would guess, since he was a natural for the role. You killed people by winking at them: they counted to five then flopped over. Anyone who thought they knew who was doing the killing raised their hand and asked for a seconder. If a seconder was forthcoming, the two accusers had to point simultaneously to 'the murderer'. If they were wrong, they themselves had to flop over.

When the time came to start 'killing' Charles winked at Neil, who keeled over with a secret smile on his face, honoured to be the first victim. Afterwards, Charles had gone up to Neil, and it was clear they must now act. 'I live in shared rooms,' Neil said. So obviously they would have to do it in Charles's rooms. Neil had taken his coat – a duffel coat, quite possibly purchased for him by his mother – and descended the staircase, obviously assuming Charles would follow, and Charles did follow, but after a slight delay, in which he said goodbye with a kiss to his host, Alistair Hart (who was in fact a viscount).

He had found Neil waiting alone just beyond the range of the single lamp that illuminated the small square in which The Annexe was housed. Some people had left the party before, and others would be leaving later. A chapel bell counted slowly to three, giving them every chance to change their minds, which they did not take, hurrying around the corner, back towards the college proper. They admitted themselves by the late gate in the garden wall, which was the way in when the lodge was locked. In the dark garden, leaves swirled; a sliver of moon was backing rapidly across the sky. A substantial branch cracked away from a tree and tried to hit them on its way down. Obviously, the weather did not approve of what they were about to do.

They crossed three unlit quadrangles. But did some light spill from Pat Price's rooms when they reached Library Quad? As soon as they entered Charles's sitting room, he stoked the fire; then they had their rapid convergence on the sofa. It was very unsatisfactory owing to the near frigidity of Neil who, immediately afterwards, tried to put everything in reverse, quickly getting dressed, retreating to an armchair on the other side of the fire, refusing cigarettes and further drink. He'd started talking – rather hysterically – about his work, trying to be funny about a certain tutor. Charles sat smoking in a dressing gown, humouring him until he realised there was no chance of round two.

He had suggested the walk as a means of getting rid of Neil, but he'd known it was a bad idea when they were back in the dark, traumatised garden and heading out through the late gate at 5 a.m. Charles's intention had been to walk Neil back to The Annexe. They had wandered instead towards the thrashing trees on the river bank. This was the real meaning of Michaelmas Term: restless trees, black river swirling. Orange leaves tumbling from the former into the latter; the night to all intents over but still no light in the day. Why were they walking to the river? For no better reason than that a gate leading to the Meadow had been left unexpectedly open. Neither knew how to get rid of the other: Charles ought to have been able to accomplish this with ease, but his worldliness had deserted him, or was it possible he was hoping for some greater thrill?

Neil was now talking about rowing, and it seemed he *was* a rower, an early morning activity that Charles only knew about from hearsay accounts. (The work ethic was so strong in these provincial types that it would spill over into their leisure time.) Well, Neil wasn't *exactly* a rower: he was the cox, the little, frequently pretty person who sat at the front, and did no work but was entitled to shout through a megaphone at the eight hulking oarsmen. They were in rowing territory now, not only the river but the college boathouses: bleak buildings that, with their flagpoles and college crests, reminded Charles of drill halls. One – towards the end of that glum parade – was in the process of being restored or rebuilt.

Neil was speaking the ugly language of rowing. His boat had recently 'bumped' another boat, which meant it had caught up with the other boat and crashed into it. The rowers might come back to college with blood on their shorts or down the back of their fat, pasty thighs – some malfunction of their sliding seats caused this. Gunshots started their races. For the winners, the trophy was 'blades', which is what they called oars. Sometimes they burnt their own winning boats in celebration. They did that at night, when they were drunk, but they didn't need to be drunk to make a lot of noise. It had been reported to Charles that after their riparian exertions they really would roar with laughter at breakfast in Hall. The slices of toast on their plates would be stacked high; they would drink neat milk.

At the river's edge, Charles was walking a little way ahead of Neil, aspiring to gradually draw away from him, as Neil said things like, 'Some of the chaps – if you look at their arms, they're nothing out of the ordinary. You see, it's all in the swing of the back. It's the rhythm, and that's what –'

'Neil,' said Charles, who was not only walking ahead but also *looking* ahead, 'I have no interest whatsoever in rowing.'

To this there was no response, only the tramp of their footsteps in the fallen leaves. Neil said:

'What you did to me back there . . . what's the big idea?'

'Well, you seemed perfectly well *aware* of the idea.'

'I'm sorry, I don't follow you, old man. You sort of jumped on me, and frankly I was in a state of shock.'

That was not the case. Neil had invited Charles's move, and he had not resisted the act, merely ensured it was not pleasurable for either party. And now he was moaning. But then Charles saw a route to the excitement he had been denied – and to a far greater excitement in fact. He had decided what he was going to do, and how he was going to do it, and the fact that he then received a violent blow on the side of his head from Neil made no difference. The blow had hurt, but not very much because the thick damp branch Neil had wielded from behind had also been rotten, so it had broken on contact with the right side of Charles's head. It – or at least the part of it that did not remain in Neil's hand – now lay on the riverbank.

Charles reached down towards the brick he'd spotted – which had been made available by the rebuilding of the boathouse. He hadn't thought he had a problem, hadn't realised he was unhappy, until he'd been pounding that pretty head for a full minute, during which he ceased to be unhappy, but became his true self, committed to the remarkable project of taking a person out of the world: it was like sending them into orbit, rubbing out the sky, or turning yesterday into today. When the work was done he looked with fascination at his achievement: the head was actually bigger than it had been before, and an entirely different colour, and Charles was being vouchsafed many congratulatory messages and insights. All those black-tie cabals of Oxford – they were like so many youth clubs. How could he have thought he was destined for anything other than this? He had a heart and it was a good one: he could finally feel its bold, pounding march. There was blood on his hands. He wiped them with his handkerchief, with the satisfaction of a workman washing his hands after a job well done.

The night was lifting – he could tell by a curious development in the sky over towards Cowley. But there was a more profound clarification inside his head. It was as if the dial on the wireless had at last found the right spot after years of interference. He was no longer numb, cold or hungover. He rolled the head (and the body attached to it) into the river. Then Neil was deep in the dark water – it was the duffel coat that was sinking him, its various grotesque pouches (hood, outsize pockets) filling with water, and many leaves were falling in on top of him, confirming his death like flowers thrown into a grave. Charles picked up the brick again, because he must get rid of it. He looked away, towards the dark boathouses: this was – or would soon be – Saturday morning, and the rowers would be coming. Yes, it was necessary to consider what happened next. It didn't much matter, since he had written the perfect poem and it could not be unwritten, but the aftermath ought to be conducted gracefully.

Very well then. It was necessary to return to college before the day started. He walked quickly through the Meadow with his head down. Somebody was coming, a sort of yokel or farmer plodding towards him along the mud track that Charles was on. To the left were trees; to the right the Meadow was becoming more evident as the morning mist rose. One of the trees seemed to beckon to him, and it was as though he was in some phantas-magoria of childhood. The tree was both a tree and a friendly giant. It was an oak, very ancient and wise, and there was a hole in the trunk that was becoming a letter box as Charles stared at it. The oncoming plodder – a man from at least a century ago – was about a hundred yards off. He looked completely innocent and rather poignant, like a shepherd who had lost his sheep. Charles realised he still held the brick and the bloodied handkerchief. It was natural – and amusing – to wrap the one in the other, and to post them through the hole in the tree, which seemed to welcome them with a graceful swoop of the lower branches (although a good firm shove was needed to get the brick through). The yokel had not apparently seen Charles do this, and he gave very little indication of having noticed Charles at all as they crossed on the track.

The late gate yielded easily to his key (it had been a little stiff the previous two times). He walked again through the quadrangles. But when he reached his own, a neat rectangle of light occupied a quarter of the square. Charles didn't need to lift his head to know that it corresponded to the room of Pat Price. He stopped and listened at Price's door, hearing no sound. When he gained his own sitting room and was staring at himself in the mirror over the fireplace (he was *totally* white), he tried to think about what exactly that light in the quad had signified: everything about Price was odd, including the hours he kept. He must have woken early, to solve some equations or compose a string quartet; or had he just come back from London, on the very late train that came into the secondary station, the one formerly belonging to the London Midland & Scottish Railway rather than the more popular Great Western? But Price could do what he liked. Charles was going to kill himself, and as he looked at himself he winked. Funny to think that his wink to Neil had proved fatal after all. He imagined the inverted commas around the word 'murderer' turning into little wings and flying away.

He stoked the fire, arranged for himself a Woodbine and a glass of Bell's Scotch. He sat at his table and began writing. He didn't want to think of it as a confession because that was a word that a weak or contrite person might use. He wrote the date and after some thought a colon, then, 'My actions this night'.

Starting with the party in The Annexe, he described them in detail over the length of an essay – or four Woodbines and two glasses of Bell's. But he was drinking in a new way: alcohol wasn't an absolute necessity, but a useful ally, like a cup of tea. He was very careful to state that he had murdered Neil. There had been no question of provocation in spite of the blow he had received. *Anyone* might be provoked. As he worked, he kept looking up at the wooden beam that traversed his ceiling, because his was a gable room, and a very old one. He had a bottle of barbiturates – Amobarbital, prescribed for sleep – but only a couple were left so he was going to have to hang himself.

Halfway through the writing, he got up to put the kettle on the spirit burner for a cup of tea; and he lit the fire, because his writing hand was going numb, and he might as well use up the remaining coal. He folded the several papers and wrote on the blank back of the topmost one: *To Whomever Finds This.* He did wonder about the grammar of that, but he was stuck with it now. He wondered about an appendix, a little jokey will: he would leave all his remaining coal (because there was still half a bucketful left), his caddy full of tea and his two bars of Cadbury's chocolate to Pat Price, because whereas Charles always had plenty of these rationed items – owing to certain favours done about town – Price was forever scrounging them off him, in return for which he would usually offer to pay. Ought he to leave a special note for his mother? No; impossible to find the right tone, and she would despise any sentimentality.

Seven chimes of the chapel bell. He was going to have to go to Mullarkey's, the hardware shop in the covered market, to buy some rope or a clothes line, but it wouldn't be open for a couple of hours, and that period of time would best be obviated. He opened the window because the room was smoky; a draught immediately came in and began doing battle with the fire. He watched the flames, amused. He walked through to his bedroom and took one of the two pills that remained. He set his alarm for nine o'clock and went to sleep fully clothed beneath the sheets.

When the alarm went off, everything was different. He found himself crosswise over the bed, and only half under the sheets. The room was full of friendly sunlight and the college chapel bells were ringing tumultuously, because it was ringing practice on Saturday morning. He remembered immediately that he was a murderer, and there was only the slightest flicker of anxiety before the pride of the previous night reasserted itself. He had reached the peak of excitement, and in the sense that it had not been a sexual peak but an existential one, he had none of the usual hungover recrimination. He walked through to his living room, and the document he had written was not on the table where he had left it.

It must be on the floor. The breeze coming through the open window was the obvious culprit. The newspaper that remained on the table was fluttering under its influence. But the papers of the document were not on the floor. He turned towards the fire. A small remaining redness fluctuated within the coals according to this same breeze from the window. Was it possible that the breeze and the fire had formed an alliance, by which the breeze blew the papers into the fire? The table was only about four feet from the fire. It would have needed more than a breeze, but perhaps the breeze had worked itself up to a proper gust at some point as he slept? He took the poker and distributed the remains of the fire across the grate: there was burnt paper in there, but then he'd used paper – some old correspondence, including a long letter from his mother – to get it going. Now that he thought of it, he *had* once lost a piece of paper to the fire. He had been using it as a bookmark, and when he created a breeze of his own, by closing the book, the paper had swooped elegantly into the fire, which had swallowed it whole. But surely it couldn't have swallowed four sheets in their entirety?

Charles moved to the window. A giant shadow, like that of a

mysterious airship, was moving down the spire of the chapel; it was now flowing over the chapel roof, crossing the bright green lawn of the quad, which seemed to be left even brighter after the shadow. But it was only a windblown cloud. What a very peculiar day this was.

He closed the window and searched throughout the sitting room for five minutes, then did the same with his bedroom. He sat down on his sofa. This was very nearly funny. It certainly made things interesting. He walked over to the door, which was unlocked. It was always unlocked, even when he was 'on the job', to use the currently fashionable Oxonian term. (He assumed everyone found fucking more enjoyable if there was the possibility of some authority figure blundering in.) His scout, Bill Duggan? No, because Bill didn't come on Saturdays.

Pat Price?

As he formulated the name, he felt – almost heard – the jolt that started his heart pounding; and this rhythm was changing his mind, energising it. He was no longer so sure that he wanted to die, not while there was thinking to be done. He stood up, and he was walking around the room as he considered Price and the missing papers.

Price would often visit Charles, which was just a matter of turning immediately left out of his door then climbing a dozen dusty stairs. He always knocked, of course. Was he likely to come in uninvited? Price was a combination of academic remoteness and provocative familiarity. He was certainly queer, so perhaps he was in love with Charles? Was it possible that he'd come into the room, read the document and decided to save Charles from himself? Price was not conventional; certainly not morally so. He was known within the college to have had a terrible High Table row with the chaplain.

65

,.. Or was he now delivering the document in person to the police station on St Aldates?

There was another possibility. That Charles's subconscious had stepped in; because he had a history of sleepwalking. Once, as a boy, he'd been found by the family maid sitting on the garden wall at 4 a.m. 'Sitting there like Humpty Dumpty,' she'd said, rather cruelly, Charles having been a portly child. And there had been other nocturnal expeditions ever since. If he *had* sleepwalked, the document could be in the river with Neil, or lying in a road in Cowley. He recollected the cloud sweeping over the quad. Things came and went in much that sort of way. Quickly. And surely there would now be a fleet – or a squad or whatever they called it – of police cars parked outside the lodge?

He put on his coat and descended the stairs. In the quad, he saw that Pat Price's curtains were open, but there was no sign of the man himself through the windows. He saw only Price's double bass and the surrealist paintings, the possessions, surely, of a man who might do anything at any moment. Charles walked to the lodge, where he saw no one but the porter. In the pretty, cobbled street beyond stood a milk float with a milkman inside it. Parked over the road was a coal merchant's lorry. He turned into Logic Lane, which was a reminder to be logical. He had left the party five minutes after Neil. Nobody except the two of them knew what had happened next. Pat Price might have seen Charles returning alone to his own room, but what did that prove?

On the High Street Charles turned right, coming to Magdalen Bridge, which was as festive as ever: rowers going along beneath, with the morale-boosting shouts of the little coxes ('Looking good, Oriel!'); bells ringing; earnest, tweedy tourists already in the botanical gardens. It was nine o'clock, a new day, and Charles was happy because he was not, after all, going to die this day. He walked on, reaching Cowley Road. 'Town' began to supersede 'gown', hence scruffier shops, the horse and cart of a rag and bone man. He passed a pub. It was not yet open of course, but it had a message for him, provided by the beer advertisement over the door: TAKE COURAGE. He was discovering a bonus to having committed a murder: the challenge of getting away with it.

He headed back to the middle of town. On the High Street a bus went past, bearing the familiar advert: WILSON'S, FOR MENSWEAR OF QUALITY. After having coffee and a bun in Queen's Coffee House, he walked to Wilson's on Turl Street to do something you probably wouldn't do if you'd just killed someone: he asked to be fitted for a suit. It was about time anyway that he replaced his baggy demob two-piece, which made him look like Al Capone. A single-breasted light grey worsted would be just the thing, and the tailor heartily agreed. At first, he was ingratiating. 'Ah, the greyhound breed!' he said, verifying Charles's thirty-inch waist, but he gradually became silent as the penny dropped about Charles, which was not that he was a murderer but something worse in the eyes of that silly man.

Back at the college entrance, not only had the milk float and coal lorry gone, so had the porter. Charles was very aware of the beating of his heart when he saw that a Roneo'd leaflet had been placed in every pigeonhole. But it was the compelling rhythm, proof of life; the thing he'd been missing all along. The message was from the Domestic Bursar. He regretted to announce that the body of a student, Neil Lindsay, had been discovered in the Isis (which was what Oxonians called their bit of the Thames) at Christ Church Meadow. Foul play was suspected. Lindsay had last been seen at a party . . . etc. Any student who could throw light on his subsequent movements was requested to attend the Middle Common Room between 1 p.m. and 4 p.m., where investigating officers of the Oxford police would be taking statements. Charles crossed the Front Quad in order to return to his room. Presumably Price had not declared his possession of Charles's statement (if he did possess it), otherwise half a dozen giant constables would now be wrestling him to the ground.

On the way, he passed the porter, who said, 'Bad show!' cheerfully enough. It was only natural that college servants should welcome any misfortune befalling the privileged fops to whom they were enslaved. Pat Price's room still showed no signs of occupation. Perhaps he was in London, looking for trade?

After lunch, when it had begun to rain, Charles went to the MCR. There were two detectives lounging, oddly enough, in armchairs rather than sitting at a table. They were youngish, possibly quite sophisticated in tweeds and flannels, and with A4 notebooks on their knees, so they could have been a couple of young dons composing lectures. But Charles told himself their sophistication could only be relative. They were not *at* Oxford, they merely *lived* in Oxford. One of them pulled up a chair for Charles, and offered him a cigarette, which he accepted. After ascertaining the basic facts about the party – the most basic of all being that Neil and Charles had not left together – he said:

'Tell me, was Neil Lindsay homosexual?'

'I don't know,' said Charles. 'Certainly, *I* am homosexual.'

'*Yes*,' said the second man, emphatically. It was the first word he had spoken.

'I suppose you think it takes one to know one?' Charles asked the first detective.

'Something like that,' he said, smiling – almost laughing – really quite charmingly.

Charles was enjoying himself, as if he was doing an exam for which he was well prepared for a change.

'I used to think he might be, yes. A bit anyway. Because it's usually a matter of degree.' This was said to annoy the other detective, whose expression remained neutral. 'It's hardly an established rendezvous, you know,' said Charles, 'the riverbank in the middle of the night. I would have thought the poor boy was more likely to have been attacked by someone who hates homosexuals, rather than one *of* them.'

The detectives looked at each other. One of them said, 'Do you know the police station at St Aldates?'

Charles did (it was a miracle he was so far unacquainted with its holding cells, or whatever its dungeon was called).

'We might need to see you there later on.'

'I look forward to it,' said Charles, and he genuinely did, because he was now in a game with them. They were reasonably proficient opponents, which would make his victory all the sweeter.

When Charles returned to his room, he thought *fingerprints*, and he used a shirt doused in water from the kettle to clean any surface Neil might have touched. An hour later, when he was lying on his bed smoking and listening to the wireless, there was a knock on his door. It was the second policeman. He was friendlier than he had been earlier. On the other hand, he was asking Charles if he would mind 'attending' the police station at St Aldates at six o'clock for a second interview. He gave Charles his card, as if he were a salesman. His name was slightly curious: Warwicker.

Over the next hour, whether sitting down and smoking, pacing the quads, or drinking a half pint in the back room of the King's Arms, Charles felt as if he were having one of those dreams of flying, but with none of the usual fear of falling. There was only the exhilaration.

It was raining more heavily and already dark when he reached St Aldates, and now he felt he was in a film: something about the blurred lights of the cars, and the swishing of the wipers on a big black, lacquered police Jag. It was rather a good film, and he was curious to know how it would end. He was led into a heavy wooden room, rather church-like with a good coal fire burning. This time there *was* a table, and Warwicker took the lead. He began with all that 'Whatever you say may be used as evidence against you' stuff, but by increasing the stakes he had only increased the excitement. Charles didn't deviate from what he'd said; he knew they had no evidence. He could only be undone by his own weakness.

After about forty minutes, he said, 'I have a party to go to. May I leave?'

'By all means,' said Warwicker, who thanked him for 'attending'. He had not been charged. As he walked back towards his college, he experienced another great surge of satisfaction, although he was exhausted. It had been an extraordinary, precipitous feat, akin to high-wire walking in that one slip would have finished his life.

Charles always had a mantelpiece full of invitations, but there was no particular event that night. In college, he rounded up some of the others who'd been at the Annexe party, and they convened in the college bar, which they usually spurned, it being the haunt of future bank managers or headmasters: stolid, plodding, pipe-smoking types. Then they crossed the Front Quad, a dark cabal in their black gowns, heading for the dining hall, where they constituted the top table – at least in their own minds, being the bohemian elite. They received many awed glances across that candlelit hall. Any one of them, after all, might have done for Neil Lindsay. It turned out that two of the group aside from Charles had been questioned formally: the host, Alistair Hart, and the man who'd left just before Lindsay, a fellow called Ralph, unknown to Charles. The rumour was that a tramp had been arrested and was likely to be charged. This must be the yokel that Charles had seen plodding towards him over the Meadow at dawn. Apparently, he had a criminal record involving violence. It was unfortunate for the man. But it would be quite grotesque for Charles to speak out in his favour. By the end of dinner they were laughing about the whole thing. 'But it's nervous tension that's making us laugh, you see,' the viscount explained to his latest catamite.

Charles slept well that night. There had been something so perfect about the sequence of events.

At ten in the morning the rain was continuing. From his window, Charles watched it generate a kind of fog on Christ Church Meadow. It would do that when it was coming down hard enough. The cattle were all standing under the trees, and there was something beautiful about it all. Charles had decided he would be leaving the University, and the means of doing so in a non-suspicious manner had been presented to him by his tutors. Having done so little work in the previous term, he had been 'awarded' (that actually was the term) 'penal collections' – 'collections' being the quaint word for a test. The penalty for failure would be temporary or permanent banishment, and in the case of a long-term recidivist like Charles the latter was more likely: he would be 'sent down'.

The midday bells were jangling as Charles crossed Front Quad beneath an umbrella. He was heading for a pub (The Bear, on Alfred Street), then the phone box in Oriel Square. Pat Price was coming the other way in his grubby mac. He wore a sodden trilby and carried a thin leather briefcase, perhaps a music manuscript case. As they converged, they smiled. Charles had seldom felt more alive. It was a shame he'd had to kill somebody to achieve this.

Price opened with, 'How's life in Darktown?'

It was a typically oblique remark, but it could be decoded. 'The

71

Darktown Strutters' Ball', as recorded by the Dixieland Jazz Band in about 1918, was a song Charles might play a dozen times a day on his gramophone, and Pat Price heard it through the floorboards every time, as he had once pointed out, mildly enough. (Rather than apologising, Charles had asked him what he thought of it. 'Out of tune,' Price had replied.) 'Darktown', in the current context, might be taken to mean Charles's louche, jazz-fancying milieu or it might mean something darker. Charles smiled. He said, 'I might ask you the same question.'

'Oh?'

'Haven't you just been to London?'

'Ah yes. Wigmore Hall for a spot of Elgar.'

But it was only a short walk from the Wigmore Hall to Soho. Charles said, 'You were in college the night before, though?'

'Yes! And I'm afraid I would have no alibi to offer the investigating officers. I was simply working by myself all night. I barely slept.'

Charles said, 'I was at the party where he was last seen — Neil Lindsay.'

'Then it must have been a very *good* party.'

The rain clattered down on Charles's umbrella. Pat Price stayed just beyond its range.

'I came back a bit squiffed,' said Charles, 'and I began doing a bit of writing, oddly enough. Then I somehow lost it, this . . . this document I was working on. I might have been sleepwalking. I don't suppose you . . . '

'What sort of document?' said Price. 'Can't have been an essay. You never write any essays.'

'It was a kind of letter, possibly rather ill-advised.'

'My dear Charles, *Ill Advised* will be the title of your autobiography. If you live long enough to write it.'

'I wondered if you'd somehow come across it, perhaps lying on the staircase, and decided to .... well, to keep it, you know, to save me from myself.'

Pat was giving Charles a fascinatingly ambiguous look.

Eventually he said, 'A lost cause, I fear. But I am flattered that you see me in that paternalistic role. In the States, we have this thing called A Nice Guy. It never occurred to me that I might be one.'

'Well, I wouldn't rule it out.'

Pat Price gave a single bark of laughter. 'Thank you, Charles. Thanks very much indeed. But I'd better get along to the Music Room, otherwise the St Peter String Quartet will be performing as a trio.'

On his way out through the lodge, Charles saw one of the chaplain's unpleasantly neat notices: there would be a special service of Evensong that night. Somebody called Glen would be speaking about his friend Neil. It occurred to Charles that they might be gearing up to having the funeral service in the chapel. The college was good at ceremony.

Charles drank a pint in the small, steaming front bar of The Bear. It was packed with Christ Church hearties, all of whom – like Charles himself – were there illegally according to the University Laws. Those laws were being rewritten, and students would be freer in the future, but never as free as Charles himself. He finished his drink and walked to the phone box. The rain on the glass made the back gate of Christ Church go blurred in various interesting ways as he listened to the ringing.

Finally, his mother picked up. He didn't call her Syl in those days, he called her Mother; but she was becoming less his mother now that his father had died, and more of a friend – a reliable ally against external threats. Her voice echoed in the cavernous sitting room of what had once been the family home. Leaving out his own role, he told

73

her what had happened, and she said she'd read a paragraph about it in one of the Sunday newspapers. She said, 'Did you know him?'

'A bit, yes.'

'Was he one of . . . you?'

'Sort of. Maybe. Does that matter?'

'It might.'

A great deal was not said in the next couple of seconds. Charles resumed with, 'I have these bloody penal collections coming up. I'm going to fail them.'

'I'm sure that's right, but can't you be a *bit* more optimistic? You're a perfectly clever boy, Charles, and you did get a scholarship.'

'What I mean is that I *intend* to fail them. I want to leave. I think we should move to Paris.'

They'd been talking of doing that ever since the death of Charles's father. He'd hated France to the extent that it seemed natural to consider moving there once he'd died. And the list of things they wanted to escape had been growing: austerity, rationing, arterial roads, ribbon developments, mock-Tudor pubs.

Charles returned to his rooms, to gaze at the melancholic meadow. He decided to organise a little party for the evening, and at three o'clock, he distributed notes to a select few. The amazing elation of the act itself was now being replaced by the subtler excitement of conducting himself in a manner befitting the type of person he had become: a person beyond conventional morality.

So he enjoyed his final week in Oxford. The vagrant was arrested and released without charge – this happened twice over, so the coppers evidently thought he was the one. In any event, Charles had heard nothing further from them.

*

74

Down below, a train came, drawing a curtain across the Oxford scene. The train was very bright, flickering. His angle was too steep to see through the windows, but he somehow knew it must be empty. It was still too early for people.

He was not remotely tired, and he realised he was not about to jump out of the window, because he had regained the energy of his last Oxford days. He was *not* scared by the anonymous cards. It was truer to say that he was galvanised by them because whoever sent them knew what he had done. The sender had the advantage of him, therefore, but the effect of the cards had been to reawaken the old, dangerous Charles, and it was he that Howard – the boy in the Cave – had encountered rather than the subdued Parisian Charles. On the face of it, the boy was an innocent party, caught in the crossfire. But that wasn't quite right, because Charles *wanted* the boy to be caught in the crossfire. Did he 'want' him full stop? Perhaps not in the purely erotic way; but he wanted to tangle with him, to perpetuate the connection. Was he punishing the boy for having watched him too closely? There was an element of that. But was it Charles's fault that the boy fitted his requirements to such absolute perfection?

He was the ideal person to send after Pat Price. The boy was intelligent – and that was the sine qua non. But he was also not well off, so he would do things for money as long as they squared with his conscience. For all his affected standoffishness, he was malleable. The romantic aspect of the job would appeal to him. He would intrigue Pat Price if they came face to face, and Charles believed that Howard would be able to give an accurate reading of Price's character and mental state. Then again, Charles did not believe that Howard would discover what had happened in 1951. Price would not tell him; otherwise Price would be sacrificing the uniqueness of his position. If the boy did find out, then Charles believed he would not necessarily turn difficult, and if he did . . . well then, the boy would have to be taken in hand, and Charles was perfectly capable of doing that.

It was half past five. He was booked on to a train that would be leaving at 12.16. Charles dressed and descended to the deserted lobby. In the street, he turned to look at the peeling orange paint of the hotel façade. *Leprous*, that was the word, and it struck him that he was a leper too; an outcast certainly. A well-dressed one though, he liked to think. He wore his linen jacket, because even Nice was cold – as well as dark – at this hour.

Avenue Durante became Avenue Baquis, where Charles turned right. The street lights were still on but beginning to look superfluous. One café was open, and Charles ordered an espresso. There was an English newspaper on the bar – a leftover from yesterday. The proprietor was about to dispose of it, but he indicated by a gesture that Charles could look at it if he wanted. It was *The Times*, which Charles had avoided all week. He glanced at the front page, which detailed the economic troubles of the homeland and the somehow complementary heatwave, which had brought a plague of ladybirds. Also, a couple of murders had occurred in central London. He indicated to the proprietor that he didn't want the paper, but the proprietor – who was reading a paper of his own – didn't appear to notice.

Charles took the packet of Gauloises from his pocket and tipped the remaining cigarettes onto the bar top. Seven left. He put them in his other pocket and returned the empty packet to the first one. He drained his coffee and left fifty centimes – which would more than cover it – on the counter top. He called a good morning to the proprietor, who looked up and smiled. At that time of the morning people were either very cheerful or very miserable, and the café proprietor had been the former. He did not deserve to forfeit the price of the coffee, but as the man returned to his reading, Charles swept up the money and put it in his pocket. This was for the enjoyment of seeing what happened as he walked towards the door – and nothing did happen.

On the pavement, Charles hesitated, to prolong the risk. But still nothing, only the gradual dawning of this beautiful day in Nice. He began walking, turning right. Even during his long hibernation in Paris, he would quite often walk out of a place without paying. He had to prove to himself that he was willing to take risks, to keep his hand in, so to speak, for situations such as the one that had now arisen.

A street sweeper was approaching – a beautiful African. He was using a long broom to encourage a flow of water along the gutter of Boulevard Victor Hugo. As he and Charles crossed, Charles said 'Bonjour,' and after walking for five minutes along the stately Boulevard, he was in the Jardin Alsace Lorraine, where amazingly tall palm trees coexisted with genteel shrubberies and a children's playground: there was no grass (the French found the English love of the stuff bizarre), only gravel between the vegetation, and there were no people. The place was preparing to be hot. Charles approached the first bench inside the park gates, and the litter bin that was alongside it. He would now set a clock ticking.

About six hours later.

Nice

The one exciting thing about the script of *The Car* was that Emma had scrawled her telephone number on the front page of it. Unfortunately she shared this number with the author of the script, Fabien. The piece seemed composed entirely of the kind of lame lines Howard would bash out on the Remington just in order to progress to the next bit, with a note alongside that read *CBT*, meaning *Come Back To*. But Fabien had had no second thoughts about lines like, 'You are in love with the guy. It is obvious, so don't deny it.' There was absolutely no humour yet people kept saying things like, 'What's so funny?' and 'I'm only joking around.'

Emma had dropped the script off very early in the morning, or at least before ten o'clock when Howard had got out of bed. She'd posted it by hand through the letterbox in the lobby door. She had not buzzed up so that he could let her in, which was just as well. There would have been bottles of beer to clear away, and the ashtray full of dead Black Cats. It was possible she would be impressed by the typewriter on the kitchen table, but not by what he'd been typing – about a hundred letter t's. He was having trouble with that key, which he would need pretty often if he ever thought up a story to write. She might like the art on the walls . . . or did posters for exhibitions of modern art really count as art? What would she think of the bookshelf? Would she mind that his editor could veer from Leon Uris to D.H. Lawrence? There was a lot of Lawrence – whom Howard thought creepy – but no Chandler, Hammett or Hemingway, all of whom he loved. So why was he being published by this guy in the first place?

If she went into the kitchen, she might be amused by the Englishman-in-exile trappings: Ty-phoo tea, cans of beans and a bag of Golden Wonder crisps. (He had finally found some proper crisps in the Union Jack Pub that disgraced a certain alleyway in the Old Town. It was a shame about the beer though – Worthington E – but then it was a shame about the beer in most pubs back home as well. Howard was developing an interest in the large bottles of wine offered in the supermarkets of Nice for not much more than the large bottles of mineral water – because it seemed the French *bought* their drinking water rather than getting it from the tap. Whether that made them more or less sophisticated than the English was a moot point.)

He turned a page of the script and came to himself: The Englishman With The Car. His interactions were with the Frenchman, Sacha, linchpin of the love triangle. The Englishman With The Car had two lines. Emma had underscored them in red using a ruler. She was a very determined person:

> SACHA (looking at the car): Hey, that's quite a beast.
> But is it broken down?
> THE ENGLISHMAN WITH THE CAR: A little
> trouble with the spark plugs. Nothing too serious.
> SACHA: Is it for sale?
> THE ENGLISHMAN WITH THE CAR: Are
> you joking?
> SACHA: I'm serious! I'll give you a cheque this minute!

The actual deal was done in the background, so to speak. Because now the two women took over with their own scintillating chat.

> CHARLOTTE: Is he really going to buy that thing?
> NICOLE: Why not? That's Sacha for you. He's crazy,
> you know! Besides, it will be useful to have a car.

But the French could get away with this peculiar dead tone they went in for, by virtue of everyone involved being tremendously good-looking.

Howard looked at the phone, which was suddenly ringing. This would be Emma, asking whether he'd got the script.

But the call was from a box.

'Good morning,' said a cultured English male. 'This is Charles here. We met last night.'

So this was serious; and he had decided to reveal his first name.

'How are you?' said Charles.

The honest answer would have been 'nervous', but Howard said, 'I'm fine. How are you? I'm afraid I won't be able to go to Oxford to look for that person. I really do have to –'

'Do you know the Jardin Alsace Lorraine? It's on the junction of Boulevard Victor Hugo and Boulevard Gambetta. I'm sure you have a street map. If you walk through the gates, you'll see a litter bin on the immediate right. In it you'll find a crumpled Gauloises packet – I doubt there'll be more than one. In the packet you'll find two hundred and fifty pounds sterling. That's for you to do what you want with. I'd rather you used some of it to buy a train fare back to England, then to Oxford, where I would like you to spend no more than two or three days looking for a man called Pat Price. He's an academic, of sorts.'

Howard could hear a roaring down the line. 'Where are you calling from?'

'Near the railway station. In five minutes I'm boarding a train back to Paris.'

'Maybe I'll just leave the money where it is.'

'In which case, the bin will be emptied at the end of the day, and the money will be gone for ever. But you seem like a decent person, so I'm sure you'd rather do that than just take it and spend it.'

'Or I could give it to charity.'

'You're becoming more virtuous by the minute. Yes. You

could stuff it in the collection box at Holy Trinity, the Église Anglicane. They're on a fund-raising drive at the moment. Or you could spend a couple of days in Oxford doing a little light detective work. I calculate your expenses would be sixty pounds. The rest is profit.'

'You must be very rich.'

'Among the troubles I have in life money is not one, Howard.'

'What do you do for a living?'

'Oh – retired. If you do go to Oxford, please check into the Eastgate Hotel. It's on Merton Street. It's perfectly comfortable, and they always have rooms. You'll find a letter waiting for you there on Monday morning, and that'll give you a few leads about where Price might be found. In a minute I'm going to give you the telephone number of a bar in Paris. I'm there every evening except Sunday from six forty-five to seven fifteen. The proprietor – he's called Monsieur Bonnet – will answer. Just ask for Charles and he'll put me on.'

Howard took down the number. What was this sort of rigmarole called in the novels of Le Carré? Tradecraft. He said, 'Why don't you go to Oxford yourself?'

'I have an elderly mother I can't afford to leave. And I don't want to bump into Pat Price if he *is* in Oxford. Also, I'm sort of . . . done with the place.'

'You were there as a student, I suppose?'

'Maybe.'

'Is this Pat Price dangerous?'

'Not to you, he won't be.' Those funny French pips came down the line. 'Goodbye for now, Howard. I hope you can make it to Oxford.'

Howard returned to the kitchen table. He saw the red underlining on the script. Clearly, he was caught between two very decisive people. But this Charles person was perhaps not always decisive. If he lived with his elderly mother and did the same things at the same time every day, there wasn't much scope for decisions. Or look at it like this: he had made one big decision, which was to live a very regular life, and that regularity was now somehow threatened by this Pat Price character. It was not a money matter; it would be more serious than that. Love therefore (and Pat Price was presumably gay, just as Charles was ... presumably). Or it might be the other heavy thing: death. Perhaps Charles wanted to kill Pat Price? Or vice versa? A criminal who'd been at Oxford would naturally gravitate to the south of France. Somerset Maugham called the Riviera 'a sunny place for shady people'.

But *Howard* was in love with *Emma*, and he wanted to be near her, or at least in the same city. So he would leave the money where it was. Or he would take it, then call Charles in that bar and demand his address so he could return it to him, perhaps with a tenner withheld to cover the inconvenience of it all.

... Because Howard felt he was being manipulated, possibly even bullied. Charles had done to him what he – as a novelist – was supposed to do to others: he had read his character. He's figured out, Howard thought, that I'm conscientious; that I'm pretty straightforward, not *mercurial*. (Howard had always wanted to be mercurial. He believed very few writers were as straightforward as he. His editor had told him as much, and if it had been a compliment, it was a pretty backhanded one.) Howard went about novel writing in a very dogged way. He plotted out in detail and had files for each character, which was why his book-writing was expensive, and why he was running out of money.

He would perhaps make a better showing with Emma if he had

more money. Perhaps he should ask her what he should do. She would give him an instant answer, one way or the other.

He made himself a tea, which he took over to the window. It was open to the maximum extent, and some pigeons had been burbling loudly on a ledge. He saw another block of flats; the green dome of a church, the roof of a supermarket, but the main thing he saw was the Mediterranean, soaring up into a bleached-out sky. It was like a banner saying, *you are here to have pleasure.* But the heat militated against the pleasure. He could *hear* the heat right now: a warning thrum, like an electrical appliance left accidentally on.

Another thing Charles had worked out about him: he was inclined to be nervous, and this Howard was always trying to correct. For instance, by crossing the road towards any row or scene of violence. Perhaps all the bravest people were nervous, and that was why they were brave. But above all there was this: ever since his novel had been accepted for publication, Howard had feared he would be punished for his luck and for his presumption in writing the thing in the first place. Some of that good luck had been under-cut – by that one bad review, mediocre sales, and the unimproved advance for the follow-up – but he was still in credit on the balance sheet of fortune, and that was certainly going to be corrected. He would find himself involved in real-life danger or presented with its possibility, which amounted to the same thing. Because he would not be able to refuse.

The phone was ringing again.

It was Emma, also from a public phone. His heart was beating at such a rate . . . he might have been running.

'Hi,' she said. 'Did you get the script?'

'Yes, thanks. I've just been reading it.'

'So what do you think?'

An opportunity to be sardonic. That was his natural tone; he ought to use it. 'I think it's as flat as a pancake.'

An awful silence came down the line, so he instantly went into reverse. 'I mean, look ... I don't know anything about film. And perhaps something's been lost in translation.'

'Well, I translated it.'

'I do think it's good *in a way*.'

'No you don't!' And she laughed, thank God. 'Why *exactly* do you think it's bad?'

'Well, perhaps we could meet, and –'

'Yes, yes of course. But tell me now.'

He went on too long, so she had to top up the call just as he was saying, 'As for the characterisation ...' When he'd finished, she said, 'OK, thanks. I'll tell Fabien what you think.'

'Now hang on a minute –'

'Of course, I absolutely must because the film is a democracy. Fabien is an auteur but he is not a dictator. He's with me now. We're in the Canne à Sucre on the Promenade. We're having coffee, then I'm going swimming.'

That would be a post-coital coffee, no doubt.

'I'll see you on the beach,' she said, 'opposite the Palais. Can you be here in half an hour?'

'Yes,' he said, then he hated himself for asking, 'Will Fabien be there?'

'No. He's going off to a production meeting in a minute.'

After twenty minutes – mostly spent in front of the bathroom mirror – Howard stepped out into the sunlight. Every time, he thought it would be different. He would not be immediately gripped by the threat of a migraine; not be awed by all these people doing, in ninety degrees Fahrenheit, the things people did back home in sixty degrees: driving and parking cars, walking dogs, laughing. And some of them were rubbing it in by roller skating (there was a lot of that in Nice), bicycling or playing tennis on those broiling orange courts. Maybe if he stuck it out for long enough, he would become like the Frenchmen, with a leathery brown go-anywhere complexion instead of accursed pinkness. He would wear his shirt open to his waist and would not need a jacket for his notebook and pens. He would just *remember* things. Or maybe he would buy one of the little leather bags they carried, held by a wrist strap. No: he definitely wouldn't be doing that. He took his heavy denim jacket off and swung it over his shoulder. He was standing next to a hat shop. His father, who had inflicted his own problematic combination of black hair and rubicund complexion on his son, had told him to 'Get yourself a hat,' but he hadn't yet found one that suited him. Any hat he put on always looked like somebody else's hat. Most of the hats were white, and the whiteness dazzled him.

After turning two corners, he was walking through the gates of the Jardin Alsace Lorraine. He immediately saw the litter bin. A father and son – English – were sitting on the bench right next to it. The kid was saying, 'Dad, do you like the smell of petrol?' the whimsicality of which suggested they were in no hurry to leave.

He looked around for another bench to sit on until they'd gone, but none of the others had any shade, whereas the bench they were on was half under a palm tree. Howard sat down in full sun. He commenced to burn. It was five minutes from here to the beach; in ten minutes he'd be late for Emma.

Now the father began reading a newspaper, while the boy tried to attract the attention of one of those elegant little French cats that made the English ones seem so lumbering and un-catlike in comparison. Most French cats seemed to have been on a crash diet, just like most French women. They were posh, this pair on the bench, like Charles. Howard was suddenly disgusted at being inconvenienced by people of a higher social standing than himself. He quit the park.

He was soon on the Promenade des Anglais. Over the road and below a white wall was the beach. It was a stone beach, therefore grey, and about as beautiful as a rough road. But the people on the beach did not need sand, only the sun. Some had towels beneath them; some held little books, or cigarettes, but none was shielded from the sun. This stretch, opposite the defunct Palais de la Méditerranée, was a public beach. To left and right were hotel beaches, and here were hundreds of regimented blue and white sunshades, most going to waste because it was still early in the season. It slowly dawned on Howard that the woman washing her feet at a standpipe near the white wall was topless. In fact, about a quarter of the women were topless. What if Emma was topless? That would be a test of his nonchalance, his *savoir-faire*. The bloody French had gone out of their way to invent words for all the qualities he lacked.

He saw her then, walking out of the sea. She wore an orange bikini, and it was like watching a fashion shoot, except that he was involved. She seemed to be pointing with amusement at his feet, and it turned out he was standing next to her towel, which was a good omen. As she approached, he wondered: are we going to kiss? It would not be up to him of course. Yes, they were, because she turned her cheek towards him. Was there glitter on her skin? No, it was only the effect of sea water on her – a kind of blessing. He watched as she towelled her hair in vigorous bursts. Every time she stopped, she looked great in a completely different way. And she was speaking a language he could understand. Here was his very own English-French person.

'Did you not bring your swimming things?'

'I don't really have any swimming things.'

He had some trunks, which he couldn't bear to mention. She looked him up and down, and the sight couldn't have met with her complete approval, because she said, 'We'll go and buy you some new clothes.'

She put on a short dress – which was more like a fast, free-flowing sketch of a dress – and some flip-flops; picked up a skimpy bag, and indicated the stone wall: a thoughtful gesture because it gave a little shade. 'You sit on my jacket,' he said, which she ignored. She took a tube of sun cream from her bag. 'You need this all over your face, nose especially. Rub it in fast.'

'Why fast?'

'So we can get onto more interesting matters.'

When he'd finished with the cream, she said, 'You keep it.' In return, he offered her a Black Cat, which she accepted. She said, 'I told Fabien what you said about the script.'

'I wish you hadn't.'

'Your point about it not being funny – he said your approach is unsophisticated. That you have no understanding at all of the difference between the absurd, and absurdism. Anyway, he'd like you to do him a favour. He wants you to look at the car.'

'Look at it?'

'Make sure it's OK.'

'I'm not a mechanic, you know. Where is it?'

She jerked her thumb in the direction of the town. 'In a garage – a second-hand car dealer's. We're hiring it. It's a sports car, pretty cool.'

Howard slid the picture card from today's packet of Black Cats. It was from the Modern Car series. 'Not one of these, I suppose? It's an Aston Martin Lagonda. Some people think it's very ugly.'

'Including me.'

'But I like it.'

'Why?'

'Partly the name: Aston Martin Lagonda. Also, it looks like a razor. And see – it's got pop-up headlamps, like a Lotus.'

'Or a frog. How old is this car?'

'Do you mean when did it go into production?'

'Yes, obviously.'

'Last year, I think. It has an LED display dash. It lights up, and some of them have TVs. *Colour* TVs. One in the front, one in the back.'

'Fabien would hate that. He never watches TV. He says it employs a debased visual language.'

'The Lagonda's very popular in the Middle East.'

'Which is why an Englishman With A Car wouldn't have one. I've remembered the make of ours now: it's an MG.'

'An MGB?'

'I think it's just an MG. What's an MGB?'

'The follow-up to the MGA.'

'Let's go,' she said, throwing her cigarette onto the hot stones. 'We'll have lunch, then get the car.'

As they walked through town, Howard didn't know where they were going, and he didn't mind. She was asking him about writing, so he began explaining his theory that whilst he never had writer's block, he was sometimes blocked about *living*. That was what he used to say, but now he was blocked on both fronts; and the line was too cute anyway, so he wound it up quickly.

Most of the populace was eating on café terraces. They sat down at one themselves.

'How's your French?' she said, picking up the menu. She put on glasses to read it, which was immensely touching. He was discovering a lot about this person he wasn't going out with.

'It's not just that I can't speak French,' said Howard, 'I can't *behave* in a French way.' She failed to refute that, and when a waitress was approaching, she said, 'Give me your notebook and pen. You order and I'll note down your mistakes, then tell you them. I would like a Croque Monsieur and a Coke.'

At least this way his ineptitude might entertain her, and as Howard interacted with the waitress, Emma made notes fairly continuously. When the waitress had gone, she read them back: 'You never just say *bonjour* on its own; it must always be followed by an honorific.'

'I gave one at the end, when I said thank you. I called her Mademoiselle, was that right?'

Emma made a fifty-fifty gesture. 'Didn't you see her wedding ring? Anyway, you don't pronounce the first "e".' She consulted her notes again. 'You asked for *café au lait*. If you want to be taken seriously, you must say *crème*.'

'And of course it's very important to be taken seriously when one is ordering a frothy coffee.'

As they ate, they speculated about the other diners. Howard had an opportunity to tell her what Somerset Maugham had thought about the Riviera. Then he told her what *he* thought of Somerset Maugham, which she didn't necessarily want to hear. Afterwards, they walked to a big barn-like shop where lazily turning fans stirred the smoke from joss sticks and cigarettes. It was like a hippy jumble sale but the second-hand clothes piled on the trestle tables were not so cheap. Records were also on sale, and a drowsy Stones song was playing as Emma wandered away. 'You Can't Always Get What You Want'. Howard assumed she was shopping for herself, but she came back with a question for him. 'Would you wear a shirt with a number on it?'

'Depends what the number is.'

'Thirty-seven.'

'Definitely not.'

She carried a bundle of men's clothes. She held the items up against him one by one, hitting him quite hard every time, which he liked. Four things did not survive this process and five remained: a white, unlined cotton jacket, some blue linen trousers, a cheesecloth shirt and two T-shirts. They walked to a table loaded with shoes, and she pointed out some blue and white Adidas trainers. He knew she was right on every count. The T-shirts had long sleeves, to stop his arms from burning, and the blue trousers were straight-legged. (Howard had been increasingly conscious of the irrationality of flares.) The only trouble was the cost: 180 francs, and as he handed it over, he thought again of the cash that might be in the litter bin.

They walked back towards the Prom, and the derelict Palais: to the rear of it. There was an alleyway – about the width of a car – between a bar and a shop that seemed to sell only sunglasses. In a courtyard overlooked by the backs of hotels were four sports cars: two black Porsches, a yellow Alfa Romeo and an MGB, which was brown with a soft top. The top was down, so the red vinyl of the seats would be very hot. There were no people: only the heat, and the muffled sound of traffic on the Promenade.

'That's the car,' said Emma. 'Do you like it?'

'It's a funny colour. But yeah.'

A small, oily man emerged from the gloomy recess of a workshop. He was darkly handsome yet completely bald, and he was smoking; the index finger of his right hand was missing. Emma began talking to him in French. He offered her a car key, and she indicated Howard, who received the key. They got in by opening the doors, but they needn't have bothered, the top being down. Howard chucked his bag of clothes in the back. The seats were almost unbearably hot and sticky, so Emma reached into the clothes bag, and gave them both a T-shirt to sit on. Howard liked the idea of Emma's bum being on his shirt. He also liked the wide wooden steering wheel and the offset ignition. He'd learnt to drive in a Morris Minor, with the ignition pedantically centred on the dash beneath the big speedo, which looked like a clock on an old-fashioned mantelpiece.

'Where to?' said Howard. He'd always wanted to say that.

'It's a test drive, so anywhere you like.'

'Doesn't he want to see my licence?'

But the man had gone back into the workshop. Howard did a three-point turn – rather well, he thought. He pointed the car at the alleyway and drove a bit too fast along it.

'Careful,' said Emma, and Howard found himself chuckling in quite a reprehensible way. He was not aware of ever having 'chuckled' before, and he was on a high, so when they came to the junction with the quiet road, he said, 'Just remind me. Which side do they drive on here?'

'Don't be silly.'

He went left, filtering on to the Prom, where they joined the holiday cavalcade. They were in one of the nicest cars, and Howard had the best passenger of all. He began changing gears unnecessarily.

'*Why* do you like it?' she said.

'It's a sports car but roomy – at least compared to the MG Midget; it's comfortable and very driveable.'

'You're a funny sort of novelist, I must say. You sound more like a car salesman ... There's not much room at the back.'

'That's to discourage you from having children.'

'Will it go fast?'

But Howard was concentrating.

'I said will it go fast?' Emma asked again. 'What are you doing?'

They were at a red light, and he was bringing the clutch up slowly.

'Putting load on the engine,' he said, and they were moving again, heading for Castle Hill. 'If there was anything wrong with the big ends, you'd hear a knocking.'

'Oh, for God's sake. And did you?'

'No. And there's no backlash on the diff.'

'I honestly think you're making these words up. How fast will it go?'

'Be interesting to see. Probably get a ton out of her.'

'You sound just like The Englishman With The Car.'

'You might want to make notes as I speak. It's a pretty big engine, like I said. Maybe seventeen hundred – eighteen hundred cc. I learnt to drive in knackered old Morris Minors, and they maxed out at twelve or thirteen hundred. And look.'

'What?'

He indicated a place under the steering wheel. 'The overdrive switch – gives you a boost when you're in top gear.'

'How childish,' she said.

With a vague idea that things were going too well, that he must now pay the price for his perfect day, he turned left away from the sea, until the Jardin Alsace Lorraine came into view. Howard drove a little way beyond, then stopped the car outside the hat shop. 'Remember the posh Englishman from last night?' he said, and he told Emma of the proposition Charles had made.

She listened with folded arms. 'Why didn't you take the money?'

'People were looking. It was embarrassing.'

'Nonsense,' she said, as they climbed out of the car.

They walked through the gates of the little garden, which now smelt very strongly of a certain blossom – a soapy smell. As before, the bench was occupied, this time by a French couple, smoking and talking, possibly arguing.

Emma said, 'Is that the bin?' and she was immediately reaching into it. Insofar as the French couple noticed what she was doing they didn't mind, and it was either the case that a young woman who looked like Emma could get away with anything, or that any act performed with sufficient boldness seemed reasonable. If any embarrassment did attach to Emma, she transferred it to Howard by putting *two* crushed packets of Gauloises into his hands. One held three cigarettes, the other a roll of bank notes. Howard had finished counting the money when they returned to the MG.

'Two hundred and fifty pounds,' he said. 'Do you think I should go to Oxford?'

'What would your man Marsh do?'

Howard could have answered that question at length.

'Marsh wouldn't be in the south of France in the first place. More likely in Scarborough, in his caravan.'

'He has a caravan?'

'Yes, but even so he's a man of action. So he would probably go.'

'Obviously he would go, and so must you.'

'But the film.'

'Today's Saturday. We don't need you until – say – *next* Saturday.'

They climbed into the MG. 'You could probably buy this car now,' she said. 'By the time you come back to Nice, you could be The Englishman With The Car *for real*.'

The same Saturday afternoon.

London

Naked Lee was stretched out on the bed, alongside the green suit, which had been lying there all week – lying, so to speak, in state. In desperation he'd had a good go at the sleeve with half a packet of Square Deal Surf, but the jacket was a *Dry Clean Only* item, and he had reluctantly concluded that it would never be the same again. So it would now be disposed of – probably cremated with full honours. He would drive back to Devon in order to do that. You could burn an entire wardrobe in that tangled, steeply walled garden and nobody would know.

Lee rolled over and thought about his week.

On coming back last Saturday, he'd showered the peroxide out of his hair and gone to bed with it wet, which showed how tired he was, because normally he spent half an hour under the dryer. He slept very deeply from two to ten, then dozed as the sunshine mustered beyond the closed white curtains. The extensive parquet floor, on which the clean white shag rugs had seemed to float like little clouds … The tan leather armchairs suggesting civilised conversation … That had been a good moment. It had been worth spending such a large part of his inheritance on the short lease. Lee had felt himself to be as elegant as the room – he had felt it before, but now there was the bonus element: he was finally important! Or would be. For the first time in years, a new song had begun to run through his mind, and he'd *let* it run, which he could afford to do, now that he'd liberated himself from his own fear. It was a very pretty thing but with only two words so far: 'Super-Duper'.

His hair had looked funny when he'd climbed out of bed that morning: mussed and skewed, and unexpectedly dark. Touch of

94

the Roy Woods. To think – he had weaponised his right eye. He was the Six Million Dollar Man! In front of the mirror, he'd closed that special eye slowly then opened it in like manner, because it was important to keep it in good working order – rather as his old man had greased his guns (or whatever it was he did to them) before going off shooting.

The week since had been a bit of a comedown. In spite of the heat, he'd stayed mostly indoors. But he'd done an errand in support of the programme, touching up the sub-plot as it were. He realised he was interested in small actions that had a disproportionate effect. This was the basic appeal of the trademark, which after all was a tiny thing, almost . . . subliminal.

Every day he'd bought the papers. The *Evening Chronicle*, being a London paper, had done the initial honours in both cases, although what they reported as the first 'find' ought really to have been the second. On the Monday, 'A murder hunt has been launched after the discovery of a young woman in an alleyway off Oxford Street . . . ' On the Tuesday, 'The body of a young woman has been found in Chelsea.' The death was 'being treated as suspicious'. God, they were slow, these coppers. On Wednesday they were 'comparing the files of the two cases' and a manhunt 'was being launched'. A certain Detective Chief Inspector Wallace – whose suit might have been created to show the perils of buying 'off the peg' – had appeared on TV, wanting to hear from anyone who had seen anything suspicious. For heaven's sake, Lee had ensured that the trademark had been witnessed in both cases! But no mention had yet been made of this.

Lee went back to the mirror and began experimenting with a side parting. Looked OK. Keep it there with a dash of product? The knock-off Ray-bans lay on his bedside table. He reached for them and, yes, they worked with the side parting, giving a sort of West Coast Beat Poet vibe. He put the glasses down. Then he looked towards the dark and quiet TV, which sat – just then – on the coffee table. It was only a twelve-inch screen, a white Iconic portable with push-button controls and the Space Age look. He'd gone for a small set, so as to be able to stow it in one of the many fitted cupboards, because TVs had always seemed to Lee to be working for the enemy, boosting the nobodies; but now this little box would be his ally.

He switched it on. For a Space Age product, it was very slow, but the BBC globe was gradually emerging from a greenish fog. As it turned, a man was talking about what was 'coming up'. He sounded very authoritative but, in reality, he had no idea what was coming up. Precisely one person knew that: Lee Jones. He had been talked of on TV many times already that week, but only he knew it. The blare of a sports programme now began, because this was a Saturday afternoon. He turned the TV off, put on his dressing gown and walked over to the window. It was very easy to launch a manhunt, it seemed; it would be equally easy – he had little doubt – to evade it, but the difficulty lay in getting any credit for the uniqueness of his style. It had been the same with Picture Show, the music's delicacy overlooked by public and critics alike.

Abi was hanging around, pen poised.

'Do you feel underrated, Lee?'

'Well of course, it's not for me to say whether I'm underrated. If I did say it, the implication would be that a few nice mentions in the press could rectify the problem. It is possible to be underrated even if you're highly praised, you know. There's a case for saying The Beatles are underrated, I think.'

'So you're saying you could never be praised enough?'

'Oh dear. I can see I'm going to emerge from this article as quite monstrous.'

He walked over to the window, which had the effect of dispelling Abi. The window was amazingly clean – hardly there at all – and the pillar box down below was incredibly red in the bright sunshine. It was like an acid trip, not that he'd ever been a big one for drugs. 'Too much going on up here as it is,' he would say, pointing at his head when they were offered, or the subject was broached. Directly opposite, but a long way below, was the newsagent's. Next week all the little people – because they were *very* little from this height – would be coming out of there holding newspapers in which his further actions would be described and speculated upon.

As usual there were women marooned on the traffic island. (Perhaps the men just walked straight across the road.) One was a particularly nice redhead in hot pants. Sometimes, when Lee saw a woman with really good legs he would hear music: some kind of short-circuit in the brain, and in weather like this, when a lot of revolting men were presuming to wear shorts, the percentage of him that was gay would drop. Even so, the next phase in the programme would be with a man, to show his versatility; and he would wear his white suit, his second-best one (not the Cerruti – the Cecil Gee) in case of further staining.

The phone was ringing, and Lee was amused at his own reaction: a suddenly racing heart, an almost ticklish tingling. Proof of life. What if this was Detective Chief Inspector Wallace? He almost hoped so. He was tired of having to invent conversations.

But it was only Geoff, who said, 'Hi Lee. It's Geoff.'

'I know.'

'Hot enough for you? I was wondering if you wanted to meet up.'

'I'm busy tonight.'

'Doing what?'

'I don't know.'

'Tomorrow, then?'

If Abi really had been in the room, Lee would have rolled his eyes at her.

Saturday evening.

Nice

Nice Ville railway station, two miles inland, was a sullen place apart. The night train – the so-called Blue Train – was battered and only partly blue. It departed at 9.14 p.m. – a bloody silly sort of time, Howard thought, but then he didn't want to be on the train at all. The compartments were weird. He had one seat, facing the wrong way, so that he must watch Nice recede, as though to underline the wrongness of his departure. Next to him, and getting in his way, was a diagonal steel ladder that led up to his bed.

The night on the train was hot and dirty. There was a bar car with too much dead blue carpet on the floor, and only one other paying customer: a sweating businessman drinking beer. The Rhône Valley was a succession of shadowy poplars, like factory chimneys. The sky was dark blue and moonless. Anything could be in preparation out there, and anything could happen tomorrow. He hardly slept, because he knew that, whatever the nature of the connection between Charles and Pat Price, it could not be a healthy one.

Slightly earlier the same evening.

London

Lee entered Soho, then walked clean out the other side, boosted on his way by the sound of Abba's ballad, 'Fernando', on one pub jukebox, and 'Me and You and a Dog Named Boo' by Lobo on another – two songs he hated almost as much as 'Chirpy Chirpy

Cheep Cheep'. The pubs were all inside out, with doors and windows gaping, and as many people drinking on the streets as at the bars. Plenty were gay chaps of course, but he couldn't find the right sort of place. The old trademark might go unnoticed in the jostling crowd.

He walked east until he came to The Salisbury on St Martin's Lane, where he entered that kaleidoscope of ornate Victorian mirrors. It had been a semi-gay place in his previous London days, and that still seemed to be the case. So there was only a frisson as he walked in, rather than a clamour as would have occurred in, say, the Golden Lion on Dean Street, which was exclusively gay. The bar in The Salisbury was curved, so you were looking at a selection of punters rather than just the barman.

He ordered a white wine, and immediately spotted a potential partner over the barman's right shoulder. He was a middle-aged guy. He had longish sandy hair but was balding, so the hair was combed over. Jeremy Thorpe MP was responsible for popularising that abomination. He wore a big-collared mid-blue shirt and, it being Saturday night, the top two buttons were undone. His chest was hairy and he was probably drawing attention to that, but he hadn't had the nerve to add a medallion. He was with a couple of mates, about the same age. He kept stealing glances, but daredn't look directly at Lee for any length of time.

After five minutes, the discrepancy between the shyness of the guy and the boldness of Lee, who had begun staring at him, became amusing. So Lee laughed; the guy smiled bashfully and the two mates, who'd been monitoring the flirtation (one of them rather crossly, presumably jealous), were starting to realise that their pal had actually pulled.

He looked over again and that was it: trademark. All three clocked it, and the guy went red. As Lee moved in, glass in hand, the other two retreated, and one of them – the one who hadn't looked cross, so the nicer of the two – put his hand on the chosen guy's shoulder as if to say, 'Good luck, mate.' He might also have given him a quick word of warning. The chosen guy was certainly looking nervous as Lee smiled and said, 'Hello.'

That was enough. After the excited introductions – Lee called himself Andy, and the guy was Kenneth – they fell into easy conversation. Lee played it cool but kind, whereas Kenneth would talk in excited flurries before going red and apologising. He was perpetually on the brink, Lee felt, of saying, 'This is amazing; I can hardly believe my luck,' and for this Lee found that he rather liked him.

Lee said he was in the fashion business.

'Yes,' said Kenneth, 'I can see that. I dread to think what you must make of my outfit.'

Kenneth was fey but not stupid, so Lee would resist the temptation to tell him that his shirt matched his eyes. 'Clothes are overrated,' he said. 'It's the person that's important.'

Kenneth worked for British Rail. He was 'in costings at Euston', and it wasn't necessary to talk about this, thank heavens.

'Where do you live?' Lee asked.

'Oh, way out. Wood Green I'm afraid. What about you?'

'Marylebone,' said Lee, because while Kenneth was flirting with Lee, Lee was flirting with danger.

'Marylebone's nice,' said Kenneth.

'It's a decent flat,' said Lee, 'but small, and I'd better not live too long, because the lease is pretty short!'

Lee's heart was making its presence known – that pleasant, fluttering sensation that came when he said things that could give him away. But he couldn't take Kenneth back to the flat, so he said, 'I've got the decorators in at the moment.'

'You can come back to mine if you like,' said Kenneth. 'Just don't expect too much.'

When they came out of the pub, Kenneth led Lee to what turned out to be a bus stop, and Kenneth fitted into the bus queue quite naturally, which Lee in his white suit did not. Kenneth was saying, 'It's the number twenty-nine we're after. The frequency's pretty good. It terminates at a pub around the corner from my place. We can pick up a bottle of wine from the off sales. Or I have some home-brew if you can stand it.'

Kenneth's a very old-fashioned person, thought Lee. If he could go home on a tram, he would do. The bus was possibly late. The queue kept getting longer, and everyone in it was staring at Lee, as being so obviously not a bus person, which was exciting in a way – because he was the star of the queue, and everyone else in it was a potential witness against him. But there were limits, and he was being not merely fancied but closely scrutinised by a cross-section of Londoners. Kenneth, who'd been nattering away about the heat – 'Hotter than Honolulu!' – realised Lee's discomfort.

'We can take a cab,' he said, 'if you prefer.'

'Right you are,' said Lee. 'I'll pay.'

'We'll go Dutch,' said Kenneth.

But then the bus turned up.

'Can you bear it?' said Kenneth, for whom money was clearly tight. Lee nodded graciously (he thought), implying that it would be interesting to see how the other half lived.

On the bus, Kenneth kept giving Lee sidelong glances as they sat side by side, but these stopped when Lee put his hand on Kenneth's upper thigh. Kenneth became too excited to look at Lee after that. Lee could almost feel – relayed along the grubby cushion of the shared seat – the pounding of Kenneth's heart, whereas his own had gone back to sleep. As they were going past the grotty hotel-land of King's Cross, he gave himself a jolt of adrenalin by slipping the folder from his trouser pocket and glancing down at it.

When they reached the terminus, Kenneth had to adjust his trousers on rising to his feet. Lee smiled at him and stroked the back of his hair, even though the only other person left on board – the bus conductor – was staring at them.

A minute later, as they were walking down some incredibly hot, battered street, whose inhabitants seemed keen to flaunt their overflowing dustbins in their front yards, Kenneth was laughing. He said, 'I'm not sure I'm going to be able to show my face on the number twenty-nine ever again!'

'Don't your straight friends know you're gay?'

'Not a one,' he said, in his quaint way.

They didn't bother picking up wine, since Kenneth remembered he had a bottle of claret, which he'd earmarked for his sister's birthday, but he could get another before then. As they walked, Lee noticed that Kenneth wore a pair of high-waisters whose flares stopped well short of the tops of his two-tone brogues. He would look much better in the kind of sober suit he presumably wore to work.

The flat was small, so Lee complimented the house it was in – which was big, if crumbling, and with an exceptionally fine display of dustbins out front. Kenneth led Lee straight into what was really the only room apart from the kitchenette. The odd thing was that Lee couldn't see a bed. The room was neat, old-fashioned, predominantly brown with not one but two heavy sideboards, each with many framed photos on top.

'Family,' said Kenneth, seeing where Lee was looking.

'Do *they* know you're gay?'

'I think my dad does. For years, he would ask if I had a

girlfriend, then he just stopped asking, so I think the penny had dropped, and he didn't want to pursue the matter because then it might drop with my mother as well. What about yours?'

'Both dead,' said Lee, with satisfaction. 'My old man knew and hated it. My mum didn't seem to mind. She thought I was a genius, and geniuses are allowed to be gay.' Lee wondered whether this was the wine talking. It was good wine and he was enjoying the conversation. Kenneth was sitting on the sofa.

'Please sit down,' he said.

Lee took the opposite armchair. Then they both laughed, and he moved next to Kenneth, who said, 'Your mum thought you were a genius at designing clothes, did she? Or were you just an *all-round* genius? My money would be on the latter.'

'She thought I was a genius at music,' said Lee.

'Music? You *are* a dark horse.'

'I used to be in a pop group, and I wrote songs.'

'Ah! Now, I'm afraid I don't know much about the pop scene.'

'The group was called Picture Show,' said Lee, sentencing Kenneth to death.

'I'm afraid I'm rather fuddy-duddy in my tastes,' said Kenneth, indicating the record player on the floor, with LPs propped along-side. The uppermost sleeve showed a man leaning on a piano – a man very ill-advised in his choice of sweater. It was one of those 'Fred Smith plays Bach' deals, and Lee never knew whether you were supposed to be buying the record to hear the one or the other. Lee thought classical music was overrated, while pop – especially his own – was underrated.

Kenneth said, 'Trevor, who was one of the two chaps with me in the pub tonight, is always going on at me to listen to Bob Dylan.'

'I wouldn't bother.'

'You don't like him?'

'I don't. His songs just seem to go on for ever. It's all ... declaiming. It's really completely exhausting.'

'I tend to agree. You're looking at the bookshelf?'

'You ever read any French philosophy?'

'Gosh.'

'Ever heard of Situationism?'

'I'm afraid not. I tend to read a lot of rather trashy fiction.'

Lee rose to his feet, glass in hand, and there was a gasp of disappointment from Kenneth. He looked on apprehensively as Lee glanced into the kitchenette. It was odd not to see a white space with a breakfast bar. Instead there was a single heavy chair facing a small but very solid brown table. Lee turned away. Crossing the main room, he looked at himself in the mirror – one of those fake Edwardian ones – and played with his hair for a second. He wasn't sure about this side parting after all. The wallpaper was woodchip, painted a kind of flesh colour. The only art was a framed poster, advertising a concert by the Allegri Quartet. There was a grey wall-phone. The room was over-carpeted.

'Love the rugs,' said Lee, returning to the sofa, and receiving a second helping of claret from grateful Kenneth.

'Oh, thanks. I make them myself.'

Lee frowned. 'How can you do that without a factory?'

'Ever heard of Rug-Plan? Something to do on the long winter nights.'

After a moment of reverent silence, Kenneth said, 'You know, it sounds silly, but I feel honoured to have you here.'

'Don't say that.'

'But don't you think I'm just terribly old?'

'Not for a minute,' said Lee (because the antiquated phraseology of Kenneth was proving contagious). 'Honoured, indeed! You make me sound like the Queen ... rather than just *a* queen.'

'But you must have a bloke of your own? Then again I suppose not, or else you wouldn't be here. Oh, I don't know, Andy. Tell you what . . . I'll just shut up, shall I?'

'Yes, Kenneth,' said Lee. 'You shut up,' and he kissed him, which became a snog.

'Shall I make up the bed?' said Kenneth after a while.

'Where is it?' said Lee.

'We're sitting on it – this is a sofa bed.'

'Probably not necessary,' said Lee, and the folder was unfolded in his hand.

As Lee walked away from the house, heading for Tube or taxi, a succession of cop cars went screaming past in the hot night.

Kenneth was surely the one who would tip the balance. Lee had done his bit, and now it was over to the two fellows who'd been in The Salisbury, one of whom was called Trevor. Surely they were conscientious fellows? Surely they would report that the trademark had been given?

Sunday.

Paris and Oxford

On Sunday morning in Paris, Howard joined a bleary crowd on the Metro for the change to Gare du Nord. On the terrace of a café opposite that station, he ate two fried eggs and drank coffee amid traffic fumes. Approaching the train to Calais, which waited in a cloud of subtly different fumes, he picked up a paper off a newspaper trolley.

He found a compartment that was empty – it was also dusty and blue – and opened all the windows. Then he unfolded his paper. The *Continental Daily Mail* was the emissary of much bad news, perhaps even more than usual. Two women had been found murdered in London – one in Chelsea, one off Oxford Street. Police were 'comparing notes' on the files of the two murders. The novelty of the heatwave had definitely worn off. Four hundred people had been treated for exposure to the sun. Houses were cracking and crumbling. There'd been a row at Lord's cricket ground about whether or not jackets could be dispensed with in the pavilion.

. . . Which reminded Howard of his new, cool clothes. He kept glimpsing himself in the grubby glass of the train window, and he congratulated himself on having been transformed by the magic touch of a glamorous woman. He was like Leo, the young errand runner in *The Go-Between* by L.P. Hartley, who was relieved of his heavy tweeds and relaunched for the hot summer of 1911 by the beautiful Marian. (The pair of them were heading for disaster, of course.)

Southern England was oppressed both by sticky heat and the fact of Sunday. The train to London seemed to be toiling uphill all the way. Howard crossed the city in a smoking carriage of the Circle Line, and he killed time before the Oxford train by walking the scruffy streets. Every car, moving away from every set of lights, seemed to give him a black smoke kiss-off. And he kept seeing punk rockers. He'd forgotten about punks. There'd been none in Nice. They seemed naturally to congregate near litter bins and scenes of dereliction.

On the train to Oxford, he thought with resentment of his destination. It threw down its gauntlet to any intelligent young person: to apply for a place or resist its lure. Its agents – usually old Oxonians – were abroad in the world, and they would try to flog you the Dreaming Spires fantasy.

The Eastgate Hotel was mock-baronial, with exposed wood

beams, swords and shields over the fireplaces. He spent the night in various pubs, where alcoholism went hand in hand with a certain formality. In an ancient, tiny pub called The Bear – presumably built at a time when people had been much smaller – he heard a fat, perspiring vicar begin a sentence with the word 'Thirteenthly . . . '

The colleges were pretty, but the grass was dying on the lawns, and where the rooms were uncurtained there was a kind of hospital light. In the hotel, Howard didn't sleep much: he missed Emma (an emotion to which he felt he was not entitled) and he was worried about the letter he was destined to receive from Charles. Maybe it would never arrive, and he could go straight back to Nice.

Sunday evening.

London

Geoff knew of a pub that suited Sunday. It was in one of those little streets between Baker Street and Marylebone where every day, in effect, *was* Sunday. It was small and dark with a melancholy old man vibe, and Geoff liked it for the depressing reason that it served cheap beer: 31p a pint. (If you stuck to revolting Watneys.) There was a big ugly TV on a high shelf, and one of those Sunday melodramas was playing with the sound turned down. A sign on the door said NO DRINKS OUTSIDE, so you were trapped.

Geoff was indicating some small cuts on his big, bass player's hands.

'Been laying crazy paving all week. It's something Pam's always wanted for the back garden. You know, forget about planting any actual plants. You'd think it'd be a doddle, laying crazy paving.

The name – crazy paving – makes you think it's just a random process, but very far from it. Imagine if doing a jigsaw was really back-breaking work. That'll give you some idea.'

The weather had put paid to Geoff's usual donkey jacket, thank God. But he'd turned up in a tartan flat cap, which had also – in combination with a lot of sweat – flattened his hair. Lee himself was wearing a cap: a Breton fisherman's cap, technically speaking, but everybody now called them Donovan caps. Lee didn't care for Donovan. *They call me mellow yellow?* It wasn't what Lee called the whimsical twit. He was be-hatted because he didn't know what to do with his hair post Kenneth. A new look was required. Maybe get a perm, like Bolan or that bloke who fronted Mungo Jerry? But perms were for footballers. Meanwhile, it was very fortunate that his drinking companion wasn't too observant.

Geoff was eating a bag of crisps. They were round – Discos, they were called: *The new kind of crisp.* He offered one to Lee, who shook his head so Geoff finished the crisps by up-ending the packet into his mouth. He folded the packet into a ribbon, tied a knot in it, and put it into the ashtray, on which was printed BEN TRUMAN, EXPORT DRAUGHT, and just when Lee thought Geoff couldn't possibly get more annoying, he cracked his knuckles. *If he does that again*, thought Lee, *I'm off.* He wondered why Geoff kept bothering to maintain the connection, given Lee's discouragement, but he knew the answer really: *Geoff is fascinated by me. In all his years of making music, I'm the only person he's met with any talent.*

It was Lee's turn to buy the next round. He didn't like going up to the bar in this pub. The landlord – who was the main server – clearly thought he was a weirdo and the barmaid didn't fancy him, which was quite unusual, but then she was kicking fifty with a beehive hairdo, so she probably went for the older gentleman.

'Tell you what,' said Geoff, when Lee returned with the drinks, '. . . made a bit of a musical breakthrough this week.'

'What are you on about?' said Lee. 'You're not playing any music.'

'Well, not as such, but I give lessons on the bass, as you would know if you'd been paying attention. Remember how – when we were doing the album – I was going for that really woody bass sound McCartney gets on *Rubber Soul* and *Revolver*? And we just couldn't get it on the old Fender Precision? You remember I was moving the pick-up about when you were doing the backing vocals on "Perplexity"?'

'Yes, which you were supposed to be helping with.'

(The one graceful thing about Geoff: he could harmonise nicely.)

'Well, the answer,' he said, 'is flatwound strings used along with this baby.' He produced from his pocket a soft, outsize plectrum. 'Felt. And the key is to play it just behind the split coil pick-up.'

In protest at this muso tedium, Lee took his very latest pair of sunglasses from his pocket and put them on.

'New shades?' said Geoff. 'They're kind of . . . I don't know . . . streamlined.'

'Geoffrey,' said Lee, removing the shades, 'do me a favour. Buy yourself a thesaurus.'

'I've got one, mate.'

'Then bloody well read it.'

They drank in silence for a while, then Lee said, 'What do you make of the punk rockers?'

'Not much,' said Geoff, and he cracked his bloody knuckles. 'Hitch saw one outfit at the Marquee last week.' (Hitch – aka Donald Hitchens, ex of about fifty boring bands – was another

bassist.) 'They were called . . . I don't know. The Fucking
Idiots or something. Hitch said they were about as tight as a
circus net.'

'But I think they've got something – the punks in general I mean.'

'Like what?'

'Energy. The ability to disrupt the Spectacle, create a Situation.
You ever read any Guy Debord?'

'No, but I've heard you banging on about him. Guy De*boring*
I call him. Let's face it, dude, you only like the punks because
they're slagging off all the people you're jealous of: the Stones,
Roxy, Bolan, et cetera.'

Lee shook his head, although this was quite correct. The landlord now stepped out from behind the bar and turned up the TV.
It was news time, and everybody in the pub watched.

Lee was annoyed to see that he did not make the headlines.
The US Treasury was now warning about the state of Britain's
economy. The heat came next: trees dying off, threat of a water
shortage. Obviously, the cops hadn't found Kenneth yet. Well,
the poor guy had as good as said he was lonely, and that wouldn't
necessarily end just because he was dead. Five minutes into the
bulletin, Detective Chief Inspector Wallace turned up in his
dreadful suit and polyester tie – somebody should tell the guy
that a tie knot was supposed to be generously proportioned. It
seemed he had moved on from 'comparing notes' about the killings of Victoria and May. A 'joint incident room' had now been
set up. It also seemed that a man had come forward to report his
wife missing. Maybe she'd been killed by the 'homicidal maniac'
suspected of having done for the other two; and there was a picture of this bird – a complete stranger to Lee. It was all becoming
rather a mess.

The TV news gave way to the sport, with footage of what seemed to be tracts of desert, but then the pavilions would come into view, and you realised they were cricket pitches.

But after the sport, there was an unexpected return to news. There had been a development in the murder hunt, and here was Wallace again, giving a press conference, which required other men in cheap suits to sit alongside him, sweating silently. Another body had been found in a flat in north London: 'a male in his forties'. He was believed to have been murdered by the killer of Victoria and May. *How have they worked that out?* Lee wondered with fast-rising excitement.

Here came the explanation. 'The man we are looking for,' said Wallace, 'encountered all his victims in a social situation prior to the killings and they left that social situation in company with him. In every case it appears that he initiated the contact by winking at the person concerned.'

It was as if he were reading from a script written by Lee himself. And just look at the effect: the entire pub was rapt!

Geoff leant forward. 'Guess what they're going to be calling this guy?'

Lee, smiling, said, 'You are now going to make a very obvious remark.'

'The Winker. I bet he's pissed off about that. I mean, it's only one letter off *wanker.*'

'. . . Which *you* undoubtedly are, my friend.'

'Well, needs must!'

The news was now over, so the landlord was back at the set, turning it down.

'You can see the logic, I suppose,' said Lee.

'Eh?'

Lee wondered whether he should elaborate. In the end, he

couldn't resist. 'Well, he kills them twice. Or it's like a sentence of death, then the sentence is carried out.'

'What's logical about that? The cat must be mentally ill.'

'One thing I'm curious about,' Lee said happily. 'Why don't they produce a photo-fit picture of this guy?' He thought that Geoff, as an employee on a Sunday paper, albeit a part-time and half-arsed one, might have an answer to this conundrum.

'They might publish one internally in Police Reports,' Geoff said. 'But if the cops don't trust the witnesses – say they think they were drunk, or something – then they don't bother putting out a photo-fit that's probably inaccurate. I mean, that would do more harm than good, right?'

'Right,' said Lee. 'Or if they suspect they guy of changing his appearance on a regular basis?'

'Yeah.'

'Hey,' said Geoff, 'it was *your* thing, wasn't it? Winking at the chicks in the audience.'

'The old trademark, yeah.'

'My shout,' said Geoff.

'No, I'll get 'em,' said Lee. 'Tell you what, I could go for a bottle of bubbly. Will you join me?'

'Christ almighty, what's going on?'

'Oh, nothing much. I think I'm going to start writing again.'

'Songs, you mean? Ace. Good on you, Jonesy! I sometimes play our demos to the kids who come in for lessons, and I tell you they're blown away, man. Blown away every time.'

The beehive lady, being quite thick, was nonplussed when Lee ordered the bottle. She had to go into the cellar to fetch it, and she came up flustered; had to get the landlord to uncork it and then couldn't find an ice bucket. He had shaken her up, and this was the whole point. He would be shaking somebody else up in the next couple of days – an old enemy he'd never met – and this would require a little trip out of town. It was all part of the sub-plot; a sort of spin-off from the programme.

When Lee set the ice bucket down on the table, Geoff said, 'Right on!' He cracked his knuckles in pleasurable anticipation, and Lee didn't mind. All bass players cracked their knuckles, and they did other oafish things like shivering their legs when they were sitting down. They didn't know any better, so you just had to put up with it. The evening ended in a cordiality that had not existed between them since the formation of Picture Show, and this was all down to the programme. Hitherto, he and Geoff had been two failures. Now, only one of them was a failure, because Lee had broken through at last.

Monday.

Oxford

The letter from Paris didn't arrive until mid-afternoon. The desk clerk who passed it to Howard wore a twisted grin, as though he knew it spelt trouble for the recipient – and the letter *was* irritating. It was signed simply *Charles* and with no address, but only a repetition of the phone number of the Parisian bar. The letter was full of confidence that Howard would be in Oxford to receive it, with the two hundred and fifty pounds (or what remained of it after his initial expenses) in his pocket, and there were thanks for his compliance, which only increased Howard's feeling of having been manipulated. The letter began with general instructions. He was to find Pat Price, then assess his character and state of mind either by direct contact or external indicators. In the most patronising sentence, Howard was urged to use his novelist's skill to extrapolate from these. It would be equally useful to Charles to know whether Pat Price was washed up or prospering, in good health or steady decline. Above all, did he seem mentally stable? And Charles would be grateful for any practical details about Price. Was he still working, and if so where? Where did he live? With whom did he associate?

Then came some sparse facts about his quarry.

Pat Price had been a postgraduate student of mathematics – in Oxford on some bursary or scholarship from the States – who had possibly become a teacher or an academic. Howard had never heard of the college Price had attended (which he assumed was the same one Charles had attended), but – with the letter in his hand – he quickly verified that it occupied a prestigious enough plot south of the High Street. He watched people walking through the main gate, which, being medieval, was too small for most of them. It was as though they were going in and out of a portal to the past. It seemed that Charles had already discovered, over the phone from France, that the college no longer held any address for Pat Price. (There would also be no point looking for him in the telephone directory; he was not in it, as Charles had already verified from Paris.)

The letter informed Howard that, as a musician, Price had performed in the Holywell Music Rooms on Holywell Street. Insofar as he used a regular pub it was the Turf Tavern, for which no address was given. Howard was advised to ask after Price at something called the Mathematical Institute on St Giles. A brief description of Price was supplied. He was – or had been a quarter of a century ago – something over six foot tall, burly and dark featured with thinning black hair. He was scruffy; he tended to wear a mac of the usual beige colour, dark trousers and suede

114

shoes. He always carried a thin music manuscript case. He was from New York and spoke with that accent. By now he might be Dr Pat Price, since he had been working on a PhD; he might even be Professor. He would be in his mid-fifties or pushing sixty. Charles conceded that Price might no longer be in Oxford at all, but it seemed he had loved the place as much as Charles had hated it and that he had – as a young man – disavowed any intention of returning to the States.

It seemed to Howard that he was entangled in the whims of two over-intellectual men. But he began trudging to the Mathematics faculty – which turned out to be a modern building with a rustic-sounding, un-modern doorkeeper, who transcribed the address of some woman that Howard would have to write to in order to pursue his enquiry. Asked whether he himself had ever heard of Pat Price, the man shook his head, not so much saying 'no' as refusing the question altogether.

Howard decided he was not going to proceed via mathematics. He embarked on aimless wandering, although telling himself he was looking for Price. The colleges were like little collections of churches, and – he was getting the hang of things – they were guarded by porters in lodges. He was beginning to see a lot of students in black suits and gowns. When you got into Oxford, you were in effect given a ticket to a fancy-dress party – and the usual accessory was a bottle of champagne. These people so attired were exam finishers. A little way out of the centre, he saw a clutch of the female equivalents: you noticed the blondes, because their hair offset the black gowns so well. If he talked to anyone from the university, Howard was going to find it very hard to avoid saying he'd got a first; and there was always the novel to bring in.

Everything in this town was a cut above, and there were a lot of interesting cars. He saw a silver Bentley and – outside an exceptionally big college – a really stunning dark green Citroën DS, which was shaped like a diagram of wind flow over something highly aerodynamic – and it was one of the later ones, with two headlamps under glass on either side. The indicators, set high on either side of the rear window, were like rocket thrusters. He imagined himself, in this town, driving that car, a bestselling author.

Howard's sixth-form English teacher, Mr Cassidy, a graduate of Balliol – the top college, he always implied – had encouraged Howard to 'have a go' for Oxford, and this had had the opposite of the intended effect. It had been Howard's cue not to apply, because he had taken Mr Cassidy's encouragement as an indication that he would have got in, and it was not necessary to put that to the test. (Whether cowardice had come into it . . . he did not care to think about that.)

It was half past two, and extremely hot, so Howard bought an ice cream from a high-minded corner shop that sold *Le Monde* and the *New York Times*. The Oxford evening paper was piled up next to the till, andhe front page was odd: an illustration of a pair of eyes, one of them closed, and the word KILLER. But Howard didn't usually bother with the papers, certainly not local papers. Trudging on, he saw a bookshop: Blackwell's. He'd rather not have noticed it, because now he was obliged to enact a ritual that always ended in humiliation. He walked in and marched up to 'M' on the fiction shelf. His book wasn't there. *Accept the fact and gracefully retreat*, commanded a sensible voice in his head, but he ignored the voice, as he always did. He went up to the counter, where he asked the assistant in an aggressive tone: 'Have you heard of a book called *Marsh*?'

'Doesn't ring any bells. What kind of book is it?'

'Fiction.'

'Oh, I was thinking natural science.'

Howard was braced for the standard humiliations, but there would always be these unexpected refinements.

'Do you know the author?' enquired the assistant.

'Howard Miller.'

Even that triggered a sceptical look, as though the name didn't ring true, but the assistant was now leafing through an enormous volume familiar to Howard: *Whitaker's Guide to Books in Print*. This would tell him whether *Marsh*, by Howard Miller, had been published, a question to which Howard already knew the answer. 'Not to worry,' he said, 'I'll try elsewhere,' and, turning away, he saw Pat Price.

He was browsing in fiction – but then why shouldn't a mathematician read novels? He didn't wear a mac, but nobody would in this weather. He wore a fawn cotton jacket over a white shirt; black trousers and ... not suede but soft shoes nonetheless. He was certainly scruffy and balding. Wait though: surely a man balding twenty-five years ago would be *bald* by now. But Howard had already asked, 'Excuse me, are you Pat Price?'

The man turned and smoothly said, 'No, I am not,' as though he were often asked that question. But that wasn't the end of the matter. He was looking at Howard with interest. 'Pat Price?' he said. 'Musician?'

'Amongst other things, yes.'

'I think you'll find him in the King's Arms.'

'Really?' said Howard, realising he was being churlishly sceptical towards this helpful stranger. 'I was told the Turf Tavern was his pub?'

'Nope. He's a regular at the King's Arms, or he was in my own drinking days.'

So Charles's letter had misdirected Howard: his resentment of

117

him deepened. Outside the shop, the man pointed towards the King's Arms: it was at the end of Holywell Street, whereas the Turf Tavern was *off* Holywell Street. Howard felt that Pat Price was near at hand, but it was too early to go into a pub, so he resumed his roaming for a while.

At six o'clock he was in the King's Arms, along with the increasingly raucous exam-finishers. The men relished the contrast between their modernity – as expressed by long hair and side-burns – and their old-fashioned examination garb. A lot of them seemed to be equipped with pretty girlfriends. Maybe Howard would have been so equipped had he gone to Oxford. As he waited to be served, he pictured himself whimsically dressed on the campus at York: he'd worn a bus conductor's cap for the best part of a year. He winced at that – and when recalling the wintry morning he'd spent in the middle of the town, selling white poppies to show off his moral superiority. The most embarrassing memory was of his association with a campaign to get condom machines put in the gents' toilets. His bravado had been checked by a brutal law student called Armstrong who'd asked, 'Why are *you* so bothered about this?' Howard was not often seen in the company of women. He knew he was thought to be gay, the option of heterosexual ineptitude having been – perhaps quite charitably – ruled out.

He realised he was in the secondary bar of the King's Arms, a sort of snug. The evening sun didn't belong here, but it was stealing in. Over the bar counter, you could see the action in the big room, but it seemed far off. In this back room were many photographs of people drinking in the same back room, which was obviously a quasi-club, an inner sanctum. There were about a dozen drinkers, mainly men. They tended to be either balding hippies or tweedy, older men who tended not to be balding, which must irritate the hippies.

Howard took a high stool at the bar, next to a hippy who was smoking a roll-up and reading a paperback. Howard lit a Black Cat. He always tried to see what books people were reading, and he always disapproved when he found out. In the case of this guy, he suspected something pseudo-mystical: Herman Hesse, say. But it turned out – when he laid the book down to order another pint – to be *The Collected Dashiell Hammett.*

'Hammett's great, isn't he?' Howard said.

'Yeah.'

Howard had his opening, better capitalise: 'He's more elegant than Chandler, I think. Tougher.'

That was a wanky thing to say, but he'd got away with it, because the guy said, 'Yeah. I'm on *Red Harvest* just now.'

'My favourite's *The Glass Key.* I didn't understand the plot though. That business about the missing hat.'

The hippy was reading again. The opening seemed to be closing, and Howard was quite glad. He was like a detective in reverse, in that he didn't actually want to find Pat Price. He wanted to be able to say he'd done his best, though, so he gave the hippy one more chance.

'I'm a crime writer myself,' he said.

'Yeah?' said the hippy, looking up from Hammett.

'Well, I've only done one book. It was called *Marsh.*'

'Read it,' said the hippy, and he put the Hammett down. Howard had now completely forgotten about Pat Price. He was waiting for the guy's follow-up, because sometimes people would say they'd read your book, then immediately drop the subject. The guy was taking a long pull on his pint. If he was going to say he liked the book, he was certainly taking his time about it. The drunken students had left the main bar, but it was still raucous in an older way. A tarty middle-aged woman was being approached by the barman. Howard could see his back, and her face. She winked at the barman, who said, 'Now I've read the news and that's not funny, love!', causing Howard to recall that day's *Oxford News*.

'Yeah, *Marsh*,' said the hippy, 'about the retired copper who keeps a file of old cases in his garden shed.'

'His *garage*. And it's really only one old case.'

'That's it. Which he investigates by going around the country in his old caravan.'

'The Astral Scout.' (Howard liked proper nouns: if they were good they were more vivid than the generic word for the thing described, and if they weren't good there was a poignancy about them.) 'Marsh used to go on holidays with his wife in it, but then she was killed. So that's the –'

'It's interesting to have an unsympathetic hero. I mean, the guy's right wing.'

'He's conservative with a small "c".'

'And anti-social, ugly – bald. And violent, with that pistol he keeps in the glove compartment of his motor.'

'The Browning nine millimetre, and the car's a Volvo.'

'Course. The Volvo. Like I say, I've read the book.'

Come on, thought Howard, *you can do it: say you liked it.*

'Yeah,' the hippy slowly said, 'it was good.'

'Do you want another pint?' asked Howard, elated beyond reason.

'I'm fine,' said the hippy, slightly bewildered. 'I've just bought one.'

But Howard insisted, and the thing now was to drop the subject of the book before the guy could backtrack on his approval, because people would add riders like, 'Obviously, you had a problem with the ending.' Howard said, 'You don't happen to know a guy called Pat Price, do you?'

The hippy was glugging beer again. 'Price?' he said eventually. 'I did know him a bit.'

'He's left town, I think?'

'You could say that.'

'You mean?'

'This is a bit like the sort of conversation your man Marsh gets involved in, isn't it? I hate to break it to you if he was a friend of yours, but Pat Price died about a year ago.'

Howard's notebook was in front of him, but he'd look stupid if he wrote that down.

'Do you happen to know what of?'

'Natural causes – if that's what you call cigarettes. No, sorry, it was the pipe that killed him. Throat cancer.'

'Could I ask . . . How do you know this?'

'Hearsay. Pub gossip. Of course, if you really were a friend of his, you'd know yourself.'

So there was a bit of steel to this hippy, who was indicating the photographs: 'If you're a regular here and you die, they put your picture up there.'

'It's some compensation, I suppose,' said Howard, looking at the photos. He might be able to pick out Price from the description Charles had provided, but he'd better not prolong the bluff. 'He's more like a friend of a *friend* really, and this person's asked me to find out about him.'

The hippy obviously didn't think much of that, and Howard pocketed his notebook, to show he could take no for an answer. The case was closed, he could go back to Nice. But he remembered he was supposed to report back on the guy's character. It would be good to throw in that detail: last known state of mind. So he said, 'What was he like, just out of interest?'

'Seemed a very nice guy. Bit nutty in a mad professor way. The man was gay of course. Tell you what, there's a cat over there who might be able to throw a bit of light on it all.'

The hippy was pointing into the main bar, and he did seem to be indicating a human cat: a small man wearing green shades. His face was perfectly symmetrical, and he had a hell of a lot of black hair, possibly dyed. It was the sort of face that must determine his profession, in which case he was an actor or male model. Or he might be a pretty jockey. He wore a loose white suit with double-breasted jacket, offset by a tight green T-shirt: a confident Mick Jagger outfit, playing with formality. It was hard to believe there wasn't some chic female in his immediate vicinity, but he was apparently alone. He was looking in the general direction of Howard and the hippy, although it was impossible to say *exactly* where he was looking. But then he lifted the shades and propped them in his hair. He was staring back at Howard – and the revelation was that there was no revelation: his eyes were as green as the shades had been, and Howard and he were in a staring match, with the hippy looking on.

'Well, you've caught *his* attention,' said the hippy.

Howard was finding it hard to look away. There was something doll-like about the man: a ventriloquist's dummy, with the same kind of emptiness; yet also a kind of glitter – a potential for surprise. He was now lowering his sunglasses, drawing down the blinds.

'Who is he?' said Howard.

'A musician, maybe. He's still watching us, you know. He used to come in here a bit with Price. It was a while ago, mind – maybe five years, but you don't forget a face like that. *You* won't forget it either, will you?'

'Bit odd,' said Howard, thinking aloud, 'that he's here after all that time just when I'm looking for Price.' (The hippy said nothing to that.) 'So he was Price's boyfriend?'

'Could be. A bit out of Price's league as a physical specimen, but maybe Price was his, you know . . . '

'What?'

Howard had to wait, because the hippy was drinking again. 'Sugar daddy,' he said eventually. 'If you want information on Price, he's your man.'

But the doll-like man was heading for the door. Excusing himself to the hippy, Howard was after him, but he was checked by bumping into a woman in the saloon (apologies were required), and on stepping out of the pub he saw nothing but an empty road in the continuing heat. He looked right just in time to see his quarry – two hundred yards off – stepping into a car, and it was the beautiful green Citroën of the afternoon. Clearly, the little bloke had a thing about green. Howard should have been running towards the car, but he was hypnotised by the sight of the thing rising from its rear, like a sprinter going into the 'set' position before the start of a race. This was the hydraulic system being pressurised. Everything in that car – steering, brakes, gears, suspension – was powered by hydraulics, and the stuff that powered the system was itself green, Howard believed: some kind of vegetable oil. And now it was off: like a horizontal space rocket. Howard couldn't make out the registration. He walked back into the pub where the hippy was drinking and reading at the same time.

'Missed him.'

'Too bad.'

'You don't know where I might track him down, do you?'

'London.'

This was where Howard was supposed to say, 'London's a big place.' But the hippy was trying – slowly – to help. 'I think he was in a band rather than solo, because I remember Price saying,

"There's one real musician in the ensemble. The fellow on the bass." The bassist could read music, or something.'

'What was the style?'

'Probably not anything prog or heavy, otherwise I'd know of them.'

'A pop band then?'

'Yeah. An unpopular pop band, operating about five years ago, and maybe still. I think they had a record out in 1970, '71, but it stiffed on release.'

Howard drained his glass. 'Thanks, you've been very helpful.'

'You got a phone number?' the hippy asked, unexpectedly. 'A couple of people who come in here might be able to give you a better steer.'

After consulting his notebook, Howard gave the hippy the number of the flat in Nice.

The hippy said, 'You bringing whatsisname – Marsh – back for another outing?'

This checked Howard. 'No,' he said. 'He died at the end – killed himself after nailing the main villain.' In view of the man's kindness, it would be churlish to add ' . . . if you remember.' But he was cross, so he did it anyway.

'Yeah,' said the hippy. 'Course he did.'

Out in the street, the light was beginning to fade. Howard could tell, because a phone box on a lonely corner was just beginning to glow. It called Howard to his duty and he walked slowly over. Inside, picking up the receiver, he thought: *I can pretend I've seen nothing. I can sign off from the whole thing by saying 'Price is dead.'* He dialled the number in his notebook, picturing the Tabac de la Jardin: the cabinet labelled CAVE A CIGARES, the fag ends and bent Metro tickets in the ashtrays (because Parisians stubbed out their Metro tickets as well as their fags), the chubby barman with a towel over his shoulder and pen behind his ear. When you paid him, you put the money in a little plastic tray, and when he extracted the money, he flipped the tray like a conjuror. You weren't supposed to put money directly into people's hands. It was another trap the French had set for the un-French to fall into. But he wanted to go back there. Perhaps Nice would become his home. There would be a slow acclimatisation to it, and to Emma. He pictured the dust jacket of a bestselling novel: *Howard Miller is married with two children. He divides his time between Nice and . . .*

The phone was still ringing. Perhaps it would never be answered. Howard pictured himself writing regretfully to Charles care of the *tabac*: 'I tried calling again and again but there was never any answer. Regarding Pat Price, I regret to have to tell you . . .' But suddenly he was listening to the clamour of happy hour in the Tabac de la Jardin. It was presumably the proprietor who had picked up, and he was now saying something in French, naturally enough. It didn't matter what. All Howard could say was, *'Je voudrais parler avec Charles,'* which was not at first understood. He attempted to modify the phrase, only to be interrupted by the shout: *'Charles! Telephone, s'il vous plait.'*

'Allo. Qui est la?'

'It's Howard.'

'How are you?'

'I'm fine. Pat Price isn't though. He's dead.'

Howard had put it that way in revenge for the telephonic humiliation he had just suffered. He immediately regretted doing so – it had been unworthy to try shocking Charles in that way. He might be upset at the news of Price's death; or then again he might be delighted. As Howard told what he knew – and of course he told everything – Charles gave no clue as to his emotions. His reaction was muted and reserved, indicative – unfortunately – of a man planning out his next move, which would in practice be Howard's next move.

He listened to his new set of instructions.

Monday evening.
Paris

In the Jardin du Luxembourg, the little sailing boats on the pond swooned and swayed, as though defeated by the heat of the day; or of the evening, since it was now nearly seven o'clock. The average age of the sailors, Charles thought, was about nine. When the boats came too close to the stone banks, they prodded them away with bamboo canes, but sometimes they prodded too hard, and the boat drifted towards the turbulent waters around the central fountain. Some children panicked at this – the ones who didn't know that any boat bobbing away would eventually bob back.

The crime he had committed twenty-five years ago was now bobbing back towards Charles. Pat Price, being dead, had not sent the cards. Somebody had inherited the secret of 1951 from him, presumably a lover of his, and they had shown themselves to be a less benign custodian of it. At best they were trying to inflict psychological torment. At worst, blackmail was the scenario, and they were working up to a demand for money. Charles wondered about the character in the King's Arms the boy had described: the musician. Many a young creative artist emerged from the Soho demi-monde of which Pat Price was a part-time member, and perhaps Price had embraced it more fully in the years since Charles had known him, becoming more reckless. This was indicated by his gravitation towards the King's Arms, and its rogues' gallery.

The boatman of the Jardin was now reclaiming his boats and loading them onto his barrow. Some of the little yachts had already been abandoned and left to dry on the gravel around the pond. With their sails spread out, they looked like so many dying swans.

Charles lit a cigarette.

Was he suffering psychological torment from the sending of the cards? The matter was certainly dominating his thoughts. For example, he knew that his copy of *The Times*, folded on his knees along with Syl's copy, would go unread. He assumed this week's news would be starting much as the last had ended, with unemployment and inflation rising, the murders of those young women unsolved ... and the amazing heat to keep the pot boiling. The news would have agitated him more if his own private drama had not seemed to be occurring in parallel.

But he was not suffering torment. What was happening attested to the importance of the original act, of which he remained in a way proud. It was the sole distinction he had achieved, and the secret knowledge of it had maintained his morale during the years of exile rather than undermining it, as the average armchair psychologist might have assumed. (He felt no guilt, in other words.) This pride would seem callous to the psychologist, but it wasn't pride in the killing of Neil so much as in the mental strength involved in doing the act and surviving – and getting away with it.

Now he saw that he had not necessarily got away with it, and there was more at stake than in 1951, which would only increase his pleasure at winning for a second time. The main things at stake were his pride and dignity. His pride would not survive an arrest let alone a charge and conviction. He was one of those murderers – the majority of them, he imagined – who favoured the death penalty, and he felt a frisson every time he read of a guillotining in France. But he would be charged and convicted under English law, and there would be the sordid matter of – what? – the last fifteen years of his life in prison. There was also the matter of his freedom. He needed that to look after Syl, but equally or perhaps more important was the aesthetic aspect of life, symbolised just now by the sight of the model boat man trundling his barrow down the avenue of chestnut trees, in the direction of the setting sun. Charles didn't want to lose that, any more than he wanted to lose his solo walks along the Seine, lunches at La Coupole, long – ideally rainy – afternoons in the Musée d'Orsay. In 1951, he'd fought against the stasis of his Oxford life; now he would fight equally hard to *maintain* the stasis of his Parisian life, and he would relish doing so.

Monday evening.

London

Driving back from Oxford, Lee had all the day's papers on the passenger seat. He was on every front page, and nobody knew it. This was true mystique. He knew he had been carrying himself differently all day. He'd always had the looks, now he had the presence as well. He had certainly proved an object of fascination in the King's Arms!

Lee was a good driver, and he drove fast. All the windows in the Citroën were open. To his left, the night was green and blue – green because he was passing the Hoover Building. He loved the way its neon blazed in the haze of pollution. That was real showbiz. And it was only eight o'clock; he would be home in time for a night out . . . which might end very badly for some stranger or other. But the next phase of the programme would be much harder. People would be on their guard. Anyone trademarking in a public place might be hauled in for questioning, and a beating by the cops.

So how might the next phase of the programme go? There might have to be two stages: the trademarking followed by a hasty departure from the scene; then a return to complete the job. So he would have to know in advance where the partner lived or could be found again.

He turned onto the North Circular, where the hot night sky became sooty. Glancing again at the newspapers, he tried to recall the last time he'd had another actual human on the passenger seat. Might have been as far back as 1970, when he was squiring Amanda Harvey. Squiring was the right word, funnily enough, in that they were both from the landed gentry, or that's how it appeared to outsiders. In fact, Lee was from fake landed gentry, his father having made his money in building supplies in south London ... and what a horrible collection of words that was! But Amanda Harvey ... she was practically *Lady* Amanda Harvey. Her dad had been in the government, back in the Fifties; his country seat was in Suffolk.

Amanda wouldn't have been sitting next to him in the Citroën, but in the Mini Cooper he'd bought on the strength of the album advance. They'd begun seeing each other in the late Sixties, just as Picture Show were forming. It had become evident that they both wanted to become very famous and each had selected the other as a suitable companion for that ride. Amanda had said she'd always love Lee whether he became famous or not, but she'd ditched him even before the record company when the record failed to break the top 100. She was currently hooked up with a man who presented arts programmes on BBC2. He was about as famous as an expert on paintings could be, which was not very.

Lying on top of the newspapers were a couple of postcards bearing Oxford scenes. They showed the significant territory: the vicinity of the field called Christ Church Meadow ... and the river. It was necessary to go to Oxford to get the cards, and he'd posted all three of them from there as well – for the sake of the postcode, which reinforced the message. What message exactly? That the act committed in that place by Charles Underhill had not been forgotten. That he had acquired a disciple, perhaps? But Lee had to admit that the purpose of sending the cards was not to flatter Underhill but to unsettle him. Lee had spent a lot of time thinking about the effect the cards must be having, especially now that the programme was underway. Underhill was being told that somebody knew what he had done, that the person was to be reckoned with, as they were now doing the same thing on a much bigger scale. Charles Underhill lived as a recluse in Paris, but even he must be aware of the news, and so he would be thinking about the smallness of his own achievement. But in the case of Underhill there was another, more personal consideration.

Lee had met Price in '65. Colonel Henderson was dead, and Lee was off the leash. He had never loved Pat Price. (You only had to look at the guy to appreciate why not.) But he had been kind to him, putting up with a great deal of condescension, and some downright rudeness: 'Do you ever hold a note for more than three seconds?' Price, the opera fan, had once asked him. Of course, Price *did* love Lee, but it seemed to Lee that he also despised him. He liked to bring up the subject of Lee's 'minor public school' and the 'cockney inflexion' in his speech.

Lee had tolerated all this when the release of the record was in the offing: 1970–71. But after the record bombed, the sly satire of Price became more grating. In particular, he resented Price's references to an earlier crush of his: the beautiful, wild and dangerous undergraduate he had known. He would never give his name, as if it were too sacred to utter. 'My little Byron,' he would say, which was extremely tiresome. Lee did not believe there had been anything physical between Price and his 'little Byron', but still he had come to feel second best, a poor substitute for this dashing demigod. In the end he had been provoked into discovering his identity, finding out in turn what he had done in the year 1951, which Lee did perfectly easily, being not quite as stupid as Pat Price seemed to think; and the discovery had been very fascinating to him.

Now Abigail was on the seat next to him, her little portable tape recorder on her knee.

'Haven't you been rather cruel, tormenting the poor man in that way? He must have come to absolutely dread the post.'

'Well,' Lee said, changing down as he approached a light, 'he is a murderer, Abi, let's not forget.'

'It's a little power trip, isn't it?'

'Was. Because I don't think I'll send any more cards after the one that went off today.'

'You wrote a message this time, didn't you?'

'Not exactly,' said Lee, accelerating past Wembley Stadium. 'I would like, if I may, to return to your point about the power trip. Surely I was entitled to one after so many years *without* power? And there is a certain aesthetic satisfaction in being able to trigger what is presumably quite a significant reaction by so slight a thing as a blank, or – in the case of today's – a nearly blank card. I think Underhill's pulse will certainly have quickened when he received the cards, just as it presumably did when he played the original game and did the original deed. I think perhaps he likes that feeling.'

'You're not about to blackmail him, I suppose?'

'Has money ever been my motivation, Abi? My aim has always

been the same: to affect people in the profoundest way, whether through music or otherwise. To make them *realise* about where they stand in relation to their fellow beings just as I find my own *realisation.'*

'But surely,' said Abi, 'what you are doing is somehow a betrayal of Pat Price?'

'Are we not becoming somewhat pompous in our line of enquiry?'

'If we are, it's obviously catching in your line of answering.'

'Professor Price was . . . a good friend of mine, but as to whether I owe any obligation to his memory . . . I sometimes wonder, Abi, whether the most fundamental point of the programme has been lost on you.'

'That is possibly true. Could you remind me?'

'Like a rocket bursting free of the earth's atmosphere, I have escaped the obligations of conventional morality.'

'I see,' Abi had time to say before disappearing.

Monday evening.

Paris

When they were on the balcony, with their red wine and cigar-ettes, and the bowl of mixed nuts between them, Syl, who had been reading her copy of *The Times*, turned to Charles and said, 'You don't appear to have opened yours.'

'Not yet,' said Charles. He was looking down into the unfre-quented, yet familiar, part of the Jardin du Luxembourg, where the two statues – made rather turquoise by verdigris – conducted their staring match in the hot gloom.

'You're thinking.'

'Yes.'

'What about?'

'Nothing in particular.'

'Well, here's something in particular.'

She passed her newspaper over – an unprecedented act. The main headline concerned the travails of Chancellor Healey. It was the headline of the second story that provoked Charles's heart into beating a tattoo: POLICE HUNTING WINKING KILLER. Charles read the known facts of three killings, then came an interview with a Detective Chief Inspector Wallace. 'My attention has been drawn,' he said, sounding just like a policeman, 'to the existence of a party game known as Wink Murder. It seems the man we are looking for is playing this for real.' With a rather delicious sense of deepening danger Charles handed the paper back to his mother. By extrapolation a two-column crime report on the front page of *The Times* signified mass hysteria in the other press.

'Of course, *you* played the game for real as well,' said Syl. 'The third person killed was obviously a homosexual man. You yourself are a homosexual man.'

'The word in 1976,' said Charles, 'is *gay*.'

'There's nothing gay about it.'

'I hope you don't think,' he said, admiring his own control, 'that I've been nipping across the Channel to play Wink Murder for real.'

'It did cross my mind. But as far as I can gather, the dates don't fit.'

'All that time you spend reading detective novels has obviously not been wasted.'

'But is the one sending the cards the person who's doing the killings? I mean, is it Pat Price?'

'Pat Price is dead,' said Charles. He then told her all about Howard, the commission he'd been given, and the report he had just filed by telephone – all of which she clearly found very engrossing. After nodding her head for a while, she indicated the newspaper. 'But you didn't know about this when you spoke to Howard?'

'No.'

'And what is he supposed to do now?'

'It doesn't change anything. I told him to go to London and try and find this character in the white suit – this "funny little bloke" as he put it in his artfully bluff way, or anyone at all who knew Pat Price. Soho would be the focus. He's going to call me tomorrow evening and tell me what he's found out.'

'Has it occurred to you that he's stringing you along?'

'Why would he do that?'

'The money, obviously.'

'He was very reluctant to take on the job in the first place and he told me just now that he didn't want any more money. He has a room in a flat in London. It's sub-let so he can't go there, but he wants to pay his hotel bill in London from the original amount I gave him.'

'Sounds as if you like him.'

'It doesn't follow.'

'Have you told him about the cards?'

'No. Not yet.'

'Why not?'

He sat back, and closed his eyes, a signal for his mother to shut up. He was thinking about the confession he'd written in 1951, which might have come into the hands of Pat Price. If that had occurred, where was it now that Price was dead?

Later the same evening.

London

When he got home from Oxford, Lee poured himself a glass of champagne and took the Tanglewood out of what was in effect the broom cupboard. If he'd had an attic, that's where it would have been, because he'd never been quite able to get rid of it. It was a couple of years since he'd played it though, and he recollected now that the top E was missing. But you could get by without a top E. He hauled the guitar onto his knee – with affection, as a father might with a child.

It was a lovely thing: satin tobacco sunburst. Those words suggested the American continent. Almost the only interesting thing about his deadbeat ex-manager, Peter Naughton, was that he always called America 'the American continent', as if the importance of the States demanded extra words. Had Naughton really paid for that billboard on Sunset, Lee wondered as he tuned up the Tanglewood. Surely that was just the standard managerial bullshit. But then again, Naughton was too boring to have lied about it.

Lee wasn't boring. He had proved that pretty conclusively these past couple of weeks. And the return of a sense of pride was liberating his music again. He began playing around with 'Super Duper'. He found the chorus quickly: a pretty thing revolving around A minor, but it was a bit dangerous to get the chorus first. You had to work backwards to the verse, so to speak. Unless of course you made the chorus the starting point, as in 'She Loves You' or 'Na Na Hey Hey Kiss Him Goodbye' by Steam, which was one of the most underrated tracks ever, to Lee's mind. Starting with the chorus was a way of getting the flow – the momentum you needed to carry you into a verse.

Lee realised he was telling himself this out loud, giving himself a masterclass in songwriting. But he would come back to 'Super Duper'. Another phrase he'd had in mind was *apple pie*: the love object being compared to apple pie – not too literally of course! They were just two nice words. And this one started in the right place – the beginning – without any trouble and yet with odd chords, which was always a good sign. He was starting on C7 and going to A. Hardly a textbook route, but it sounded great with a slightly psychedelic vibe, and these words:

> If I go drifting on the seas of fantasy
> Will you come along and rescue me?
> I think you probably would
> I think you probably would now

A word like *now* – a word of energy – didn't arrive by accident. It proved there was energy in the piece. Some words you didn't want, *just* being one. *Just* didn't mean anything; was always filler. This time around Lee got the chorus straight out of the verse: both were catchy but quite involved. Bit of a challenge for the guitar-playing kids who liked to work out the chords to their favourite records, cracking the code of genius.

He sang it again, got it wrong the second time. Third time he found it again. Better scrawl down the chords. No, record it. He'd sold his four-track, but he had his little Bush portable, and he had a few blank C60s lying around. If not, he'd record over something else. He liked to switch the Bush on sometimes when he did his interviews with Abigail.

Lee poured himself another glass of champagne, and unwrapped an Old English Spangle. It was the treacle flavour, which went well with champers. He found the Bush and a mainly blank cassette . . .

and another song was immediately incoming! 'Spotlight' was what it wanted to be called:

Spotlight will shine upon the chosen one.

No wonder that word had come to him. The programme, he now understood, might not be as prolonged as he had originally thought. It was being displaced by a different aspect of his creativity. More and more, the correct order of priorities was becoming clear. First music, then clothes (and appearance in general), then fame, then people. He could only handle the people if he had the first three right. He had the programme to thank for clarifying these thoughts, and for giving him the self-esteem to find his way back to the thing that had always been his personal number one: the music.

But he must consolidate his success by trademarking again – and in the full glare of the spotlight. He was thinking of the headlines on those newspapers heaped on the sofa in the other room. And having made that resolution, Lee sang, played and talked 'til the batteries of the Bush ran out.

Tuesday.

London

Howard began the next stage of his enquiry in Berwick Street, which featured on his personal London map (as yet rather underdeveloped) as the place to buy second-hand records. Howard wasn't very into music – which was to say that he liked the Beatles and the Stones – but when he did buy records, they were second-hand.

The record shops shared the street with a fruit and veg market operated by noisy cockneys. They were in the overspill from Soho, and there was a good-time, rackety vibe that suited Howard's mood. The death of Pat Price might be the start of something, as in *A Christmas Carol* ('Marley was dead, to begin with. Of that there is no doubt whatever'). But it was far more likely to be the end. It seemed to Howard that the matter would be prolonged only if he found the little green-eyed fashion freak of the night before. He didn't *want* to find him, but he would try his best to do so and he'd promised Charles he'd spend two days on the job: today and tomorrow.

Tomorrow evening he'd head back to Nice, where Emma was waiting for him, as he liked to think. He had mentally scripted all sorts of rows between her and Fabien, in which she said things like, 'Why can't you be more like Howard?' (only more subtle). Since he had apparently been overpaid for the work – a situation completely unprecedented in his life – he was thinking of returning by the Night Ferry, which in spite of its name was a famous *train*, and one he'd never taken before. Michael Caine, as Harry Palmer, took the Night Ferry in the film of *The Ipcress File*, although not in the novel itself. The train departed for Paris at about 9 p.m. from Victoria, and that was going to be Howard's cut-off point as far as the job was concerned.

He entered a record shop, and the shouting of cockneys gave way to horrible, heavy rock played at top volume: possibly Led Zep if the screeching of the singer was any clue. The people who worked in record shops would always subconsciously – or consciously – punish the customers with the music they played. In this shop, he wouldn't even start on a tortuous enquiry about a minor pop group with a small creepy-looking singer. So he tried the next one along, which was quiet with a few studious browsers.

138

There were two men at the counter, both reading what appeared to be music papers. It was as if playing music would detract from the study of it.

Howard said, 'Excuse me,' and one of them looked up. 'I'm trying to find a certain LP, but I don't have much to go on. It's from about five years ago. It's a group, and it's pop rather than rock. The singer's a little dandyish guy with a lot of hair. He likes wearing sunglasses.'

'That's about three-quarters of 'em,' said the one who'd looked up.

'He has very green eyes.'

At this, the second bloke looked up as well. 'Sounds like a job for Dan Weller,' he said.

'Dan's the man,' said the first, so this was some sort of in-joke.

Howard said, 'Who's Dan Weller?'

The first one said, 'He has a column in *Music Mirror*. It's called "Dan's The Man". You write in, and he answers your questions about music.'

'I haven't really got time to write in.'

The first man shrugged (the second one had gone back to reading). 'You could try giving him a call, I suppose.'

Howard thanked them, and walked around the corner into a Wardour Street newsagent, which was about the one shop in the road not selling hard-core porn. It sold a lot of soft-core porn though, and it took Howard a few minutes to locate such a relatively innocent publication as *Music Mirror*, which was a big-format magazine with Eric Clapton looking wasted on the cover. Howard found 'Dan's The Man', which had a photograph of a bikerish bloke wearing a deliberately incongruous mortar board and studious half-moon glasses. The first enquiry began, *Dear Dan, Knowing you are a veritable professor of pop, I wonder if I could trouble you with a small query regarding two Humble Pie B sides . . .* The next one began, *Dear Dan, I wrote to you six months ago, and you proved you really are The Man by your deciphering of the great Zim's lyrics on 'Hurricane'. I now beg your indulgence once again, on the matter of . . .*

It seemed flattery was required in the court of King Dan. There was no phone number, only the address, which was presumably the address of the magazine. It was on Lexington Street, a walkable distance. So Howard walked.

It was nearly midday. With luck, Dan Weller would be in a pub, or standing just outside one along with most of the population of Soho. But nobody at *Music Mirror* would know which pub, so Howard would be entitled to draw a line under this enquiry. Things were progressing ideally so far in that he was keeping busy and using his initiative in an impressive way, whilst discovering absolutely nothing.

Music Mirror was at the top of a dirty staircase in a big Victorian house on Lexington Street. The reception was a depressing room that had been painted too many times in off-white. There were magazines everywhere – *Music Mirror* and its stablemates – lying in or out of cardboard boxes, as if some archive had overflowed. The receptionist was eating chocolate, smoking a cigarette and talking on the telephone, or listening to someone else doing so. There was a yellow plastic bottle of Skol Suntan Crème next to the phone. When Howard asked to see Dan Weller, she pointed with her cigarette towards a broken sofa with magazines underneath and on top of it. Eventually, she hung up the phone but carried on with the chocolate and cigarettes: Bar Six and Kensitas. She was now reading a magazine. There was a sink in the room with crockery on the draining board. On the shelf above was the biggest tin of Nescafé Howard had ever seen, a jar of Coffee-Mate (apparently empty and minus its top) and a packet of Sugar Snaps featuring a picture of Mr Spock, some of which had spilled onto the floor. Next to the sink was a poster of David Essex, and another showing Concorde cutting through the clouds. The receptionist had started on another Bar Six. She was quite dishy but wouldn't be for long at this rate. Howard thought he'd better mention the name of Dan Weller for a second time.

'Oh,' she said. 'I thought you were going to wait for him.'

'Where is he, exactly?'

'It's lunchtime so he's probably at lunch. He doesn't usually take long. Probably be back soon.'

I'll gave it ten minutes, thought Howard. After that, he could be absolved. Meanwhile, he said to the girl, 'I want to ask Dan a question.'

'That's what he's there for.'

'I want to find out about a singer in a group. They were pretty obscure. Had a record out five years ago or so, but it didn't do anything. The singer was small and had very green eyes.'

'Lee Jones?' she said. 'I used to love him.'

'Maybe,' said Howard. But he knew she was right. The little man in Oxford had been a 'Lee' all right. Any novelist could have told you that. He was hedging his bets as usual though, so he said, 'What does he look like?'

'Like you said. And gorgeous. I was reading about him the other day. A real blast from the past.'

'Where?'

'In a magazine – an old one.'

She came out from behind her desk. She was tall, or maybe that was the effect of her denim maxi skirt, which had some badges down the side. They were ironic. One was a *Blue Peter* badge, another read I AM A MEMBER OF THE TUFTY CLUB. Still smoking, she knelt down in front of Howard, and began pushing her long hair – which was quite nice – out of the way, by hooking it behind her ears, which were touchingly not up to the job, being very small. Howard liked this girl. The room was depressing but she wasn't. She reminded him of Emma.

'It was in *Christabel*,' she said, dragging a box out from under the sofa.

'What's Christabel?'

'A magazine.' She was taking copies of that publication out of the box, flicking through some of them. After a while, she gave up. 'Have a look if you want. They're all *Christabels* in there.'

'What was the group called?'

'Picture Show. The article tells you all about them.'

Christabel was a magazine for the slightly more mature female teenybopper. Alongside pop, it dealt with adolescent emotions. *I SHOULD NEVER HAVE TRUSTED HIM . . . a reader's true experience.* Howard went through every page of a dozen copies until he came to a picture of the man who'd been in the King's Arms the night before. It was in the edition of Thursday May 13th, 1971. (Howard didn't like 1971: it was the year his mother had died.) The photo was an upper body shot. Jones wore a green shirt with a massive round collar, and he was holding – arrogantly dangling – a pair of sunglasses in one hand, and wafting a cigarette in the other. He was grinning and leaning towards the camera, and he was winking. Strange coincidence that, given the current news, which Howard had been reading over breakfast. But the fact of a winking killer being on the loose would draw attention to all instances of winking, which was perhaps why the loony murderer was doing it in the first place. (As far as he could remember, Howard had never winked at anyone, just as he had never wolf whistled at anyone; he wasn't sure he actually *could* wink or wolf whistle.)

It was only a short item, and with no byline:

Lee Jones is one of the nicest looking men to try his hand at the pop business in 1971. The other members of the group he leads, Picture Show, don't let the side down either. Drummer Bob and Crispin (on keyboards) are almost as handsome as Lee, but it's Lee who catches your eye when they're on stage. And his eye might catch yours at well, because he has a habit of giving a wink to audience members . . . if they are of the female persuasion, of course!

'It's become a bit of a trademark, I must admit,' he tells me over the phone from the studio where he and the group are putting the finishing touches to their debut LP. 'But I won't be pictured winking on the cover of the album because that's a serious business. I don't mean that the songs are not enjoyable, it's just that we don't want anything to detract from the quality of the music. We've worked really hard on the album and we're very proud of it.'

The word on the grapevine is that there are some really lovely songs on the record, and it's tipped to be riding high in the charts this summer.

'But Lee,' I say, 'can we just go back to the winking for a minute?'

'If you like,' he says, laughing.

'It must have got you into terrible trouble,' I suggest. 'Some guys must have thought you were trying to steal their girlfriends?'

'Oh, I've very often been in terrible trouble,' says Lee, still laughing. 'I've had to run for my life on many an occasion. Fortunately, I'm in pretty good physical shape.'

All of us here at Christabel *certainly agree with that!*

Howard thanked the girl. She had – unfortunately – been very helpful.

Armed with the name of the group, he walked back to the second record shop, which was busier now, and with some hypnotic instrumental playing. Every browser was smoking sleepily, and one of the two assistants was taking all the records out of the window, presumably because they'd started melting. Howard flipped through the LPs under 'P' and there was Lee Jones again: one of four hairy blokes sitting in the lower branches of a tree. He gave the same double impression here in the photo as he had in the pub: a pretty person but compressed, like a focusing of something unpleasant.

The group was called Picture Show, whereas the record was called *The* Picture Show. So that was pretty affected, unless it was an oversight.

On the reverse side were the credits:

Picture Show are
   Lee Jones (vocals, guitars, percussion)
   Geoff Hudson (bass, backing vocals, organ on Blue, Blue Day)
   Crispin Philips (keyboards, marimba on 'Perplexity Jane')
   Bob 'Basher' Barton (drums, percussion)

Also on the back was a transcription from an interview with the band conducted by somebody called Mick Tavener, for *Record Times* in July 1971:

On first making the acquaintance of London-based hopefuls, Picture Show, your eye falls naturally on an elfin figure in tight green loon pants and red silk shirt, with unearthly looks reminiscent of David Bowie. This is Lee Jones, vocalist and principal songwriter. While the other three band members are tucking into the red wines and nibbles laid on by their manager, Peter Naughton, in the polished pine kitchen of his Finchley home, Jones is not partaking. He smiles when I open the conversation by suggesting that the imminent release of the combo's debut long player, The Picture Show, *is surely reason*

*for a little celebration. 'Oh, I wanted to keep a clear head.' 'Why?'
I wonder. 'For you, Mick. I don't want to seem overly pedantic but
I wanted to be quite specific about what we're trying to do here.'*

*Lee (as immaculate in his speech as in his dress) explains how,
while he has no time for 'the somewhat overblown complexity of
progressive rock', song structure is very important to him: 'I think
you'll find that every cut has a middle eight. And while my acoustic
cross-picking is somewhat foregrounded in the mix, and we were
photographed in a forest for the cover, we're not folkies by any stretch
of the imagination! In fact, on some tracks we really boogie on down.'*

*The other band members begin to interject. Amiable bassist Geoff
Hudson offers me a vol au vent while saying, 'We like to think
there's something for everybody on the record.'*

*Pianist Crispin is rather reserved. Asked for his keyboard influ-
ences, he blushes and mumbles satirically, 'Oh, I'm a great fan of
Mrs Mills, you know.' Drummer 'Barto' seems the extrovert of the
group: 'Can I just get something straight?' he says. 'The forest Lee
mentioned was actually more of a copse, and it was on Hampstead
Heath, since there was a train strike on the day and we couldn't get
out of London. As for "boogying on down", I prefer to say we rock
out. Ask me my musical influences.'*

'Consider yourself asked.'

*'I've no politics in terms of musical appreciation. My tastes go
through all sorts from Stockhausen and John Cage to Frank Sinatra
and Ella Fitzgerald. As for drummers, I love Charlie Watts, but
most of the guys in the Top Forty couldn't swing a sack of sh —'*

*At which dangerous moment, Lee Jones judiciously interrupts,
asking his bandmate, 'Would you like another bottle of wine, Bob?'
before turning to me and giving a confiding wink. He asks if I've
had the chance to listen to the record. I tell him not yet, but I've
heard good things about it. He presses a copy on me, asking very*

politely if he might have my phone number so he can call and find
out what I thought. We arrange a time three days hence, and sure
enough he calls to the minute, obviously anxious in case I have
disapproved of the platter, but I am able to put his mind at rest. I
report to him, as I now report to you the reader, my opinion that
The Picture Show *is well worth one pound seventy-five of anyone's*
money: really nice in fact, and with its engagingly loose feel, and
Beatley pop sensibility, it ought to do something to lift the band from
the hard grind of one-nighters and doing it the hard way.

The repetition of 'hard' was a bit jarring, Howard thought. In fact this guy Tavener seemed to go completely to pot at the end of his piece. Howard himself had been well reviewed in indifferent prose, which tended to undermine the commendation. But you couldn't go back to the critic, requesting they couch their praise in slightly more elegant terms. Howard took the record out of the sleeve to inspect the label. He read, *All songs, music and lyrics, written by Lee Jones.* So there was no question about *that.* Howard saw that *The Picture Show* was *a Peter Naughton production for Moreish Records.* He checked the sleeve again and was relieved to see there was no small print giving the address.

The album had been repeatedly marked down, and was now 55p, so Howard would buy it. It would make a good offering to Charles, tangible proof of the effort he'd put in. If Charles wanted to pursue Lee Jones, here was a lead for him to follow up at his leisure. The assistant who was not in the window was still reading at the counter. He recognised Howard from an hour before. 'So you remembered the name?' he said, as Howard counted out 55p.

Howard nodded. He would quit the shop as soon as the guy put the record in a bag. But then – as the record was handed over – he thought he owed it to Charles to ask a couple of questions.

'Is this any good?'

'Yeah.'

'I don't suppose you'd know how I can track them down?' he said.

'They don't exist any more. Not as a band anyway.'

'But as people.'

'They do exist as people, as far as I know. One of them, Geoff Hudson, gives bass guitar lessons.'

'Oh. Where?'

'At his house, I should think. Try the small ads in *Melody Maker*, or the noticeboards in Denmark Street.'

*

Howard knew Denmark Street by reputation as a focus of the music business. What he found was a short street of old houses with garish guitar shops undermining their dignity at pavement level. All the doors and windows were open, and as he walked along he heard a tangle of guitar noise, like abstract music, and this was people tuning or testing guitars. He walked into one of the bigger guitar shops. The guy behind the counter was affecting to play the drums with two pencils.

Howard said, 'I'm looking for a bass guitar teacher.'

The guy didn't stop drumming – he obviously thought he was very good at it – as he said, 'If you wanted to *buy* a bass guitar, I could help you.'

Howard thanked him – although he couldn't think why – and as he trudged away from the counter, the pencil drummer said, 'Check the notice board next door.'

The next-door shop contained literally hundreds of guitars but only three people – all hippies. One was playing a guitar – probably quite well, Howard had to admit – and the other two were appreciating his technique, nodding their heads, or their hair, in a reverential way. They might be sales assistants, trying to sell the instrument to the player. Nobody bothered about Howard as he read the notices, which divided into the fanciful and the businesslike. On the one hand:

YOU ARE: a Dylanesque twelve-string maestro and instinctive harmoniser willing and able to let your freak flag fly.
WE ARE: (but you already guessed) the new Byrds.

On the other hand:

Friendly ex-pro offers bass guitar lessons. All styles, reasonable rates. Call Geoff.

Five minutes later Howard did so, from a suffocating call box full of dead or dying flies in Tottenham Court Road. Geoff picked up the phone after two rings and was friendly, as billed.

'I have to tell you at the outset,' said Howard, 'that I'm not looking for bass guitar lessons.'

'That's OK, man. How can I help?'

'My name's Howard Miller. I'm a writer and sort of ... researcher. I'm trying to get hold of a guy called Lee Jones.'

'Ah! My old comrade in arms!'

'You were in a band with him.'

'For my sins!'

'I think Lee Jones knew a man called Pat Price, an academic from Oxford who died about a year ago. I'm trying to find out about Price on behalf of a man who used to be a friend of his. I know this all sounds a bit ...'

'Not at all. Be happy to help if I can. I've never heard of Pat Price myself, but I'm sure Lee will tell you all about him. He'll also tell you all about himself. Look – best way to play this, given that old Lee can be a bit of a tricky customer . . . Can you give me your number, and I'll pass it on to him? I was going to call him in a minute anyway.'

Howard gave him the number of the hotel. He said, 'Trouble is, I'm only there 'til tomorrow early evening. Then I'm off back to France. I'm living in Nice at the moment.'

'Oh,' said Geoff. '*Nice* one. Pun intended, by the way!'

' . . . So really – the latest he's going to be able to call me is tomorrow lunchtime.'

'I'll tell him. In fact, I'll call him now and get straight back to you.'

Howard put the phone down, and pushed the door of the box open for some air, or what passed for it on the Tottenham Court Road. After about a minute the phone rang.

'Hi there, Geoff again. I'm sorry man, but there was no answer from Lee. I'm off into town just now, but I'll try him again later, and I'll definitely give him your message, all right?'

'That's very kind. Many thanks.'

About an hour later.

London

In the Cellar Bar of Ye Olde Cheshire Cheese, Maureen was thinking about the subject of regularity. Most of the people in the Cellar Bar were regulars – they came here every lunchtime – and most were from the offices of her own paper, the *London Evening*

Chronicle, whereas the *Telegraph* hacks, for instance, drank in the Back Bar. (It was said the 'Cheese' had many 'holes' in it.) Maureen would have interviewed some of her colleagues for the feature she was writing about people with fixed habits, except that it was considered bad form for journalists to write about other journalists. A very *famous* journalist could write a backslapping piece about another very famous journalist: that was done regularly. But Maureen wasn't famous. Not yet. Which was fair enough (she thought) since she was not quite twenty-five, and she'd only been at it for a couple of years.

Both the Cheese and the offices of the *Chronicle* were spoken of as being 'on Fleet Street' but they were both just off it: the *Chronicle* on Shoe Lane, the Cheese in Wine Office Court. But Fleet Street was bigger than the actual thoroughfare. It was 'the home of British journalism' and that had many outposts, many of them being licensed premises.

The Back Bar of the Cheese dated from 1660 or so, but it had things in common with the editorial floor of the *Chronicle*: chiefly a shortage of light and an excess of heat. There were no windows at all in the Back Bar. High in the wall was an antique metal grille that might have been intended for ventilation – it certainly provided no illumination – but the clouds of cigarette smoke that drifted past it went undisturbed. There *were* some windows at the *Chronicle*, but they were filthy, so the progress of the natural day went unnoticed. In the Cheese, the walls were of rough white-washed stone, like a medieval prison cell, and they were wet with the evaporated sweat of the hacks. What must happen to that sweat at the *Chronicle*? Probably absorbed by the crumbling grey plaster on the walls of the editorial floor – which was probably *why* it was crumbling. Everything on the *Chronicle* was grey: the metal desks, the typewriters and the copy canisters that wavered along the wires dangling from the dirty ceiling. But Maureen loved the editorial floor of the *Chronicle*. The only trouble was that she was on the wrong side of it: in features instead of news.

To her friends, it was an abstruse distinction. They didn't understand it even after she'd explained it to them. But they'd know soon enough if they met Maureen's immediate boss, Philip Lovell, Deputy Features Editor, who was sitting next to her just then, and moaning about the possibility of having to supply a new features page to the Saturday edition of the *Chronicle*.

Philip Lovell was quite a nice man, but he was a wimp. About twenty years ago he'd written a novel, and the world of journalism was supposed to be very grateful to have this 'stylist' (a word he often used, as in 'Maureen, you're no stylist, but we'll make a features writer of you yet') in its midst. 'Features' denoted everything that wasn't news. In other words, colour, humour (so called) and description. Anything that was really long was sure to be a feature. Philip Lovell was always instructing her in 'style'; how to 'evoke' things. All those parts of a novel that you skipped? That was evocation. Philip Lovell had thought she could do it because she'd read English at Cambridge, which was where *he'd* read English, as everyone who spent five minutes in his company would find out. Once, slightly drunk and trapped with him in the Cheese, she'd said, 'Philip, you're a Cambridge don manqué,' and he'd loved that, especially the word 'manqué'. He was full of bookish conversation. Regarding the accursed 'regulars' – a feature idea of his own making – he'd mused, 'You might make mention in your introduction of Sherlock Holmes' brother, Mycroft.'

'Oh yes?'

'... Of whom it was said, "He has his rails and he runs on them", and who went to the Diogenes Club every night between – from memory – quarter to five and twenty to eight.'

'Right,' Maureen had said. 'Will do.'

'Holmes himself, of course,' Lovell had continued, 'was disturbingly *ir*regular. In one of the stories – you can look it up, I'm sure – his housekeeper, Mrs Hudson, stops him when he's on his way out and asks what time he wants dinner. And what does he say?'

'Something brilliant, I'm sure.'

'"Seven thirty the day after tomorrow."'

Maureen had interviewed half a dozen real-life regulars for the piece. For example, a woman who'd been going to the same service at the same church in Kilburn for sixty years. And a man called Fred whose high chair at the bar in a pub at King's Cross read FRED'S SEAT. With so much going on in the country – soaring inflation and unemployment, the IRA bombing campaign – it seemed frivolous to be writing about people whose main quality was dullness. Maureen had at least persuaded Lovell to let her touch on the news issue of the weather – so she'd interviewed a man who went swimming at the Men's Pond on Hampstead Heath every morning at six. But according to Lovell, she hadn't evoked him properly. 'I can't see this man in my mind's eye,' he'd said, to which she'd very nearly responded, 'No, but there'll be a photograph for that.'

Lovell was still moaning about the Saturday project. 'It's going to mean a later finish for you on Friday,' he said, trying to co-opt her into his grievance. You'd think a features editor would be only too pleased to supply more features, but not Lovell, who was cruising towards retirement. 'I rather like the Saturday paper as it is,' he was saying, as they both watched the characters at the bar.

Most of the news subs – who were all men – were there. They were an unprepossessing lot physically, but they interested Maureen because they were proper journalists. She loved watching them do their quick blue hieroglyphics on a piece of copy. They started work at six and were at the mercy of events until the City Final edition went to bed at 3 p.m. They did take half an hour for lunch though, and some of them would down three or four pints in that time. They were a bit more lax in their subbing after lunch, and some news hacks would have the dubious pleasure of seeing their pieces go into print exactly as written.

Only one man at the bar wasn't a news hack. He stood directly beneath the olde worlde sign reading SERVERY. Maureen did not recognise this person. He did not work on the *Chronicle*, and she didn't believe she'd seen him in – or off – Fleet Street before. She'd have remembered. He was small and flamboyant. With slicked-back dark hair, trim red flares and a somehow flouncy white shirt, he looked matador-like. He was quite dishy but you knew he knew it, for which Maureen always deducted points.

It was now 1.15 p.m. Maureen had finished her half of bitter and ham sandwich. Although she aspired to the news desk, she did not aspire to news desk drinking habits. She wanted to get back to the office. She was having to unpick the 'regulars' feature to fit in the Hampstead swimmer. But Lovell was still droning on.

The man who fancied himself had sunglasses in his top pocket – he'd be quite capable of wearing them on the top of his head, she believed. He kept looking over at her. He was drinking a 'short' drink, and now he was smiling at her. She was flattered but looked away, encountering the reproving stare of Lovell. He'd noticed where she was looking. She ought not to be flirting while he was moaning . . .

'Most people I know,' he was saying, 'consider the Saturday paper perfectly charming in its present form.'

A newspaper – Maureen thought – had no business being charming, and to her mind the Saturday edition of the *Chronicle* was a non-event. It was largely devoted to horse racing or cricket. Reading it, you'd almost think London was a country town, and there was a long-running leisurely column called 'Sam Martin's The Week In Review', which fascinated Maureen because of the suspect grammar of that heading, and because she could never work out whether it was supposed to be amusing.

She glanced again towards the bar, and the man who fancied himself. He winked at her. Then he drained his drink and pushed his way through the crowd to the ascending stairs, the front bars and the exit. Only when he'd disappeared did Maureen remember about the wink murders, and the news stories she'd read about how certain sick individuals would capitalise on those crimes by going about winking at people just to scare them. She'd read one op-ed piece arguing that, in the circumstances, 'the harmless, flirtatious wink' ought to be re-classified as a form of common assault punishable by law, like spitting at someone.

Philip Lovell said, 'Did you see that? The fellow winked at you. That's pretty outrageous in the circumstances.'

Maureen picked up her bag and headed for the stairs. She ran out into the little maze of Wine Office Court. Then she was in Fleet Street, looking left and right. She could see no fast-moving, small, fashionable man, only a few pin-striped saunterers. The entire street seemed stymied by the heat. The traffic was hardly moving. Two lorries carrying giant rolls of paper were trapped in it. They ought to have been delivering in the early morning, not the early afternoon. A bus conductor smiled at her from the rear platform of his stationary bus. She anticipated another wink, but the conductor merely smiled. The thought flickered in her mind: what if the man who fancied himself had been the Winker? The actual one? But then she remembered the six million in London and the thought faded. The man merited anger rather than fear.

It was like when someone knocked on your door and ran away: annoying because pathetic. He had obviously crossed Fleet Street, availing himself of the barrier caused by the traffic. Or (it now occurred to her) he might have taken the other exit from Wine Office Court, heading into the mazes north of Fleet Street which housed the duller sorts of professionals: accountants, insurance brokers and so on.

Then Maureen realised her opportunity.

Five minutes later, she was walking fast across the editorial floor of the *Chronicle*. Philip Lovell, who'd evidently just returned from the pub himself, was coming up to her, but he stepped back when he saw she was bypassing the features desk and heading for the news desk and the news editor himself: Henry Meredith.

Maureen said, 'Some joker winked at me just now – in the Cheese.'

Henry Meredith, who was saturnine and fanciable – a Humphrey Bogart type – offered her a cigarette in sympathy. Maureen felt it was to her discredit that he didn't know she didn't smoke, since he was the fulcrum of the whole paper. 'I thought it might make a news feature,' she said.

Henry lit his cigarette, nodding: 'There's a lot of it about, I think. Men – it's mainly men of course – winking at women to frighten them. Even though this killer actually goes for men *and* women. Yes, there *is* room for a first-person account. What do you think? Three hundred words?'

'When for?' she said, because Henry was so laid back he hadn't told her. He glanced at the four-sided electric clock above his head. It dangled in a permanent fog of cigarette smoke, tyrannising the entire room.

'Two o'clock?' he said. 'We'll put it into West End Final.'

That gave her twenty minutes. She'd have preferred an hour to

155

write and another to polish, but that was a features desk mindset. As she turned to begin, Henry called her back.

'We'd better byline it "a *Chronicle* Reporter", don't you think?'

'Oh. Can't I use my name?'

'If the guy really is the killer – which is a million to one – he might be coming after you. So we ought not to be telling him your name.'

Maureen appreciated his chivalry. She also thought it patronising.

She knew how to type a news story from close observation of the news desk. As opposed to a couple of fluttering A4s with one carbon in between (making a copy for Philip Lovell to fret over), you made a compact sandwich of octavo papers and octavo carbons, all the ingredients being available from a wire basket on the news desk. Philip Lovell kept a reverent distance from her as she wound the papers into the typewriter. Needing as she did to interweave the fact of what had happened to her (the first-person element) with the 'issue' (the epidemic of winking) and a few flashes of style (because there *was* style in news writing, but it was subtle – a matter of economy), she had to concentrate hard. It was a shame about the lack of a byline, but the people who counted would know it was her work, including the editor himself.

When the twenty minutes were up, she wasn't happy with her intro but was pleased with the pay-off:

Those who amuse themselves by scaring others are not (except in the case of one deranged individual) The Winker, but they are something approximating to that designation. It is simply a matter of substituting one vowel for another.

She kept one copy for herself and began distributing the others. She loved doing this. It felt so munificent, like giving out party invitations. Unfortunately, on this hot afternoon, there weren't many people to distribute *to*. She gave one to Lovell (as a courtesy), one to the only news sub not in the pub. He was an old guy, but new; he'd been a big shot on *The Times* and was working out a kind of part-time semi-retirement on the *Chronicle*. She couldn't remember his name. She gave the other three copies to Henry Meredith, who nodded thanks and began reading the piece immediately while smoking in a way that almost made her want to take up the habit. He read fast, which was just as well, since she was desperate for his verdict. He looked up. 'Just the ticket, love,' he said. 'You should do more for us.'

Now she watched as the elderly sub began reading the piece. He wasn't as stylish a reader as Henry, and after a couple of seconds, he groped for his blue pen. He didn't use it though. Instead, his phone rang and he answered it. But now Henry Meredith was strolling over to him, and he was required to interrupt his call – with hand over the mouthpiece – as Meredith whispered some instruction to him. The sub returned to his call, and Meredith to his desk, where he did not sit down but merely put out his cigarette and stooped to collect his attaché case. Because of the weather there'd been no coat or even jacket to collect but he was undoubtedly knocking off for the day. Maureen slightly regretted that he hadn't given her one final word of congratulation before departing.

She ought now to be getting on with her 'Regulars' feature since that would be 'going to bed' later today, even though it was not required for tomorrow, Wednesday, but for Thursday when it would have the honour of constituting the pedantically named 'Thursday Feature'. But she couldn't get down to the fiddly business of fitting in the Hampstead swimmer.

The elderly sub was finishing his phone call. Now he stood up. He was coming over to her, with the piece in his hand. Was he going to countermand Henry and reject the piece by simply handing it back to her? He might be allowed to do that – because of his track record in the profession.

'Terrific piece,' he said. He was quite posh.

'Thanks.'

'Sorry, but I think Henry said you didn't want your byline on it? I was on the phone, and a bit distracted.'

Maureen said, 'He suggested we should go with "A *Chronicle* Reporter".'

'Right,' said the sub, scratching his hair, of which there was only just enough to do that. 'Well, it's up to you really.'

'In that case I'd like a byline.'

He nodded, with a charming smile: 'You're going on the front page, you know.'

Five minutes later, she watched the canister with her piece inside wavering along the wire to the end of the room. Here the wire became vertical and dropped through a very literal hole in the floorboards to the composing room, where men who sat at typewriters far bigger than themselves created pages of steel. She returned to futile fiddling with her feature. Then she heard the surging roar from below that always made her think she was on a great liner whose engines had just started, but which meant the presses were running for the West End Final. As far as Maureen was concerned, the machines were printing nothing but her piece. It was impossible to continue with the feature. She wanted to be on the street – any street – so she could walk into a newsagent and buy the paper with her article on the front page . . . Because only the best news features made the front page.

She walked over to Lovell, who'd made a point of not reading her piece. She said she had a slight headache, and could she leave early. She felt guilty about the lie, but she knew Lovell was always sympathetic to headaches. He often had them himself, especially when called on to produce any copy. There was a hesitation, however. 'I'll come in early in the morning,' she said.

'Yes, all right. It can go off on the late run at ten tomorrow.'

'Thanks. I'll come in at seven. I'm sure I can get it sorted out in three hours.'

She walked into the dirty glare of Fleet Street.

About three hours later.

London

Standing by the window in the flat, Lee was looking out – and down, at the milling, sunburnt people. Lee, who wore his dressing gown minus the belt, felt himself analogous to the sun: he created beauty for people who didn't follow through; did not appreciate his efforts or act with commensurate grace. Didn't those small pedestrians ever think how lucky they were? He could stand here at this window with a machine gun and take them out in their dozens. Instead, he had devised a more artistic scheme to bring them realisation. *Real-eyes-ation*. Because Lee had made every glance given by everyone significant. Or he would do, given sufficient publicity. But his attempt to make realisation universal had just suffered a setback.

The plan had been perfectly reasonable. Find a partner in a public place; trademark; then follow her to discover her home address or place of work – the location to which he would, after waiting patiently for the right opportunity, return with the folder.

159

He had selected the pub off Fleet Street knowing that any customer was likely to be a journalist working in one of half a dozen newspaper offices nearby. The trademarking had gone smoothly and been witnessed by the girl's fussy-looking grey-haired friend. Lee had immediately quit the pub, because anyone trademarking at the moment was likely to draw heat. He had then positioned himself on the other side of Fleet Street from the alleyway that housed the pub, waiting for the girl to emerge, and ready to follow her whether she went left or right. But then a giant lorry carrying paper – like so many enormous toilet rolls – had parked bang in front of him, and that must have been the moment when she came out. He'd lost her, anyway.

But all was *not* lost. He was pretty sure – from what he'd overheard – that the woman worked on the *London Evening Chronicle*.

Turning away from the window he saw the Tanglewood on the sofa. He could hardly bear to look at it. Any writing was out of the question until he'd found that journalist again.

Something made him turn back to the window – a flicker of movement from over the road. He saw that the little newsagent had emerged from his shop carrying one of the display boards used to advertise a paper. Lee couldn't read what the board said, but he sensed this was going to be significant, as when a new set is about to be revealed at the theatre. The newsagent propped the thing against the shop's front window and Lee saw that the placard advertised a story in that day's *Chronicle*. As the little scene shifter retreated into his shop, Lee read AN ENCOUNTER WITH THE WINKER?

Lee began dressing rapidly – not the clothes he'd worn in Fleet Street, obviously – and he'd just scooped up enough change from the bedside table to buy the *Chronicle* when the phone rang. Could this be a call related to the *Chronicle* story? In which case it spelt the end of the programme, just as it had really started. It would also be the end of his freedom. He did feel a sense of fear, but also a great sense of importance as he walked over to pick up. But it was – of course – only Geoff Hudson.

'How's it going, man?' Geoff said. 'I have a message to pass on.'

'Yes?' said Lee, and he had spoken in a much more vulnerable tone than the one he normally used with Geoff. Perhaps this *was* about the *Chronicle* story after all?

'I had a call from a guy who wants to speak to you.'

'What about?'

'A sort of interview.'

'Are you taking the mickey?' said Lee, but he still wasn't sure this was the usual sort of Hudson triviality.

'I knew you'd be pleased. It's actually concerning a guy he thinks you know. Guy called Pat Price. Ring any bells?'

It rang many, and they made an interesting rhythm with the fast beating of Lee's heart. Who had connected him to Price? Could this be related to the sending of the postcards? It couldn't be related to the *Chronicle* story.

'Anyway,' said Geoff, 'here's the guy's number. He's called Howard Miller, and he's staying at a hotel 'til tomorrow night, then he's off back to Nice in France, where he's living. He's asked if you can call him by lunchtime tomorrow. Got a pen?'

'No. Just tell me the name of the hotel.'

Geoff obliged, as he always did. Then he said, 'Just had a bit of good news.'

'What?'

'Had a call from the reviews editor at *Melody Maker*. He wants a thousand words on the new Alice Cooper. *Alice Cooper Goes to Hell*.'

'Right. Well, he did that a long time ago. I have to go now.'

Lee couldn't wait for the lift, so he ran down the stairs and over the road.

In the shop, he realised he'd better buy something else along with the *Chronicle*, to blur the issue, as it were (because the little bloke did know Lee slightly). He picked up the *Radio Times*, which had the Two Ronnies on the cover, and Lee had the strange and very exciting thought that he was actually more famous than them because when, after all, had the Two Ronnies been on the front page of a newspaper as opposed to a showbiz magazine? But as he emerged from the shop with the paper in his hand, he realised it wouldn't do to read the item in detail. His eye had caught the words ... *a creepy little would-be Lothario in red loon pants* ...

Her name was Maureen.

It really ought not to be so easy to manipulate the world! thought Lee, throwing the *Radio Times* in a bin. It had only been vaguely in the back of his mind that he'd find a partner who would broadcast the news of the trademarking. That hadn't been the purpose of going to Fleet Street, but Maureen had done him proud with a front-page article. He began heading towards Oxford Street, with no purpose except to use up the energy burning away inside him. As he stood at a junction, he watched the passing pedestrians for any sign of recognition. He half wanted that, and half didn't. Perhaps he should be wearing shades? But recognition would surely be unlikely on the strength of Maureen's article. Lee was now wearing his faded Levis, not the red trousers, which he never would wear again; and Maureen had not been generous enough to mention the most salient detail about Lee, which was that he was incredibly beautiful.

Anyway it didn't matter what people said about you, he reflected, as he crossed the road, as long as they said *something*. Oscar Wilde had expressed the thought rather better, he believed. On Oxford Street, he was heading rapidly east. The placards seemed to appear every few yards. AN ENCOUNTER WITH

THE WINKER? It was cleverly put. The *Chronicle* would definitely outsell the *News* and the *Standard* this evening, and Lee was finding that all the things that usually brought him down – Rover cars, men in shapeless desert boots, girls with Bay City Rollers scarves, the very sight of the His Master's Voice shop (a publicity event for Picture Show had been cancelled there, back in '71) – were not having their usual effect. Vandalised phone boxes were another downer (not so much because they were vandalised as because he sometimes had to use them), but the one Lee stepped into now was only vandalised to the extent of a few cigarette burn marks on the receiver. Its full set of telephone directories was completely unscathed.

He looked again at the front page of the *Chronicle*. Maureen made up for the dullness of her Christian name with an exotic surname, which was probably Greek, comprising a jumble of p's and s's. There ought not to be too many in London, and in fact there were only four, of which just one was prefaced with the initial 'M'. In his head, in that hot box, the music was beginning to flow. He was itching to get back to the Tanglewood. The number called 'Apple Pie' was in his mind, and he was now thinking of it as a slower piece, with brass – that sort of stately, Stax vibe. Yes, once he'd taken the folder to Maureen he could perhaps consider the programme concluded. Because at that point, the publicity would be absolute. Hysteria would reign! Then he would be back to music full-time.

Back at the flat, Lee tuned up the Tanglewood and began messing about with a riff on the bass strings, thinking as he played. Then he took a shower and poured himself a Coke with the towel round his waist. No booze, because he would be driving, and he'd better get started. But he couldn't resist the pull of the music. He wanted to get the riff down on tape.

Abigail was standing near the curtains.

'It's nice,' she said.

'Thanks Abi. I'm now hearing it on a clavinet. Ever heard "Superstition" by Stevie Wonder?'

'Course. What are you up to tonight?'

'If you're after a date, forget it.'

'Going out trademarking, I suppose?'

'It's a secret.'

'Not for much longer, I think. Various people are on to you, I would say.'

'Perhaps. But they might not last very long. One of them, name of Maureen, is currently embarking on her last evening.'

'The journalist.'

'She's a journalist, yes. Like you. So watch out, love!'

'She'll bring the tally up to . . . what?'

'It's not about numbers, Abi, as I have explained before.'

But she was already gone, and the keys to the Citroën were waiting for him on the bed.

*

Maureen lived far out in east London. But even this part of town had its sunshine, and Leytonstone turned out to be a surprisingly pretty spot, almost semi-rural. The road he wanted was a small one, and the house was a sleepy villa with a monkey puzzle tree in the front garden. There were three doorbells, signifying three flats. The road was off Whipps Cross Road, which bordered a big green that Lee's *A to Z* told him was called Wanstead Flats. He parked the Citroën at the junction of the

164

two, placing the folder by the *A to Z* on the passenger seat. It was five o'clock.

There was a boating pond on Wanstead Flats, with happy East Enders rowing into each other and shouting apologies – so it was really more like bumper cars. There was a car park near the pond, with an ice cream van parked in it, and a long queue of people waiting to buy. The queue was ... disproportionate. All over the dead grass of the Flats, people were stretched *out* flat as if they themselves were dead. In the distance was a building that looked like the Tower of London, and it seemed to be floating in the heat. He picked up the *A to Z* again and saw that this was Snaresbrook Crown Court. The words on the page excited him, because that was just the kind of place he must not end up in. He had the window on his side wound down, and two women walked past very close. One said, 'I'm taking cold baths on a regular basis. Sometimes in the middle of the night.' He realised that neither he nor the car ought to be on public view. He drove away.

An hour later he was back, going slowly along Whipps Cross Road. People would tend to clock the Citroën: men especially, who would be either jealous or impressed. But again ... the risk was quite exciting. There was very little difference about the scene on the Flats, except more people stretched out and a hint of yellow in the sky as well as the grass. The sun was still high in the west – over Leytonstone. He drove down the little road again. He couldn't tell whether Maureen was in her flat (Flat C, according to the telephone directory) because it was not yet necessary to switch on lights, and it wouldn't be necessary for several hours. Maybe he should come back in the morning, which was going to be Wednesday? She would leave for work at ... what time did a journalist on an evening paper have to be in work? If he turned up at six, that would encompass any possibility. Then Lee had an idea. He didn't know if it was a good one, but it was certainly bold.

He could park the Citroën some distance away, walk back and ring the bell for Flat C. If she answered, he'd introduce himself and apologise for having trademarked her. It could be done in quite a jocular way: 'I'm not really a would-be Lothario, you know, and I assure you it was done in all innocence. I'd completely forgotten about this madman on the loose!' Of course, he'd have the folder behind his back.

But when he drove up to the garden again, he didn't fancy it. It seemed, from her article, that she was not the type you could charm. He drove away for a while, then drove back. It was now eleven o'clock but no light in *any* of the flats, for heaven's sake. She might have come in and gone to bed while he was away.

He drove away once more, and eventually slept in his car at a place that was possibly called Theydon Bois. He was near an Underground station that was not underground; and the night was very hot, so he did not sleep much.

Early Wednesday morning.

London

It was five thirty when Lee woke up. He could hear birds singing, a horrible racket – birds could *not* sing – that confirmed his own superiority. He peed in a cluster of ill-looking trees that had once been a wood, and now formed the border to a supermarket car park. He had to get this over with quickly, and he would do. He was impatient to begin his true fame – and he had plans for the

166

rest of the day. They included calling this Howard person who wanted to speak to him. He was very curious about that.

He drove back to Leytonstone, which was already waking up. He parked outside Maureen's garden. At six o'clock exactly a light showed in her flat. Her alarm must have gone off. She came out at half past, nicely dressed and made up for work. He turned the car round as she stepped out of her garden. Accelerating, he mounted the pavement so as to nudge her, trip her up with the front bumper of the Citroën, but he must have been going faster than he thought, because he had evidently knocked her out, judging by her lack of resistance as he was upon her with the folder. The ease with which he brought her into the programme proved the validity of the programme. As he drove away, Lee was deeply happy – which was sad in way, because he realised the feeling was completely new to him.

About seven hours later.
London

Howard met Lee Jones in the scruffy wooden cabin that was the French House pub. It was presumably home territory for Jones, and Howard felt he'd been watched for a while before Jones walked up and shook his hand.

Howard had – with embarrassment – described himself to Lee over the phone. It had seemed the only alternative to saying: 'Don't worry, I know what you look like' and he didn't want to say that because it would suggest that the meeting was going to be focused on Jones, whereas it was supposed to be focused on the late Pat Price. Only when he had finished shaking hands with

Jones – an experience he did not enjoy – did Howard realise the further implication of his move, namely that he hadn't seen Jones in the Oxford pub two days before, whereas in fact he had. But did that matter? Had Jones connected him with the Oxford pub? He was now frowning in a half-amused way while studying Howard. *He does recognise me from there*, thought Howard. *I'm going to have to put the record straight.*

'Of course in a way we've met before. On Monday, you were pointed out to me in a pub in Oxford as being someone who'd known the late Pat Price.'

Lee was nodding.

'You might have seen me looking over,' said Howard. 'I hope I didn't seem rude.'

Jones made no answer at all to that. But he was now smiling and changing the subject:

'Really nice jacket,' he said. 'It's a bold move to wear an unstructured item but it's the only way to go in this heat, and you've got the figure to pull it off.'

The words *Hollywood smile* came to Howard. He'd known he wasn't going to like Lee Jones, and he *didn't* like him. He wore his black hair slicked down. His clothing was restrained – correctly faded Levis, pristine white shirt – but you sensed he was just taking a breather between more flamboyant outfits. He spoke precisely, as though always on the record, and he was consciously charming and would often touch Howard on the arm. He was quite camp, but tough; and he was bright.

He'd called at the last possible moment, running right up against Howard's deadline, as relayed to the bass player, Hudson. It was a familiar tactic among those who sought – or maybe possessed – mystique. Then again, he had agreed immediately to a lunch within the hour. 'We'll find a caff,' he'd said, 'but first we'll have a drink,' and he'd suggested this place, which he familiarly called 'The French'.

'You a regular here?' asked Howard, when he'd bought a couple of wines.

'Used to be. I practically lived in Soho at one time.'

'That's when you knew Pat Price?'

'Yeah. Let's get that side of things out of the way, then we can have a nice lunch. What do you want to know about Pat?'

'I have to admit that I'm asking on behalf of someone else, who's being rather cagey with me. I'm sure it's nothing too heavy, but he doesn't want to be identified, so it's going to seem a bit furtive.'

Lee Jones looked at Howard in a way Howard didn't like; then he laughed, and if there was such a thing as a Hollywood laugh this was it. 'Sounds about right. Pat was a man with many double lives. No, that's wrongly phrased. You can only have one double life, but you know what I mean, Howard, I'm sure. Cards on the table. The guy was gay, and he used to come up to London for sort of . . . adventures, if you get my drift. Or does one go *down* to London from Oxford? I assume you were at university there yourself, right?'

'I was at York.'

'Well, you're one up on me, man. I left school at sixteen, and it was a very bad school; expensive but bad. If I did get an education, it was partly through knowing Pat. He could talk about absolutely anything. He was a mathematician as you might know, but also a musician, which is the line I happened to be in at the time.'

That's a bit disingenuous, thought Howard. He produced the Black Cats.

'Cool packet,' said Lee Jones, but he wouldn't have one. Looking after that perfect little body maybe. 'Pat wasn't into pop of course, but he'd tell me things about my own music. All sorts of stuff I didn't know I was doing.'

'Like what?'

'He'd tell me what key my songs were in, which I never really knew, believe it or not. After a while I'd have to tell him to back off, because when I write I take an instinctive approach, and I wouldn't want to lose that.'

'I bought one of your records this morning. Would you sign it for me?"

Jones was nodding, looking at the sleeve warily. This record meant something complicated to him, and Howard felt he'd made another mistake. 'You're a clever boy to find that,' said Jones, and Howard thought for the first time about how this guy had fifteen years at least on him. He'd done a lot more in life and had a lot more to regret. He signed the record when Howard produced a pen, but dismissively, almost defacing the front photo with a flamboyant signature. Panicking slightly, Howard said, 'I've had a listen. I think it's great.'

'Yeah?' said Jones. 'Where did you listen to it if you bought it this morning and you're staying in a hotel?'

'They had a listening booth in the shop,' Howard lied, and he ought not to lie because he went red. Going for broke, Howard said, 'It reminded me of the Beatles.'

Lee looked at Howard for a long time. 'That's what the guy says on the back of the sleeve.' Then he relented somewhat. 'Thanks for that, man,' he said. 'It's a great compliment.'

Howard said, 'Pat Price . . . '

'Yeah. Ask away.'

Howard did his duty by Charles, asking about the character and by implication the mentality of Price, who had been, according to Jones, 'a very sweet guy, a little weird at times. Not at ease with himself. Probably conflicted about his sexuality, but quite keen to indulge it.' The implication was that he'd indulged it with Lee Jones, but Howard dared not pursue the matter.

'Did he ever talk about his friends in Oxford?'

'A bit. But he came to London to get away from ... what's it called? Academe.'

'Where did he live in Oxford?'

'North Oxford. The smart bit with all those big red-brick houses. He only had a little flat though. Full of books, of course, and ... violins.'

'Sounds like Sherlock Holmes.'

Lee Jones smiled – full beam, bringing the green eyes into play. 'Bit of that, yeah. It was the usual deal for a don, or whatever he was.'

'You went there – to his flat?'

'Once or twice.'

'Could you tell me the address?' Howard had his notebook out. He knew some people didn't like his notebook – Charles for one.

'Not offhand,' said Lee. 'Could probably dig it out if you really want. But I mean the poor guy's been dead for two years, so ...'

'Yes,' said Howard. 'Not to worry.'

'Shall we eat, man?'

They found a caff: a hot noisy place, what with crowded tables of red Formica, a hissing prima donna of a coffee machine – the centrepiece of the counter – and Radio One turned up quite loud. Howard knew the song that was playing when they walked in: 'Car Wash', American disco music; it suited the heat. The seat on which Howard proposed to sit had a newspaper on it. So he lifted it off, and laid it on the next table, which was waiting to be cleared. Lee Jones watched him do this. Then they picked up the red plastic menus. The place seemed to dictate burgers and chips, so that was what they ordered.

'But tell me about yourself, man,' said Lee.

Howard talked about his novel, which became a matter of moaning about sales. Lee seemed to listen quite sympathetically, but with a touch of impatience; and he was clearly aware of getting looks from a couple of women.

'It's a blessing to be creative,' said Lee. 'It's also a curse. I know that very well.'

He didn't seem to listen to the radio, even when that certain jingle was played – 'Radio One remembers . . . ' – by which the station boasted of its mental capacity and called up an oldie or two. It might one day preface the playing of one Lee's own songs, but not in this case.

As they were reaching the end of the meal, one of the women came over. To Howard, she said, 'Excuse me.' To Lee Jones, 'Are you Lee Jones? Can I have your autograph?' She proffered a scrap of paper and a pen.

This was clearly not a common occurrence, and Lee seemed rather dazed . . . until Howard realised he was not dazed but trying to listen to the news, which was being announced by another breathless jingle. Lee was actually blanking the woman, concentrating on the bulletin, which was about rising inflation at first; then – with much more enthusiasm but no new facts – about the hunt for the winking killer. The woman – attractive, a bit overweight in too-tight denims – was losing her nerve, seemed on the point of withdrawing. Howard was thinking he ought to somehow intervene. But as soon as the news finished, Lee Jones signed her scrap of paper with the flourish Howard had already seen.

'Second time today!' Lee said, flashing a conspiratorial smile at Howard.

The woman was now burbling on about how her brother had bought her *The Picture Show* for Christmas five years ago. 'I just can't understand why it's not better known. Do you think it could be one of those slow burners?'

Lee, smiling, said, 'Anything's possible I suppose. It'll probably be number one when I'm dead.'

'Oh, don't say that!'

'Can I introduce Howard Miller? He's a hot young novelist. Check out his book. It's called *Marsh*.'

Howard wanted to test Jones and, as the woman retreated in a flurry of thanks, he recalled a piece of rudimentary psychology he'd made Marsh employ. You try to elicit from the interview subject a 'tell', a proof of lying. You do it by asking a question that will probably be met with a lie, and then you watch the person. It had worked for Marsh in the case of a man who'd been married twice, to women who'd ended up prematurely dead.

They finished the burgers, both agreeing that pudding was not required. Now they were drinking coffee, the taste of which did not justify the histrionics of the machine. The next question would have come better after another few wines but nonetheless Howard said, 'Did you feel bitter about what happened to the record?'

'Bitter?' said Lee, and he moved his hand through his hair, ruining the sleekness. 'Not really,' he continued, smoothing the hair back down. 'I wrote the songs. I'm proud of them. They're only three minutes apiece. They're not ... prolonged, but then a poem by Keats is not prolonged. How did you feel about *Marsh* not turning you into the new ... ?'

'The new Frederick Forsyth?'

'If you like.'

'I did feel bitter, yes.'

'Because you wanted the fame?'

'It was more the cash.'

Lee shrugged and smiled, in which moment Howard nearly

liked him. 'I've always had enough money, which has possibly done me more harm than good. But you wrote the book. You made it up yourself. I've always put a high value on making things up.'

'Yes. Why?'

'Because most people can't do it. And it takes bravery. I've never sought to be . . . equivalent to anyone else.'

Howard wondered whether the smoothing of the hair had been the tell. He would find out by eliciting another lie. Looking over at the newspaper he'd dumped on the adjacent table, and which was still there, he thought of something but he didn't *dare* ask it. So he aimed lower: 'I apologise again for being so obtuse, but I can't help thinking that the man I know who wants to find out about Pat Price might have had some reason to fear Price. Can you think why?'

This earned another long look from Jones. Eventually he said, 'Pat Price was a lovely guy. As I've said already.'

This time, he didn't touch his hair. He could well be lying, but there was no 'tell'. So much for the psychology of novelists.

Jones said, 'Where are you living in Nice, by the way?'

Howard instinctively knew he mustn't say. 'Couple of minutes from the front.'

Jones sat back: 'Most of the town's a couple of minutes from the front, isn't it? What are the happening places there just now?'

'I wouldn't know,' said Howard, and so here at last was open war.

'Lovely spot, Nice,' said Lee. 'I'm thinking of going there myself.'

'Oh. When?'

'Soon. Very soon.'

Howard said, 'Shall we get the bill?' and he said it fast, in case his voice should betray his fear.

As they rose from the table, the jingle singers on the trannie were breathlessly confiding, 'You've got a friend . . . The happy sound of Radio One.'

174

Jones left first, with a nod and no handshake. Howard reclaimed the paper he'd moved to the next table. On the face of it, this was a dead thing: a London newspaper from yesterday. He read the second headline on the front page, AN ENCOUNTER WITH THE WINKER? Then he read the whole article.

Howard had, briefly, engaged with the currency of the times. He'd written a novel, and the novel had been reviewed. Was it possible he was now more profoundly engaged; that he was actually plugged into the news?

Ten minutes later.

London

In Foyle's bookshop, Lee hunted for a while in Fiction. Then he remembered about Crime Fiction, where he found *Marsh* by Howard Miller. He read the dust jacket: 'Howard Miller grew up in the idyllic setting of a farm in Swaledale, Yorkshire. After attending the local grammar school, he went to York University where he took a first-class degree in English Literature. *Marsh* is his debut novel.'

The book was written in a simple style that Lee supposed might be taken for elegance. There was a single chair in the whole of Crime Fiction, and Lee sat down on it, leafing through *Marsh* until he found:

Marsh practised elementary psychology. When questioning a suspect, he deliberately elicited a lie. For instance, a man he knew to be a drinker and not proud of the fact might be asked, 'Do you go to the pub every night?' The lie might be accompanied by a gesture: a 'tell'.

175

By identifying a tell you could unlock secrets. Marsh was thinking of this as he took the Volvo up to fifty, checking the rear-view to make sure the Scout was still stable. He'd find a lay-by and park up. There was enough gas in the bottle to boil a kettle and fry up some sausages. He'd look over the Whittaker file and think up some questions that would be answered with lies. From what he knew of Jack Whittaker that shouldn't be too difficult. 'Are you Jack Whittaker?' would probably do it. Reaching to turn up the heater, Marsh inadvertently caught a glimpse of his own reflection in the rear-view. He instinctively looked away, as usual. But things had gone well today, and so Marsh did a rare thing: he looked squarely back at himself.

Elementary psychology. It was very elementary indeed, thought Lee.

It seemed that Howard Miller considered him a suspect. Of what? At the very least of sending postcards to Charles Underhill, who was of course the person who had sent him to enquire about Price. And the cards connected to the whole business of the trademark – at least they did to anyone who knew what Underhill had done in in 1951.

It occurred to Lee that he had endangered the whole programme by sending those cards. It had never occurred to him that he might be discovered as the sender. That he *had* been discovered was down to the sheer bad luck of having been in that pub in Oxford at the same time as Miller. But that might easily become Miller's bad luck, because Lee was sure he could correct any problem he had made for himself. He quit the shop, leaving *Marsh* on the chair.

Seven hours later.

London and the south of England

On the train that was confusingly called the *Night Ferry*, Howard stood in a compartment made of a kind of light brown plastic. It was too hot, and the window couldn't be opened. The complicated bilingual explanation was pasted to the glass – something to do with Customs and Excise.

He was leaning on the window smoking a Black Cat. It was ten o'clock and the train was still shuddering its way through the suburbs – denoted by various oblongs of dirty black, relieved occasionally by some smaller oblongs of dirty light.

Two hours ago, he had called Charles in the Tabac au Bon Vin. He had given a bland account of his lunch with Lee Jones, partly because it had seemed undignified to express the fear he had felt, and partly because that fear might be unjustified. His statement had been a kind of sign-off. He'd told Charles that Lee Jones was a minor pop singer, ex of a group called Picture Show; that in spite of his lack of success in music he appeared to have private means; that he drove a classy car; that he'd known Price in the context of gay Soho; that he'd been pretty vague in his answers about Price, describing a more-or-less amiable eccentric living a donnish life in North Oxford, and without sinister tendencies.

Charles had not asked Howard to do any further work. Whether he really wanted him to had not been clear, because he had said very little. He was probably thinking he would lose the moral advantage if he began to overtly exploit Howard. It seemed the investigation would now be wound up. But Howard knew it ought not to be wound up. It was like those times when he kidded himself he'd finished a page of fiction but knew he could go deeper and would not sleep until he did so.

Why did Charles want to find out about Price?

The reason must be an important one. It must also be a negative one. You didn't need an intermediary to say, 'How are you? Let's meet for lunch.' Howard had been thinking that blackmail might be the reason; that Price had been doing it to Charles. Any homosexual with money was open to blackmail but Price, from what he could gather, was not the blackmailing type. The hippy in Oxford had given him the thumbs up, character wise, as had Lee Jones. But whereas the hippy had not been lying, Lee Jones almost certainly had been, about this or other matters, and it was possible to go further in the case of Jones: the man was an undoubted cunt, and perhaps he had taken over from Price as the blackmailer of Charles, because Price had been dead for a while, after all.

Certainly Charles had been interested in what lay beyond Price; in his hinterland, so to speak. In other words, the death of Price had not checked Charles's curiosity, and so Howard had been sent after his friend, Jones.

Was Jones the Winker? The odds were millions to one against, but somebody was the Winker, and why not him? If Howard had been required to come up with a winking killer for a novel, he'd have invented an intelligent, narcissistic, embittered loner with a track record of winking – a history that he subconsciously wanted people to know about. The possible Winker described by the woman in the *Chronicle* ... that could have been Jones. Assume he *was* the Winker. The question then was this: was it an accident that the investigation initiated by Charles should lead to him? In other words, did Charles think Price would lead the way to Jones? And did Charles know that Jones was the Winker? The hypothesis could not (as the crime writers had it) be dismissed.

At Victoria station, the scruffy stifling waiting room for the Night Ferry had been strewn with the day's papers. In the absence of any new corpse they'd all reviewed the Winker's killings. The first had occurred on the Friday of the week before last. Charles had commissioned Howard to go from Nice to Oxford a week later, but then there would be a lag, given Charles's insularity, and the slowness of the police investigation as reported. If Charles knew that Jones was the Winker, what did he intend to do about it? Why didn't he go to the police? Was he somehow in league with Jones? Should Howard himself go to the police?

What would Marsh do? That was pretty simple to answer. If satisfied of some villain's guilt by the lower standard of proof he applied in his vigilante crusade ('balance of probabilities' rather than 'beyond reasonable doubt'), he would shoot him dead – or shoot him 'down' as Marsh always said – with the semi-automatic Beretta he'd stolen off his first victim.

Howard was not Marsh, but he was determined not to be a coward. The question was *how* not to be a coward. He found the ashtray below the window and stubbed out his fag. He climbed up to his bunk. It was like a high cot, with a little fence to stop you rolling out should the ferry, into which the train was about to be inserted, start pitching about. He had a good view of the small sink, which was incorporated into a kind of cupboard. On a shelf in the cupboard under the sink was a French potty: a *vase de nuit*. There was a trace of yellow liquid inside, which might have been detergent and might not.

A life jacket hung from the door, a very pre-war looking piece of kit, like a gas-mask bag. It would be strange to be on a train in a boat, then to be on the same train again in France. Howard was thinking about the TV puppet show *Thunderbirds*, in which

179

vehicles were always giving birth to other vehicles. On arrival at the terminus, he would have to effect the notorious 'change at Paris': Metro from Gare du Nord to Gare de Lyon where he would entrain for Nice (and Emma). He had envisaged taking a daytime service to Nice, but he could always take the overnight once again. It left Paris at 9.30 p.m. or so, which would give him time to go to the Tabac au Bon Vin, where he would see Charles and have the chance to find out more about him.

The Night Ferry was clattering over points, seemingly smashing its way through. This long and heavy French train didn't seem to quite fit the English tracks, and when it was clear of the points, there was still a loud banging of a different kind. Somebody was knocking at the door.

Opening it, Howard was confronted by a burly man in a brown blazer with brass buttons. He wanted – in French – to see Howard's ticket and passport. Howard was always flattered to be mistaken for a Frenchman, much though he hated Frenchmen. When the ticket inspector had departed, Howard stepped out into the corridor.

He began crunching through lumps of coke, spilled from the heaters at the ends of the carriages. He passed what seemed like half a mile of closed compartment doors, everyone apparently having turned in early. He was looking for the bar car, but when he got there he saw that it was closed, along with the restaurant car – owing to some technical malfunction, as another bilingual sign announced. He wandered back, stopping by a carriage door with an opened window. Fresh air; and he would watch the Dover arrival from here.

The men who worked the special train ferry dock all seemed elderly and embittered. They trudged about the dock carrying torches and shouted to one another as the train began coming apart, because it would be shunted into the boat in sections. The scene was blue-black, the sea signified by little glimmerings of white froth – phosphorescent. A small, warm wind was blowing. A car was approaching along the dock, a fast object in this scene of slow toil. It was a big Daimler – grey, a criminal's car. Two men got out of the back and ran up to an official of the train who was supervising the loading. It seemed they wanted to get on, but he wouldn't let them. A shouting match began, and Howard thought it would come to blows. None of the men with torches stepped in to help the guard. They just carried on putting the train into the boat, and Howard found himself and his carriage sliding away from the drama before he could see how it ended.

He walked back to his berth as the hold of the boat enclosed the carriage. He had a bottle of Double Diamond in his suitcase and the penknife capable of opening it. He was also reading quite a promising thriller for once. It certainly had an excellent title: *Midnight Plus One*, which was quite appropriate to Howard's situation, in that it signified a moment of danger either just past or imminently approaching.

About the same time.

London

There had been nothing on the evening news, but Lee was confident he would be starring on *tomorrow's* evening news. So he was entitled to his celebration. He began by pouring himself a glass of champagne and unwrapping an Old English Spangle: aniseed. Not his favourite flavour but he loved the green colour. He wanted to hear some music; was starting to regret binning his stereo in the depths of his disillusionment . . . and it had been a top of the range Sansui. He would get these cravings. Right now, he really wanted to hear 'Stoned Love' by the Supremes. But Lee was in the fortunate position of being able to make his own music, and it was brimming up in him now. He took up the Tanglewood and started picking out the chords to 'Stoned Love' – and it was one of those that started with the chorus: D . . . B minor 7 . . . E minor 7. 'Far out!' he said to himself, laughing, but there were also tears in his eyes because it was such a beautiful progression, and lyrics . . . so free . . . *I tell you I ain't got no other!* Who wrote it, he wondered? And why weren't they famous for doing so? But then the best people often weren't.

Then he got out the Bush and recorded full versions of the two new songs: 'Apple Pie' and 'Spotlight'. All the remaining lyrics had come to him without pause for thought and he was sure that same momentum would propel these songs to the top of the charts in a day not very distant. He then put on the Cerruti suit – which was his *best* white suit – and he loved the demo so much he put it into his pocket along with the folder. (He never went anywhere without the folder these days, because he loved that too.)

*

He wasn't a member of Zanzibar but people who looked like Lee would generally get in, and as it turned out the doormen practically bowed to him as he entered.

Zanzibar was one of the most happening places in London, and tonight it was really buzzing with its American Prohibition-era

182

vibe. The heat of the night had brought it all into focus: polished chrome and twirling fans; swirling sweating people; barmen in white tuxedos; the tom-tom rhythm of New Orleans jazz and cocktail shakers. Tomorrow, everyone here would be talking about him. Meanwhile, he walked about with his cognac and Coke and two eyes fully open, sparing life after life.

He returned to the bar for another drink. He had said 'cognac' but not yet 'Coke' when a hand came down hard on his left shoulder. Was this the end? His arrest, somehow brought about by the over-inquisitive Howard Miller? But as he looked down at the hand Lee saw that he was going to be OK. The long nails suggested a guitar picker, and the ruby ring suggested money. The owner of the hand said, 'It's Lee Jones, isn't it?'

This was John Ormond, a very smart operator indeed. Ormond was a public school product, like Lee himself only more so. He might actually have been to Eton. He was camp but straight – specialised in marrying and divorcing American fashion models. He'd written a few hits, and they weren't to Lee's taste – mawkish ballads custom-made for lovelorn ladies – but they were decent enough formally speaking. Ormond was also a manager, a music publisher and a producer with a connection to the Regent B studio.

He said, 'You got sick of your bucolic idyll, am I right? When I heard you'd moved to Devon I thought you must be going off to get it together in the country. Like Led Zep, Traffic or . . . Who else got it together in the country?'

'Nick Drake?' Lee suggested, smiling. 'Mike Oldfield?'

'That's it. But when no new product emerged I had to accept that you'd become a farmer or something.'

'I inherited my old man's place. There was quite a lot to sort out.'

'I really dug *The Picture Show*, you know. I still play it all the time. Such a drag that it didn't hit. Any theories as to why?'

'Oh, who knows? You could go mad thinking about it.'

'Maybe a bit more could have been done production-wise?' said Ormond. 'It certainly wasn't the material. Your stuff is really built to last. Proper songs with really well-constructed bridges.'

'You make me sound like Isambard Kingdom Brunel.'

'You know when you're listening to a track, and you absolutely love the middle eight, but you also want it to be over, so you can get back to the chorus? I always have that with your stuff . . . I hope it wasn't too much of a downer for you, Lee, that record not making it? You were always known as a confident young man.'

'*Cocky*, I think was the term usually applied.'

'Tell you what though: you're still *looking* great.'

Lee smiled one of his best smiles, and for the first time looked squarely back at Ormond, assessing him. He was a decent-looking bloke himself – greying, with those wings of hair above his ears like an antique dealer from Surrey. Lee knew that he could work with a man like Ormond. He always seemed to bring out the paternal side in educated, upper-middle-class types.

'As a matter of fact,' said Lee, 'I'm writing again.'

'You are? Let me get you a drink . . . '

Ormond began pushing his way to the bar, and the danger now was twofold: either he would never come back, or the subject of Lee's writing would have been dropped by the time he did come back. But neither was the case.

'Have you got a demo you could let me have?' Ormond said, handing over the cognac and Coke.

Thursday.

Paris

If you're going to kill a day, you might as well do it in Paris, thought Howard. He'd been somewhat affected by the laconic tone of *Midnight Plus One*, which had continued promising as he read it on the Gare du Nord approach. In the station, he'd carried his suitcase through the blue fumes to the bureau de change, where he changed his sterling for francs. The pound was in a shocking state as usual. He'd fought his way across the concourse to the newsagent's, infuriatingly called *Relais*. The front page of the *Continental Daily Mail* would have told him something about why he'd got so relatively few francs, since it was entirely devoted to the economy. Then came two pages on the heavy weather, mainly photographs, which might have been showing a natural disaster or the ultimate British holiday. Nothing new about the winking killer.

Walking away from the station, Howard experienced the Parisian version of the heatwave: it involved more cigarette smoke, hairdryer blasts from the Metro when you walked over certain gratings ... and the gilding on the showpiece buildings seeming to flare like fire. He walked aimlessly until the suitcase became heavy. This occurred outside a café where he drank an espresso and smoked a Black Cat on the terrace. He had laid his notebook on the table, and also *Midnight Plus One*, which he was continuing to sample. But then he began watching the Parisian cars battling their way across a cobbled square: a lot of Citroëns, but they tended to be 2CVs rather than DSs. The DS was a rare bird, even in France.

The blare of horns was almost constant, and Howard felt a headache coming on. He was sitting in full sun, and all the shaded tables were taken. When the waiter came by, he paid the bill, then walked inside the place and started again at a new table. This was a breach of etiquette, but he had lacked the language to explain to the waiter that he wanted to move into the shade. The interior – grubby red plush – was nearly empty because of the heat, and Howard sat at a table near two dangling signs that had been set swaying by an otherwise ineffectual electric fan. One said TOILETTES, the other TÉLÉPHONES.

He waved at a waiter. Unfortunately, it was the same guy who'd just served him outside. Obviously, Howard ought to have cleared off by now, but here he was, perpetuating his lack of *savoir-faire* in a different location. Howard said, '*Une bière, s'il vous plait,*' and the waiter appeared not to have heard. He did eventually bring the beer but without comment. Probably he would never speak to Howard again. The beer must have been strong, because after half a glass of it, Howard had an idea.

The waiter had attempted to inconvenience him by giving the maximum number of coins ... and there was the swaying sign reading TÉLÉPHONES, indicating a slim wooden booth. He would call Emma – for which he would need a number. After riffling through his suitcase, he couldn't find the film script on which the number was written. So he began removing the contents of the case, and placing them on the banquette – another outrageous act, judging by the look the waiter was giving him. He found the script and took it into the phone booth.

As her phone rang, he began to think this was highly presumptuous on his part. What would he say except, 'I'm on my way back to you,' which was the kind of thing said between the most cloying kinds of couples. And what if Fabien picked up?

(On the train, Howard had only slept for a couple of hours and all of that time – or possibly only a minute of it – had been taken up with a dream in which he was involved in a love triangle with Emma and Fabien. It had been a *Talented Mr Ripley* type of scenario, with a luxurious Riviera backdrop. The pale blue sea was a constant dazzling presence, and everyone had been highly sophisticated.)

Emma picked up the phone, and his pulse was set racing as surely as if someone had pulled a gun on him.

'*Allo*,' she said brightly, obviously expecting an upbeat French person, so when Howard said, 'It's Howard,' he sounded truculent with his north of England tone.

'Howard! The Englishman With The Car! Where are you? And when can you get here?'

'I'm in Paris. I'll be there tomorrow morning.'

'That's great. We want to do the car scene as soon as possible.'

The 'we' was so irritating. But then Emma would be part of a 'we' until she died. It was an absolute rule that beautiful women – the people most able to forge an existence on their own terms – were always *sharing* their lives with some horrible bloke.

She said, 'I'll call you at the flat tomorrow afternoon.'

He had been trying to think of a way of telling her about his investigation, and his suspicions, and now she provided the cue: 'So what did you discover in Oxford for the mysterious Charles?'

He told her, and kept on telling her, refuelling the phone with change on three occasions, because she did seem interested. He described Jones, stressing the greenness of his eyes, and told her of his suspicions about him. She had read news stories about the winking killer – 'Obviously. Do you think I'm a hermit?' – and when his tale was winding down, she said, 'Maybe you've really found him. Do you think your man looks like a murderer?'

'Yes.'

The pips were going, and this would be terminal because he'd run out of change. They had about three seconds left for any

187

telephonic footnotes. She just had time to say, 'I wonder if you should go to the police? I'll ask Fabien what he thinks.'

Resuming his wanderings, Howard reflected that since it didn't matter to him what Fabien thought, it ought not to matter to Emma. On the Rue de Rivoli he entered an English language bookshop. They didn't run to a copy of *Marsh* but he let them off: this place was too posh for paperback thrillers. He bought an expensive little French–English dictionary, then crossed the river, which was cloudy pale green, and seemed to be steaming between its beautiful stone banks.

He came to Notre Dame, which because of the buttresses reminded him of a ship under construction. He pushed on through crowds of tourists, drifting towards the Latin Quarter, where Paris became quite Middle Eastern, with the narrowing of the streets – in which kebabs were being cooked and hookahs smoked, adding to the hot cigarette fug. He began heading east, navigating by the burning sun, to a district where the streets were quieter, made of pure white stone with occasional tendrils of green dangling from window boxes. But he could always hear police sirens in the distance.

He entered a spartan café bar and ordered *saucisses frites*, and it turned out he'd ordered them *au comptoir*, which was cheaper than *dans le salle* but he had to eat them standing at the bar. Howard liked to read as he ate, even though – or perhaps because – it annoyed the French. He stooped towards the suitcase, fishing for the script. He enjoyed reminding himself of Fabien's literary ineptitude. But he couldn't immediately find the script. After a couple of minutes of undignified rummaging on the café floor, the verdict was in: he must have left it in the phone booth at the other café, which meant he no longer had Emma's phone number. But that didn't matter. She would be calling him tomorrow afternoon to arrange about the filming.

His food came. This place was dominated by a big, blurry colour TV, enshrined on a shelf on a kind of giant lace doily. A garish game show had just given way to the news. A report on a French crime – a shooting in Paris – was followed by a report on an English one. It became evident, even to Howard with his minimal French, that the Winker had killed again. The camera showed a newspaper office, the words over a revolving door: *London Evening Chronicle*.

So it appeared that the paper was not only covering the story but was *in* the story. One of its journalists had been killed. A certain word kept coming up: *Clignotant*. Howard took out his dictionary to confirm the meaning. It sounded more dignified than the English equivalent. Now they were showing a picture of the dead journalist, a young woman; then a photostat of the article she'd written, and which Howard had read the day after it appeared: AN ENCOUNTER WITH THE WINKER?

It seemed to him that the question mark was now invalid. He pictured himself walking into a French police station and saying, 'I know who did this.' Of course, he wouldn't be able to make himself understood, which was only one of many ridiculous things about the vision.

Four hours later.
Paris

Charles was in the Tabac au Bon Vin when Howard walked in. He had *The Times* – two copies, oddly enough – and a small white wine on the bar before him. He looked younger than Howard remembered him, and the *tabac* was somehow more opened

189

up – more exposed to the street and the park over the road; and to the heat of the evening sun.

Charles was obviously not happy to see Howard; his nod was a kind of flinch. He did not offer a drink. He said, 'I thought you were going back to Nice?'

'I am.'

'Thanks for doing that work for me. I think our arrangement is now concluded.'

Howard would have to say this quickly or not at all. 'I wondered whether you had any insights into who this London killer might be? The Winker, I mean.'

Charles drank most of his wine; looked down at the bar for a while. 'That's one of the more extraordinary questions I've been asked.'

'You set me on a trail that led to Lee Jones. I think he might be the one who's doing it.'

'Doing the winking?'

'The winking and the killing – four people.'

'I thought it was three.'

'There's been another one. It was on the news this afternoon.'

'Don't you think that if I knew who was doing this, I'd go to the police?'

'Unless you had a reason not to.'

'It would have to be a very good reason indeed, wouldn't it?'

'Yes.'

'This Lee Jones character . . . I don't follow pop music. I'd never heard of him until you mentioned him on the phone last night. You've met him – you know far more about him than I do. If you really do suspect him, you must go to the police.'

'I think I will.'

Charles said, 'What is the basis of your suspicion?' and Howard

190

was aware that he was not dismissing this subject as rapidly as he might have.

'I found him very creepy, and early on in his career, he was known to wink at people. A sort of gimmick of his. The latest victim is a woman, a journalist for the *London Evening Chronicle*. She'd written a piece about being winked at by a man in a bar, speculating that it might have been the Winker. Her description of the man roughly matches Lee Jones. And there's something else. When I was having lunch with him, a woman came up and asked for his autograph. I think he's the kind of man who lives for that sort of moment and it can't happen very often, because he's never become a star. But he ignored her. He was far more interested in listening to the radio news, which was all about the Winker.'

'It's a sensational story. A lot of people are interested in it.'

'But this man is known to be a winker.'

A bark of laughter from Charles, and Howard was suddenly furious that he didn't even know the man's surname.

Howard ordered a white wine for himself. He said, 'Will you tell me why you were interested in Pat Price?'

Charles drank from his glass, even though it was empty.

'No,' he said, after a while.

'Not even in a general way?'

'I wanted to find out about Pat Price because he'd been in touch with me in a way I found odd and, I admit, slightly sinister.'

'In touch how?'

'By post.'

'Must have been a while ago, since he's been dead for two years. It has occurred to me that he had some secret about you and was trying to blackmail you.'

'He was not trying to blackmail me.'

But his voice had lost some of its suavity, about which Howard was pleased. Charles picked up his newspapers.

Howard said, 'Will you tell me your surname?'

'No.'

'I notice you have two newspapers.'

'Yes. You're very observant. One's for my mother; I must get back to her. And you must get off to Nice.'

'Yeah. Lee Jones is going there as well.'

'He *is*? When?'

'Imminently. Said he'd been planning a trip.'

'And this bothers you?'

'Yes, it does a bit.'

'Did you make an arrangement to meet him?'

'No.'

A particularly unpleasant thought occurred to Howard: he ought to have warned Emma that Lee Jones had said he was heading for Nice. A jokey tone would have been called for, but it would have been the right thing to do. Impossible now, without her phone number. Should he attempt to retrace his steps to that café? He had no idea of its location.

Charles was saying, 'Does he know where you live in Nice?'

Howard finished off his own wine; shook his head.

'Look here,' said Charles, finding his patrician tone again. 'This man was in the habit of winking at people. So are lots of people. Anyone who seeks to ingratiate is likely to be a winker, aren't they?'

'Such as?'

'Oh . . . milkmen. They whistle and they wink. Bus conductors wink. Men in bars trying to pick up women. And I suspect it's habitual amongst – what are they called? – light entertainers. I admit, the more stand-offish types, the ones who want to appear superior or iconoclastic, wouldn't do it. I don't suppose Marlon Brando is a winker ... But aren't there pictures of the Beatles winking? They seem on the point of winking or doing some equivalent thing in every photo I've ever seen of them. Horseplay, it's called.'

This was true enough.

Then Charles said, 'Did Lee Jones wink at you?'

'No.'

Charles smiled. 'Then you're safe for now, it seems.'

They shook hands, and Howard watched Charles quit the bar, moving fast, almost fleeing the scene. And no doubt he would be taking a roundabout way home, in case Howard followed him. But instead of doing that, Howard lit a Black Cat and ordered another drink. He had a couple of hours before train time and he wanted to think.

Ten minutes later in Paris, and Friday morning in Nice

Charles entered the flat with such momentum that Syl not only looked up from her book, she laid the book face down on the table.

'What on earth's happened?'

Because Charles had walked right through the living room to the bedroom corridor. He took the terrible Bernard Buffet painting (the one Syl was so fond of) down from the wall and opened the safe it concealed. He took out a few hundred francs (no time to count them) and the Model C.

Syl was standing behind him.

'Who are you going to kill this time?'

193

He gave her the sort of dangerous, evasive answer she would appreciate. 'I don't know. Probably nobody.'

'Not yourself, I hope.'

'Definitely not myself.'

'It's to do with the cards, isn't it?'

'Yes.'

'The one that arrived today?'

'All of them.'

'I was looking at the one that arrived today. That drawing. It looks like a sort of fat spider, but I think it's a closed eye with long eyelashes.'

'Yes, it is.'

'A winking eye.'

'Yes.'

'Somebody knows what you did, don't they?'

'At least one person, possibly two. I've just seen one of the two now.'

'And you're going after him now with the gun? This must be to do with the Winker in the news?'

The extraordinary thing was that she really did seem to be enjoying this; but then again so was he, in a way. The absolute determination not to lose was filling him with a great sense of power. He said, 'I'm going to Nice.'

'Why?'

'Because that's where the two people are going.'

He gave some of the francs to his mother. 'Call Jasmine and get her round.'

'When will you be back?'

'I don't know. Not long.'

He was packing his bag: espadrilles, foldable panama; and he threw in his transistor radio, because he was going to have to keep

194

up to date with the news. He kissed his mother with a sudden surge of affection, because she was now beginning to look a little dazed and old. Her adrenalin surge was wearing off, but with Charles the case was very different, and would remain so until the matter was resolved.

'Call Jasmine,' he said again, and he was clattering down the stairs.

In Place de l'Odéon, he found a taxi. They were coming up to Boulevard de la Chapelle when the first directional signs for the airport appeared. The sight of them made him reconsider.

He leant towards the driver. *'Je suis vraiment désolé, mais j'ai changé d'avis . . .'*

He told him to head for the Gare de Lyon instead. So now the Boulevard revolved as the driver swung the car into a U-turn. They had installed an x-ray machine at Charles de Gaulle airport. Charles had read about it in the papers. Most – if not all – the luggage was put through it, and Charles had the Model C in his suitcase.

It was quarter to nine. The night train left Gare de Lyon at about nine thirty. But the roads were clear, the taxi was well over the speed limit, and Charles was actually smiling.

The illuminated clock on the tower of the Gare de Lyon pre-sided moon-like over the twelfth arrondissement. He asked the taxi driver to pull over at a delicatessen across the road from the main entrance. He made purchases duplicating – as far as he could remember – the contents of the picnic baskets you used to be able to buy inside the station itself: half a bottle of red wine, bread, cheese, pâté, a bar of the darkest chocolate. Charles would be avoiding the dining car on the train. The boy *might* be flying down, but he would probably be on the train, probably in second class, although with the money Charles had paid him he could afford first – which was where Charles would be. (And perhaps Charles was underestimating the boy's taste for luxury as he had underestimated his intelligence.)

The purported Winker, Lee Jones, might be on the train as well, but Charles didn't know what he looked like, and he sounded more like an aeroplane man. If Jones turned up in Nice, that was proof he was the Winker, and proof that he thought the boy knew his secret.

Whether Jones was the Winker or not he must be the card sender, having found out from Price what had happened in 1951. Charles had the latest card in his pocket. He took it out. It showed *Oxford, The River and House Boats*, a summer scene. An eight was pulling through the water creating a trail of circles on the surface. But this time the rear was not quite blank. Under the words *For Address Only* was the drawing Syl had described. An eye, closed but poised to reopen. The postmark and date stamp were clear for once, and this had been posted from Oxford on Monday, the day Howard Miller had seen Lee Jones in the King's Arms.

What did Jones mean by the cards? Pure mischief possibly. He might be co-opting Charles into a fellowship of Winkers, or boasting of his crimes. Above all, Lee Jones must *enjoy* sending the cards, and he would enjoy whatever he was going to do in Nice. It seemed likely the boy was in great danger ... and it was an interesting situation, in that if Lee Jones eliminated the boy, he might be doing Charles a favour, because it was possible the boy was on to Charles as well as Jones. Had he worked out what had happened in 1951?

Perhaps everybody knew everything.

The station was packed with holidaymakers. It gave Charles a quite reprehensible thrill to be walking among them with the Model C in his suitcase. The booking hall was packed, but not the first class counter. It was necessary to be in first class to have a compartment to yourself. He didn't want to bump into the boy on the train. It would be embarrassing. It would look as though he were following him, which in effect he was. If he *should* happen to run into the boy he could say with perfect truth: 'I've been thinking about what you said, and I've decided there might be something in it. I was hoping to have another word with you, and I want to track down this Lee Jones character.'

In his compartment, Charles had *The Spectator* and *New Statesman* for company (he never read novels), but he didn't so much as open the magazines. He lay on his bunk but didn't sleep. Sleep was not required. His mind was racing, but at the same time tranquil. He'd transferred the Model C to the pocket of his linen jacket, and the jacket hung from the door. He knew he was back on the sort of trajectory he'd been on in 1951. It was, on balance, unlikely that he was going to avoid firing the gun, but he would try to resolve matters by diplomacy.

At six, just east of Marseilles, he pulled up the blind. Sea and sky were grey. In the absence of sun, the swimming pools in the gardens of the villas looked highly presumptuous. At Agay, the beach was empty but the sea was beginning to glitter, and a few minutes later the platform at Cannes presented a lurid scene under bright sun: lemon-yellow booking hall; red bougainvillea; the blue and gold uniforms of the railway officials. A lot of people got off here, including the happy American family who'd been banging about for the past hour in the adjacent compartment. They represented what the world called normality, but Charles had a normality of his own, and he was once again discovering the uniqueness of it.

At Juan-les-Pins, Charles put on his jacket, and took the Model C from the pocket. Gustave had been right: it was 'nice to hold';

197

better to hold than the handle of the battered canvas demob suitcase he'd retained for perverse reasons, and which he now took down from the luggage rack. Charles had fled Oxford with most of his possessions in this case; but he would not be fleeing a second time.

Nice station was stifling under glass, but elegant, like a conservatory. Charles was one of the first from the train and into the underpass that led to the ticket hall and exit.

He crossed the dazzling square in front of the station. Breakfast in a quiet little café was required, but first he'd check into his hotel, and he did think of the peeling pale orange one just off the square as 'his' hotel. He pushed at the tall iron gate, which creaked in a melodramatic sort of way. He was about to enter the jungly garden when he looked back along the heat-buckled pavement. The boy was there, holding a plaid suitcase and darting behind a palm tree in an attempt to hide. Should Charles call the boy over and explain himself? He couldn't decide whether that would make the situation more or less absurd. He wouldn't bother. He had the boy's phone number, and he would call him when he was ready.

Charles entered the garden of the hotel. It was full of singing birds.

Fifteen minutes later.

Nice

Howard was back at the flat by nine. Unpacking was a matter of tipping everything on to the bed. He then sat down on the part of the bed not covered by his possessions. He tried to tell himself he was angry more than scared. In Paris, Charles had treated him with upper-class condescension and dismissed all his hypotheses as not only hysterical but crass. But Charles had known all along that they were right, or that some of them were. Enough to bring him to Nice. He was here either because Howard was here, or because Lee Jones would be coming. More likely the latter. But that didn't let Howard off the hook. If Charles believed Jones would be coming to Nice then he probably *would* be coming. It was no longer possible to dismiss Jones's statement of intent as mere bravado. And why was Jones coming to Nice? To get Howard.

Perhaps Charles was in town to get *Jones* and *protect* Howard. But Howard didn't see Charles as either vigilante or guardian angel. He ought to go straight back home, wherever that was. It had been ridiculous to think it might be here in Nice. He'd nearly fainted from heat stroke on the walk from the station – there had been no shady side of the street – and the day had hardly begun. He looked with disgust at the bookshelf. There was one decent thriller, *The Day of the Jackal*, but that had a bookmark protruding from thirty pages in. What the hell was he doing here? He'd typed nothing since his arrival but a row of t's. Yes, he was going to be in Emma's film; but she was just another person who was manipulating him, and was doing so on behalf of her unpleasant French boyfriend. He would never prise her away from him, and what would he do with her if he did? He ought to go back to London or Yorkshire, and instead of trying to write a book, he should buy one: *The Joy of Sex*. Because it was about time he started living.

He lit a Black Cat and surveyed his scattered possessions. He couldn't see his copy of the *Picture Show* LP. He must have left it with the film script in that first café in Paris. He blamed the waiter, who had intimidated and flurried him. Everybody intimidated and flurried him. Now that he couldn't call Emma, he would have to wait until she deigned to call him. What day was it? Friday. She'd said she would call in the afternoon about the filming tomorrow.

He opened the window: pigeons scattered, and there was the soaring sea. By the time she did call he might be dead, stabbed by Lee Jones, who might not even go to the trouble of winking at him first. Jones didn't know his address, but he'd find him if he wanted to. Charles didn't know it either, but he did know his phone number. Maybe Charles would pass that on to Jones? Because Howard had no idea which way the guy was going to jump. He shouldn't have suggested that Jones might be black-mailing Charles, because that implied that Jones had something to blackmail him about, and that he (Howard) knew what.

Wait a minute. Could Charles himself have been doing the winking and the killing? In a thriller by, say, Freeman Wills Croft – the kind of book that began with an extract from a railway timetable, by way of a warning to anyone expecting literature – Howard would consult his own timetable to discover that, yes, with the railway equivalent of a following wind, Charles could have been in Paris at all the times he was *supposed* to be in Paris, and in London in time for all the murders. (The worst example of railway mania in a thriller was *Five Red Herrings* by Dorothy L. Sayers.) But no. Lee Jones was the Winker. Unfortunately, no policeman would believe Howard if he said so, and he didn't know where Jones was – only that he was heading to Nice. Could he be here already? Yes. He'd declared his intention to come as far back as Wednesday lunchtime, so he'd had two and a half days. But Howard wasn't going to run away. It was all right to feel like a coward; it was another thing to act it. And he was in love with Emma.

So he was trapped.

There was hardly any food left in the flat, and he was down

to his last Black Cat. In the bathroom he applied some of the sun cream Emma had given him, because he didn't want to be too red when he saw her. He would go to the supermarket. It was something to do. He was almost through the door when the phone rang.

He approached the phone. This had to be Emma. She had said she would call in the afternoon, but she was very impulsive, and it was surely too early for the other, terrible possibilities. Yes, this would be Emma calling. He picked up, and the speech from the other end was already underway – a coarse shouting.

'Howard? It's your dad.'

'Oh, hello Dad,' said Howard. 'You all right?'

'Yeah. Now listen, I've had a man from your publishers on.' ('On' meant 'on the phone'; it was very important – if you were a flinty Northerner like Howard's dad – not to waste words.)

'What did he want?'

'Your address in Nice.'

His publishers had suggested that Howard should boast, on the dust jacket of *Marsh*, of having grown up on a farm in the beautiful countryside of Swaledale. The farm was in the phone book under Miller.

Howard said, 'Why?'

'Said he had something to send you.'

'Was he calling from a call box?'

'I don't bloody know. It was Clem who picked up.' Howard's 'Uncle' Clement (not really an uncle) was his dad's farm manager, or head labourer, depending whether or not Clement himself was close at hand. He was a primitive old bloke, not likely to appreciate telephonic nuance, or even to hear it. Howard's dad said, 'Why would he be calling from a bloody box? He'd be calling from his office, wouldn't he?'

'Did *you* speak to him?'

'Course I bloody did. I –'

'How do you *know* he was calling from the publishers, Dad?'

'Because he said he was, for Christ's sake.'

'When was this?'

'Just now.'

Both Charles and Lee Jones would sound like publishers to his dad.

Howard said, 'So you gave him the address?'

'No. That's why I'm calling. I couldn't bloody find it. You might want to get on to the bloke and give it him direct, if he's not called you already?'

'So you gave him the phone number?'

'Course I bloody did.'

'What was his name?'

'I asked him and he said not to bother, he'd call you. But he's your publisher, so that should narrow it down. I mean, how many have you bloody got?'

'Did he say he was my *editor*?' It was too complicated to explain that the caller couldn't have been Howard's editor; that, since his editor owned the flat, he knew its address.

'I've just told you what he bloody said.'

Howard could have asked a lot of other questions, such as 'What did the man sound like?' but that would have risked a real bust-up, and remarks along the lines of, 'I'm not your bloody secretary, you know. I've got a farm to run.' In the event, their conversation wound up in what was – for Yorkshiremen – moderate civility.

'Well, thanks for letting me know.'

'Right you are. Keep in touch then.'

'Will do, Dad.'

Howard went back to the bed, and this time he lay down on it.

The enquirer might be Charles, furtively seeking the address to go with the phone number, which he already had. He could not be doing that for any good reason. But the more likely candidate was Lee Jones, in which case Howard could now expect a phone call from a murderer.

*

Howard waited by the phone until one. Then he went to the supermarket for food, returning via the *tabac* that sold Black Cats. Throughout the afternoon he told the time by the chimes of the church bell that floated through the window together with the distant shrill screams of sea bathers. He knew he ought to be out in the sun, but he couldn't leave the phone. By four o'clock he'd smoked ten fags and read a hundred and twenty pages of *Midnight Plus One* without giving the book the concentration it deserved.

It was obvious by now that the filming couldn't be taking place tomorrow as billed. But why hadn't Emma called to say that, for Christ's sake? And what about the person who'd been seeking his address? Why hadn't he called? Probably because he'd now discovered the address and intended to just turn up. So Howard was in effect watching two phones: the actual one and the entry phone, which would buzz nastily, as he'd found soon after his arrival in Nice when a woman had pressed it by mistake, and had been indignant at his answering in English.

At six he did go out again, and he sat on the crowded Prom. He'd stopped bothering to carry his notebook. He was now in the business of trying to suppress his imagination rather than recording its wanderings.

And it was far too bloody hot. There was the accumulated heat of the day with the heat of the heatwave on top. Only a slight deepening of the blue of the sea denoted late afternoon. As he scanned the beach, he was looking for Emma but saw only lesser females. Then he stopped studying the beach, in case his eye should land on Lee Jones, who – as a narcissist – would be a keen sunbather. Howard realised he was in front of the ruined hotel, which was like a single bad tooth in an otherwise healthy mouth. He walked inland a little way, to the shadowy, oil-smelling alley leading to the courtyard where the MGB had been parked. It was parked there still, suggesting that Emma had not found a new Englishman to be The Englishman With The Car. She might be ringing him now: 'We're shooting at dawn. Here's the location.'

So far, her impulsiveness had been attractive to him, since he himself had so little of that quality. But it might become irritating if you really got to know her. Well, he would take that chance. He drank a *pression* in the Canne à Sucre and amazingly enough that turned out to be his last drink of the day, because he walked back to the flat without finding an off licence (or whatever the French called them) on the way. As the telephone kept its vow of silence, he whiled away the rest of the evening with the aid of two pots of tea, a tomato omelette, a bar of chocolate, half a dozen Black Cats and *Midnight Plus One.*

He found he could forget about the phone for minutes on end. But his relative equanimity deserted him just when he needed it most – at bed time. As he was closing the curtains on the open window and the still-hot night, he thought of one appalling reason why Emma might not have called him. She was the kind of person who was likely to be winked at.

Saturday.

Nice

Ever since arriving in Nice, Charles had been waiting for the news of a killing: the killing of the boy Howard by Lee Jones. So he had kept his radio tuned to the news while in his hotel room, to the point where the batteries had died and had to be renewed. If no fatal development occurred soon, then Charles was going to have to phone the boy and suggest a meeting to talk things over in a more honest way than hitherto. Meanwhile, he would conduct his own search for Jones, in which he was hampered by the elementary fact that he didn't know what Jones looked like.

But as he drank his mid-morning espresso on Place Masséna it struck Charles that he might look for the LP record Jones had made which, according to the boy, was done under the name Picture Show. There would be a picture of him pouting on the record sleeve. He then remembered about the record shop on Rue Cassini which he had visited with Syl, who – being operatic – liked opera.

He would head that way. He had twice asked for the bill to be brought to him by the oafish and spotty waiter who was now lounging with a cigarette on the margins of the terrace. So Charles took pleasure in sauntering away from his table with no money left upon it. He was looking for trouble all right. In his jacket pocket, the Model C bounced lightly against his upper thigh as he walked through the hot white streets. Nice was a beautiful backdrop to whatever he was going to do, just as Oxford had been a quarter of a century ago.

At the record shop on Rue Cassini, his mention of Picture Show elicited a grimace from the man in the pop music department.

But a grimace was better than a blank look. The man said that the record was *'très obscure'*, and he directed Charles to a warehouse-like place on Rue de la Buffa that retailed all sorts of hippy junk, including old records. These – it transpired – were presided over by a sinister youth with a convict's haircut and wire glasses.

He was reading a paperback as Charles approached, and he continued to read it as Charles stood before him. Charles had him down as a displaced intellectual, a veteran of *Les Événements*.

Asked about any possible record by a group called Picture Show, he stared with suspicion at Charles before announcing that he had sold his one copy of that very LP not more than half an hour ago – a fact that greatly interested Charles. He asked if he might know to what sort of person – male, female, young, old? – thus giving the youth his chance to *épater le bourgeois*: *'Ça ne vous concerne pas,'* he said, returning to his reading.

Charles had been tempted to say, 'Now you can do better than that,' whilst removing the Model C from his pocket. But in the event, he walked half a mile to the sleepy mansion that housed the Musée des Beaux Arts, which was always more or less deserted, and offered a more relaxed way of contemplating the Promenade des Anglais – as depicted in the tapestry-like paintings of Raoul Dufy and others – than the hectic reality. Had the boy Howard Miller been the purchaser of the record? No, because he already had a copy, as Charles seemed to recollect he had said. It seemed to Charles that one very likely purchaser of a record by Lee Jones was Lee Jones himself.

Charles sat alone in the cool, high-ceilinged room. The shutters of the tall windows were closed against the heat of the day, but fuzzy light seeped in around the edges, as in a Mark Rothko paint-ing. Charles had come here to think and also to do something he shouldn't. He said a mental apology to Dufy and the other Fauvists as the scenario he had envisaged – and hoped for – began to unfold. From the wide corridor beyond, he heard the voices of some tourists – English tourists. One of them, a cockney male (surprisingly thuggish-sounding, given the location), was speculating about the availability of a 'toilet'. The speaker was accompanied by a woman and at least one child. It seemed possible, as their voices became louder, that the quest for the 'toilet' would be deferred in favour of entering the room in which Charles sat. They would be in the room within a couple of seconds, so Charles brought the Model C into the open, and rested it on his knee.

He re-pocketed it the moment they entered, but it was possible that the child – a girl – had seen the gun because she suddenly broke off from recriminating about how her parents had not made good their promise of an ice cream. And so the excitement that Charles had kindled in himself had been brought to a higher pitch.

He stood up. What now? He was envisaging the derelict Palais, like a corpse at a party, and its neighbour the Canne à Sucre. The young Charles would ensure he was there very soon with a bottle of tourist's rosé on the table before him.

About seven hours later.

Nice

At 6.30 p.m. in the flat, Howard – who was quite literally staring at a blank sheet of paper – noticed that the pigeons beyond the window had started making their evening noise. He put the kettle on the gas, ran a bath. The clattering of the water began to coincide with the screaming of the kettle, but there was another noise on top. The phone. Racing to it, Howard heard the joyful sound of Emma, with other joyful noises in the background. He wanted to say, 'You're alive!' But the remark would have been otiose. She was in a bar.

'Hello, Man With Car! Get down here immediately!'

'Where?'

'The Cave, of course!'

She had sounded a bit drunk, he thought, as he hurried through the airless, crowded streets, having neither bathed nor made tea.

He descended into the golden gloom of the Cave. She sat at the usual table (the 'high table', so to speak), her skin browner than before, and her hair blacker, and very roughly gathered up into its short ponytail. The place was packed. A sort of conference presided over by Fabien was going on at the table, but Emma seemed semi-detached from it, which was promising. She rose to greet Howard with a bottle of wine in her hand and her skimpy bag over her shoulder. She offered a cheek for kissing, then the other one, which Howard took as an indication that he'd done the first kiss right. She stood on a chair, in order to signal imperiously to Eric at the bar, and he brought over two glasses. The bottle that Emma poured from was full, as if she had been saving it specially for Howard, but he must not get carried away with self-congratulation.

'They're talking about camera lenses,' she explained, indicating the conference. Fabien caught Howard's eye, gave him a grudging '*Ça va?*' It was a rhetorical question of course.

Howard said to Emma, 'I thought we were supposed to be filming today?'

'We had some problems yesterday and today but we're all set for tomorrow.' It seemed about the most characteristic sentence she had ever spoken, and Howard loved her. He offered her a Black Cat. She took one, then reached again towards the packet. She removed the picture card and showed it to Howard.

208

'Any good?' she said.

She was definitely slightly pissed. 'It's a Reliant Scimitar,' said Howard. 'Princess Anne has one. So they must be good.'

'Now,' said Emma, returning the card to him, 'I have a little story for you. We were in here last night ... '

Howard thought again how much he hated that 'we', but then he began to be worried on a deeper level.

'There was a big crowd in,' she continued, 'and we couldn't get our table – *this* table, I mean – so we were standing at the bar. There was a guy at the far end, and he kept looking over at us, or at least I think so, but he wore sunglasses, so he was pretentious ... to say the least.'

Howard wanted to stop her there; to stop time itself there. But she was relentless.

'Fabien,' she said, 'is interested in faces, as you know. He said the guy was very cool looking, and maybe he could be something in the film. I didn't exactly agree; I thought the guy was pretty, but too pretty – sort of artificial looking, and not nice. I had the feeling he would be trouble on the set. I mean, he was probably not the type to do anything in a supporting role.'

Howard said, 'Will you just tell me what happened?'

'That's exactly what I am doing. Fabien got into a long conversation with Marc, who's our cameraman.' (She indicated a man at the table.) 'So it was me and the guy in the sunglasses, and he definitely was staring at me, and then he took his sunglasses off, and he had the most amazingly green eyes I've ever seen. I was thinking about what you said on the phone from Paris about how you'd come across someone who you thought might be this winking killer who's been in all the papers, and you described the guy, and said he was small, good-looking and with incredibly green –'

'Look,' said Howard, and he was quite surprised that he'd grabbed hold of her arm (as was she). 'Did the guy wink at you?'

It was absolutely imperative that she say 'no'.

'No.'

'Good. That's very good indeed.'

'*I* winked at *him*.'

Of course – because she would always show boldness. Even so, he asked bleakly, 'Why the hell did you do that?'

'To flush him out. See how he'd react.'

'And how *did* he react?'

'He looked shocked, as if he'd suddenly become a prude, and he sort of retreated, putting his sunglasses back on and moving away from the bar . . . which might have been partly because Fabien was giving him a pretty heavy stare at this point. Then he left. So the question is this, Man With Car: was he the person you talked to in London? Was he Lee Jones?'

'Yes; that *is* the question.'

'I mean, it's interesting, but I know he can't have been really because your Lee Jones is in London, and so is the winking killer, and I know the chances of your Jones being the winking killer are tiny anyway, but it's definitely interesting . . . '

He couldn't bring himself to say that Lee Jones had threatened to come to Nice; that he ought to have warned her of this.

'So today,' Emma was saying, 'I went looking for that record you told me that Lee Jones had made with his group, Picture Show. Because it has his photo on the cover, right?'

'Yes,' said Howard. 'I was going to bring it, but I left it in a bar in Paris.' He would admit to that lapse, at least.

Emma said, 'I found the record at Hélène's.'

'Who's Hélène?'

'Oh, a *grande dame*. No, a *jolie laide*. She runs the place where we bought your clothes. She does records as well. It was cheap so I bought it.'

'And was it the same man?'

He couldn't bear to see her face formulating the answer 'Yes', so he looked away.

'Well ... I don't know. I don't think it was.'

'Are you sure? The picture on the record was taken a few years ago.'

'Yes, but the bone structure of the man in the picture was different from the man I saw.'

He wanted to congratulate her with an embrace, even though he couldn't be certain that the man she'd winked at had not been Jones. Ought he now to tell her that Jones had said he was coming to Nice? It was too late, somehow, and at this point it would seem like a gratuitous attempt to scare her, not that she had betrayed any sign of fear while relating her story. It might equally seem self-pitying because after all, the reason Jones wanted to come to Nice was – as Howard understood it – to kill Howard.

'Now tomorrow,' she said, 'will be an early start. We need you at the car place at eight o'clock.'

'Will you be there?'

'Of course. We'll drive down to the cove. I'll direct you.'

'Where *is* the cove?'

'Between here and Monaco.'

'What happens there?'

'There's a little beach, and a little road. That's where we film your scene. We want the sea in the background when you sell the car. Fabien says the shot of the sea will point up the triviality of the commercial transaction. He also wants to get a shot *from* the sea.'

For half an hour they drank wine, and she briefed him about the shoot. 'This jacket, please,' she said. 'It looks very nice.'

'You would say that; you bought it.'

'It's partly the way you wear it.'

'Well, I can only wear it in one way,' he said, whereas what he should have said, he realised too late, was 'Thank you', because it was probably the greatest compliment he had ever received.

She said, 'Do you have a plain white shirt?'

'Yes.'

'Can it be pressed?'

'It's a non-iron shirt.'

'Mmm.'

Fabien had apparently been listening. He leant over, pointing accusingly at Howard. 'And you will shave, yes?'

Howard eyed him. Eventually, he nodded agreement. Howard always shaved, whereas Fabien had his five o'clock shadow twenty-four hours a day. Fabien was now rising to his feet, collecting Emma, ready to take her away.

Howard slept very deeply that night, and when the alarm woke him at six, things were different.

Sunday.

Nice

Things were different because Howard was now The Englishman With The Car ... and it was also raining. He took a bath, then buttoned up his white shirt at the window. The weather over Nice was throwing a fit, and it was shocking to see, as when a good-natured person becomes suddenly angry. A big puddle was forming on a flat roof twenty yards to the left of the window. He'd never even noticed that roof before. There was no sound from the pigeons, only the seething of the rain.

Down on the Prom, he drank a crème and ate a croissant on the terrace of the Canne à Sucre, where he was protected from the rain by a plastic canopy of semi-transparent green. The palm trees on the traffic islands rocked in the wind, their leaves threatening to begin whirling in circles, windmill-like. At eight exactly – because he was always on time – he was walking down the oil-smelling alleyway. The brown car ('chestnut brown' would be the official designation) was waiting with the hood up; Emma sat inside with a map unfolded on her knees. As he climbed in, they did the double kiss more or less spontaneously. She wore a short white mac. Surely, it couldn't be an accident that she was his accomplice in all film-related matters? She must want the role.

It was very intimate under the hood, which gave a rubbery smell to the interior. The key was in the ignition. As he turned it, Emma half-folded, half-crumpled the map, and tossed it into the back. 'I know the way,' she said.

Howard said, 'Won't the rain disrupt the filming?'

'It'll clear up later. And Fabien always says the Riviera sky after rain has the best light.'

If he was always saying that, thought Howard, he must be very boring. As before, he gunned the engine a little in the alleyway, and the note was as sweet as before. Emerging between the bar and the shop that sold sunglasses (both of which were closed) he turned left towards the Prom – and Emma was winding down the window on her side. 'That's him!' she said. 'That's the guy I saw in the bar!'

Howard stopped the car, just before the junction with the Prom. A dirty white dustbin lorry immediately came up behind and began honking its horn. What the fuck was it doing at large on a Sunday? And the thing was bedecked – ludicrously – with flashing orange lights. There were no fewer than five rough-hewn Frenchmen sitting in the cab, as though they were sitting at a bar. But Howard wasn't bothered about them. Emma had indicated the pavement on her side – the left – and he couldn't see that properly unless he climbed out of the car, so that was what he did. Obviously, the dustbin men were furious: not only had he parked at a junction, but he had just climbed out from the 'wrong' side of a fancy car. Amid the blaring of the lorry's horn – now continuous – he crossed the road and caught up with the man Emma had identified. From the rear, he appeared well-dressed in high-heeled Chelsea boots, expensive jeans, green shirt. He was protected from the rain by a silly white sunhat, and one of those cheap transparent ponchos. The impression – from the rear – was one of slightly fetishistic camp. Howard overtook him, looked back. He had no idea what he would do if this should be Lee Jones.

He saw . . . a man who was not Lee Jones, albeit handsome in that same compressed, waxen way, and with green eyes. In his relief, Howard forgot where he was, and he apologised in English to the man for having scrutinised him so suspiciously. He ran back to the MG, and one of the dustbin men was opening the cab door while his colleague continued to blare the horn.

Howard jumped into the MG, and there was immediately a gap in the traffic on the Prom. Turning hard left onto the Prom, he said, 'You sure that was the man you saw on Saturday?'

'Of course.'

'Well, it wasn't Lee Jones.'

'Therefore it wasn't the Winker?'

'Correct.'

'I think you have a bit of an obsession with the Winker.'

Instead of being pleased, she was frowning into the rear-view. The French dustman who'd threatened to climb down when they were on the side street had now actually done so, and it was very unpleasant to see him at large. He pulled open the door on Howard's side, roaring '*Sortez!*' So Howard climbed out, obeying his own law of walking towards trouble whenever possible. He was scared of the man, but more scared of being seen to cower in the low car. Emma had also climbed out and she began shouting at the dustman while he shouted at Howard. The dustman was quite small and round; not soft though. He resembled a clenched fist and spoke with incredible force and volume, as if he were part of the storm. He seemed to be indicating that Howard step onto the traffic island for a formal fight.

After a couple of false starts, Howard managed to respond with '*Quel est votre problème?*' He said it because he *could* say it, not because he didn't know what the problem was, and it was this: he had held up the rubbish lorry for half a minute. All along the Promenade des Anglais, the traffic had stopped and horns were blaring amid the din of the wind and rain, and perhaps with the noise of the sea mingling in too. Somewhere along the line, a police car was trapped. Howard could hear its frustrated two-tone siren, which sounded absurd, since it was supposed to accompany momentum.

Emma was now in the full flow of a presumably eloquent speech, and the man was gradually paying attention to her, perhaps because she appeared to be asking him a lot of questions. Howard glanced towards the other men in the cab of the dustcart, and they were grinning, so Howard knew this situation at least would probably not come to violence. A policeman was coming through the rain on a motorbike, and Emma began redirecting her eloquence to him.

Two minutes later, they were moving again, Castle Hill coming and going in between the swiping of the wipers.

Howard said, 'What were you asking him?'

'Lots of things. Who did he think he was? (I think he found that one the hardest.) Why was he so rude? What's the hurry about collecting up a load of rubbish? Did it cross his mind that we might have had an excellent reason for causing a slight delay back there? Did he realise he had already committed an assault by threatening you? And so on and so forth. Turn left here.'

They were leaving the sea behind, climbing through the town towards the railway station. Then they were on the motorway running east, following the signs for Monaco. Road signs in France were different: the arrows were crooked, like broken branches. It was all slightly disturbing; and the hood didn't fit properly, so that trickles of rain were coming down the wrong side of the windows. But the MGB was running beautifully, and the rain was easing.

Then it stopped altogether.

They pulled over in a gravel lay-by and took the roof down: a two-person job. Below them were terraces with villas and small vineyards, and then came the sea, all smiles again, the glitter starting as though an electric current had been applied. As they pulled onto the road another MG – a white Midget – suddenly appeared in Howard's rear-view mirror. It had come fast round a bend and nearly clipped them – the driver had to swing into the other lane. If another car had been coming the other way, everybody would have been dead. The car disappeared around another bend – and these were hairpins, as on a race track.

'Bloody nutcase,' shouted Howard, because of the wind in their faces. He hoped it wouldn't make him too red; he had not thought to apply sun cream, what with the torrential rain of the early morning.

'It was a similar model to this?' said Emma, who looked very at home in a speeding sports car.

'An MG Midget. Incredibly nippy – like a roller skate. That's really the classic MG. All the racy English guys have them until they get too fat to fit in. Shall we try to catch it?'

'Don't be silly.'

But then she smiled sidelong at him, so he put his foot down, and they were both laughing, as people do on a funfair ride. Around every bend . . . the Midget was nowhere to be seen.

'Bit odd,' said Howard, in view of the fact that he'd been averaging seventy.

'Maybe he's gone off the edge,' said Emma, because it was precipitous on the sea side, with only a two-foot-high white wall. Fly over that and you'd be bouncing – probably upside down – over scrub and white rocks, then onto some taller, more villainous rocks waiting in the edge of the sea.

He said, 'Where's the cove?'

'About ten miles.'

She was adjusting her baggy trousers, somewhere in the region of her hip. His hand, coming up from a gear change, brushed hers. It seemed a significant moment on her side as well, and Howard felt emboldened. He asked, 'You live with Fabien, right?'

'Of course.'

He wanted to ask *why*. Was it possible beautiful women lived with men so as to emphasise to other men that they weren't living with *them*? In which case perhaps any man would do as a cohabitee . . .

He looked at the rear-view mirror, seeing only the road. When he looked again, a car was there. It was green: a Citroën DS, coming on like a fucking rocket.

Howard immediately accelerated, and Emma flashed him a

worried look, the first he had ever seen on her face, because this was now too fast. Whereas Howard had been taking pleasure in his driving skill, he now had no option but to drive well. He felt too scared to talk, but he owed Emma an explanation.

'He's here after all,' said Howard, nodding towards the window.

'Who?'

And for the first time he wondered if she was stupid.

'Lee Jones. That's his car. At least ... it's the same make as his car.'

But complications of light on the windscreen of the Citroën made it impossible to see the driver.

'Only the same make?' said Emma, and at ninety miles an hour he did not have the spare capacity to answer that.

She said, 'Slow down, Howard,' and it was an order.

He could afford to do nothing more than shake his head.

'He's trying to kill us.'

He was down to sixty for a bend, during which the Citroën kept up its speed. This was such a strange road, he thought, changing up again. You were going one way; the next minute you were going the opposite way. But the situation did not change as the angle of the road changed: the Citroën was twenty yards behind, and there was a permanent blinding sparkle on the windscreen.

As Howard accelerated there were mountains soaring to the left, rocks descending to the right – and another hairpin was coming up, the low wall bending with it. Howard had been changing down to third at the previous bends. Now he changed down twice – and fast – to second, slowing severely, so that the Citroën was only a few feet behind. Howard aimed at the apex, and the back end swung towards the sea. So they were sideways, and the tyres were being destroyed, but he was calm. Then he was aiming the right way, and accelerating to a hundred.

'You see, a car can go sideways as well as forwards,' he said. Ridiculous boasting, but it was adrenalin talking.

'Pull over!' she shouted, and he knew that whatever happened next, things would be different between them. Another car was coming the opposite way: a fat stately Merc. The speed of the MGB seemed to blow it towards the wall, but only for a second. The driver would be pissed off, but at least he was alive. The Citroën was further back now but gaining as another bend approached. Basically the Citroën was a more powerful car than the MGB. Howard was changing down again, and there was the Citroën right behind, but still with a driver who was no more than a shadow. Did he wear sunglasses?

Whoever he was, he couldn't drift the Citroën. It was too long: it would be like drifting a train. But the hydraulics gave the car brilliant road holding, and it squirmed its way around the corners with horrible determination.

'I'm sure it's Jones,' said Howard, shouting over the engine noise. 'I think he saw us on the Prom when we were fighting with the dustmen.'

When they were on the straight again, there was a man – an idiot – pushing a bike on the side of the road. Howard nearly blew him into the sea as well. 'That was the turning for the Cove,' said Emma, because the man had been plodding past a junction. Howard was approaching one hundred miles an hour. The faster he went the narrower the road seemed to become. The MGB wasn't made for this. Its bluff had been called. Howard remembered a magazine advert he'd seen for the marque: *It's all you need*, had been the slogan, but Howard needed something quicker. The Citroën was about fifty yards behind.

'Pull over!' Emma said again.

Howard said, 'There *is* nowhere to pull over.'

But then there *was*: a sort of stone crescent cut into the hillside on the left; a very antiquated lay-by, like a remnant of something Roman. Howard skidded into it; the Citroën flew on past. Emma was nodding, perhaps in self-congratulation.

Howard felt the need to defend himself. 'I think he was trying to run us off the road.'

'You think. Perhaps you think too much. Turn around and let's go to the shoot.'

'But what about *him?*' Howard nodded towards the bend around which the Citroën had disappeared.

'What *about* him?'

'I mean what if it was Lee Jones? The Winker.'

'Then let him go winking at people in Monaco.'

'And killing them?'

She sighed. 'Yes. You'll have to tell the police if that's what you really think. There's a village near the Cove. You can call from there.'

There was silence in the car as Howard did a three-point turn in the white dust of the lay-by. He drove at normal speed (which felt dead slow) towards the junction for the Cove. He kept checking the rear-view, but no Citroën DS appeared: only a grubby white Peugeot that kept its distance.

He turned onto the Cove road, a winding descent that seemed likely to tip them into the sea. He wanted to show he was calm, so he said, 'It's rear wheel drive, this car, so the back end always wants to step out. You might as well take the hint and go sideways. We might have a complaint from the garage about the tyres, but you do what you can when a car like that's on your tail. The Citroën maxes out at about one-twenty. Have you seen the film *Samourai*? I mean *Le Samourai*? Alain Delon is an assassin who has a bunch of skeleton keys. They allow him to steal any car as long as it's a grey Citroën DS. Everything in the film's grey or light blue, probably to match Delon's eyes. I've just thought: I won't be able to speak to the French cops. Would you mind doing it?'

She nodded, without looking at him.

'I'm sorry for the dangerous driving,' he said, 'but I had to take evasive action.'

'I'll speak to the cops,' she said, 'but what do I tell them? I mean, you thought the man in the bar was Lee Jones ... '

'So did you. That's why you winked at him.'

'Only because you'd told me about him. But it wasn't Lee Jones as it turned out, was it? And the green car – the Citroën. There must be thousands of those in France.'

'The popular one today is the SM, and the one back there was definitely a DS.'

'Oh, you and your cars. Was it the same number plate as the one you saw in Oxford?'

'I can't say.'

'That's unfortunate.'

'Well, you know. I was a bit busy trying to keep us alive.'

She shrugged. 'People drive like maniacs on that road. Everyone thinks they're – whatsisname – James Hunt on the Corniche.'

Howard was beginning to see things from her point of view. Lee Jones had said he was coming to Nice, but Nice was one of the most popular destinations for any Briton and he – Howard – had developed a complex about the Winker. He was seeing him every-where. He'd scared Emma yesterday and endangered her today. She was not impressed by his driving; his charm was wearing off, if he'd ever had any in the first place.

At the bottom of the hill, the road began running compan-ionably along next to a small white beach, but there was nothing companionable between Howard and Emma. He parked the car. About a dozen good-looking French people were on the beach.

Any one of them could have been in a film, but only three of them were – or four, including Emma.

The focus of attention, the camera, was a delicate, antique-looking thing, and Fabien – skeletal in black jeans and black vest – was in a permanent mobile conference with the man who carried it about. There was a rubber dinghy at the water's edge. The sight of it did nothing to help Howard relax because he kept thinking a wave would pick it up and take it away. A make-up station had been created on the beach. It occupied a dent in the rocks of a promontory, a shallow cave, and was inhabited by the make-up artist and another woman whose job was to hold the mirror. Emma was in the chair now. A transistor radio in a leather case hung by a shoulder strap from the back of the chair, bad French pop music leaking from it.

Howard was watching proceedings while leaning against the hot bonnet of the MG. So far nobody had really spoken to him, but Fabien was apparently speaking *about* him (or about the car) with the cameraman and others. Howard lit a Black Cat. His latest worry was about sunburn. Why must traumatised skin default to red, of all colours? Why couldn't it go sallow? Howard was always jealous of people described as 'sallow'. The word applied to most of the people on the set.

As he smoked he felt unreal. This film was by definition unreal, and his supposed 'real life' offered nothing more solid by way of contrast. The sun, his enemy, was currently bleaching the sky and the sea. There was too much light – it hurt your eyes – but on the Corniche, this same sun had created darkness, hiding the identity of the man at the wheel of the Citroën. Maybe the driver *had* been a total stranger. Howard could hear the road from the beach, and every car on it seemed to be racing. If he really had been over-dramatising, the realisation ought to be making him happy, as when waking from a nightmare, but he could not be happy because of the way things were between himself and Emma. Could a thing be all over when it had never really begun? Stepping onto the soft sand, Howard bent down to rub out the cigarette. Suddenly, he was in shadow. The man standing over him had a neat, dark beard and what were sometimes called flashing eyes.

'Hi, I'm Raphael,' he said. 'I'm also Sacha.'

He had taken the trouble to remember that The Englishman With The Car really was English. This Raphael might be playing a shit, but he seemed to be the nicest guy on the set. Howard gave him a guided tour of the MGB as Emma was being made up. She had not looked at Howard since they'd arrived. Another man came up, a sort of assistant to the cameraman – even though he was dressed in swimming trunks – and asked Howard politely enough in broken English to move the car a little way forward. Howard did so, and Fabien nodded his approval from the beach, but the nod was directed to the man in the trunks rather than to Howard, who glanced again towards the make-up chair, from which Emma had now risen. But she hadn't moved far from it. She was standing on the sand looking out to sea with arms folded: a very noble, rather lonely pose. But now she was slowly turning around and coming over.

'Rose is ready for you, Man With Car,' she said, with something of her former friendliness.

But he had perhaps gone off her slightly, and the make-up didn't help. It made her look harder and older, which was no doubt deliberate. She must appear to be the sort of worldly woman who would be in a *ménage à trois*.

Howard too was made up in the cool cave, in which the sea made the same noise it does in a conch shell. Rose was very nice as she patted on brown powder, or at least she avoided mentioning his bad

223

complexion. But the mirror girl was irritating. She clearly lacked the imagination to appreciate that not everyone would want to see their own reflection. Over at the MG, the man in the trunks was raising the bonnet, creating the broken-down car scenario.

Rose turned off her radio, and filming began. Sacha really did say, 'Hey, that's quite a beast. But is it broken down?', and Howard really did say, 'A little trouble with the spark plugs. Nothing too serious,' as Sacha, Emma and the other woman looked on. Emma delivered her lines according to the French cinematic norm: she sounded quite wooden in other words. It had clearly never occurred to anyone else how terrible the lines were, even though each one had to be spoken half a dozen times at varying distances from the camera. Howard – who tinkered with his own prose until the last possible moment – quite admired this tenacity. The only real problems, it seemed, were caused by the shadows the sound woman kept inadvertently making as she held out the boom microphone; and by the noise from the road – the screaming of cars along the Corniche. It seemed Fabien kept moaning about it, and every time he did so, Emma looked at Howard while saying things in French to Fabien, presumably along the lines of what she'd already said to Howard: that it was every man for himself on that road.

The final shots were taken from out at sea, with the versatile man in the trunks controlling the dinghy.

Afterwards, Emma congratulated Howard. 'Fabien was delighted with your performance,' she said, indicating the stringy genius in question, who was just then biting into a baguette – because a trestle table bearing what was by now a late lunch had appeared on the beach. As Emma ushered Howard towards it, she slapped a red baseball cap on his head, which was thoughtful of her, but Howard couldn't help thinking these affectionate actions were not erotically significant. 'Sisterly' – that was the word, possibly even maternal. So was there really any point in being back in her favour? It seemed to him she had convinced herself that they had not been pursued by a murderer on the Corniche, and she was now making an effort to forgive Howard for having frightened her. She was not a person accustomed to being frightened, and she must rub out the memory.

In late afternoon, the set was (Emma translated) 'struck'. The man in the trunks dragged the dinghy into the make-up cave. A couple of people turned out to have motor scooters, on which they sped away, to join the Wacky Races of the Corniche. A white Renault pick-up truck collected most of the others. Howard would be returning the car to the garage behind the derelict hotel. Emma would be his passenger once again, and it was arranged that the man in the trunks, who was now the man in shorts and cheese-cloth shirt (his name was Felix), would squeeze into the residual back seat, because it seemed he had an appointment in downtown Nice. His English wasn't very good, but still it would be awkward to revisit the subject of the Winker with him listening in.

As it turned out, most of the talking was in French between Emma and Felix. Their theme, as far as Howard could tell, was the brilliance of Fabien, and he spent a long time listening to them, because for almost all the way back to Nice they were stuck behind a slow Saab with a placard on the roof reading AUTO ECOLE.

They were late onto the Prom (where they dropped off Felix) and late to the garage or showroom, or whatever it was. A gate had been dragged across the alleyway, and very decisively locked.

'It's all right,' said Emma. 'I thought this might happen. Georges said if we weren't back by four, we'd miss him.'

'And did he tell you what to do in that case?' said Howard, hearing a new impatience with her in his voice.

'Of course.'

She directed him to an underground car park that seemed to specialise in accommodating sports cars, and she indicated a small sticker on the windscreen of the MGB that was a kind of season ticket for the place. After they'd parked, Emma took the keys and put them in her skimpy bag. 'Georges is closed on Mondays,' she said, and Howard realised she must be speaking about the car man. 'I'll take them back to him on Tuesday.' So Howard did not seem to be required again.

'See you soon,' he found the nerve to suggest.

'Of course,' she'd replied, and the closing kiss had been the most fleeting of all their fleeting kisses.

*

As he entered the flat the phone was ringing, which required him to review again the question of who knew the number. His dad; but it wouldn't be him again. Talking to his son really took it out of him, and he always needed a long break from Howard after doing so. Emma? No. He'd only just left her, and she'd probably never call him again. His editor? To ask him how things were going in the flat? No, not his style. That was all the reasonably pleasant possibilities ruled out. He had to face it: this was going to be either Charles or Lee Jones. But when Howard picked up, the voice was unfamiliar. This was a plummy, slightly louche – and possibly slightly drunken – man in late middle age.

'Hello, you don't know me, but your number was given to me by Bruce.'

'Bruce?'

'You spoke to him in the King's Arms in Oxford.'

'Oh yes. I never got his name.' (Howard had also forgotten he'd given him the phone number.)

'And you're not going to get mine either, I'm afraid. You were asking about Pat Price and I think that, by coincidence, Lee Jones was in the pub at the same time.'

'Yes. Lee Jones was a friend of Price, right?'

'Wrong. At least . . . the word friend is wrong. I'm afraid that Pat developed rather an obsession with that little bastard. He was strung along by him for several years.'

'Oh.'

'And for no other reason I can see except to play games.'

'What sort of games?'

'Games designed to leave poor Pat uncertain of his position.'

'How?'

'By the giving or withholding of affection, I assume.'

The tone of the answer suggested that Howard's question had been superfluous. He tried another one: 'Do you think Lee Jones was after Price's money?'

'Not especially. As far as I could tell, Jones had more money than Price. But that brings me to what I really wanted to say. When Price was on his deathbed at his place here in Oxford, some of us would visit him, and one day towards the end he was very distressed, which wasn't like him. Lee Jones had called around and walked away with some important personal papers of Pat's. I don't know what sort of papers, he wouldn't say. Do you have any idea what they might have been?'

As he said 'No', Howard wondered whether this were really true.

'Apparently,' the man said, in a tone now openly aggressive, 'you were asking about Pat Price on behalf of some third party. Might he know anything about what became of those papers?'

'I don't know; I don't think so. He seemed to know very little about Pat Price. That's why he wanted to find out things.' Howard then thought of a clever thing to say: 'I'll ask him, if you like.'

'Yes. You do that. Because what happened was a crime: theft – and theft from a dying man.'

'Do you want me to tell you what I find out? I'd be quite happy to do that. But I'd need your phone number.'

And by that, he'd pricked the balloon, which was just as well, because Howard would *not* have been 'quite happy' to relay information to this man.

'Well no, don't worry about that,' the man said. 'There's nothing I can do for poor Pat now, and I don't want to be involved in any way with what sounds like a rather sordid nexus.'

He was proud of that word, Howard could tell.

'I just thought you ought to know,' said the man, and that turned out to be his sign-off.

I ought to visit Charles, Howard thought, putting the phone down, *and why am I not doing that?*

The reason was cowardice; therefore, he must do it.

*

He walked north, away from the sea, entering the part of Nice that could have been any French town: people walking small dogs, sitting on chairs placed on the pavements, drawing the shutters down over the windows of pharmacies or estate agents. It was 8 p.m. The streets became scruffier, more suffocating and cigarette-smelling as he approached the vicinity of the station, and Charles's hotel.

Insects seethed in the garden as he approached the peeling doors. He could hear a station announcement reverberating. He pictured Charles in his room: elegant but dishevelled, drinking heavily beneath a listless fan – a scene out of Maugham or Greene. The lobby was dark. It took him a while to get his bearings; there was the reception desk ... but nobody at it. Then a large woman, cheerful but slouching in slippers, appeared from behind him. She'd stepped out of a room in which a TV comedy was playing, and she had perhaps only just finished laughing.

'Monsieur Underhill? I will call him. Your name please?'

So Howard had the surname at last.

She held a short telephone conversation in French. Then some pretty little lights (very noticeable in the gloom) started twink-ling above the door of the lift. Underhill did look a bit seedy, approaching Howard in his stockinged feet as if this hotel were really his house. He might have been drinking as well, because he said, 'Howard, come on up,' as if they'd known each other for years.

'How are you?' he said, as the lift doors closed. 'I was half expecting you to call.'

Howard was considering (and rejecting) crass lines such as, 'I think you owe me an explanation.'

The room was dark brown and hot – and Howard didn't want to look too closely at the furniture, because he knew he would find marks of distress that would be disturbingly at odds with the per-sona of the occupant as he understood it. Then again some of it was familiar from Howard's imaginings: on the scuffed coffee table stood an opened bottle of red wine; there was an empty packet of Gauloises, and a pretty full – and big – blue glass ashtray. There was also a transistor radio on the table. Howard was thinking, and Underhill was watching him think – and he was smiling, regaining the upper hand, in spite of everything. 'I usually stay here when I come to Nice alone,' he said.

'Why?' asked Howard.

'I want to avoid the English.' Underhill was still smiling; but now he became galvanised. 'But we can't have our meeting here.' He was reaching into a battered wardrobe for a shirt and jacket, and he didn't seem to mind dressing in front of Howard, who was reminded that the man was gay. Or this might be a public school characteristic: those types had the confidence to veer between formality and informality. They would take hold of your arm and offer amazing confidences. This was charm, possibly. Howard thought of charm as something he might get around to later, when he'd made his name as an author.

Underhill took him to a little bar down the road from the hotel. It was another Cave, but above ground and rather bright and antiseptic. They were the only people in it apart from the beaming proprietor, who had supplied them with a bottle of white wine despite obviously being in the process of closing up.

'Cheers,' said Underhill, and Howard did not feel obliged to respond. 'I must be starting to appear rather disingenuous,' Charles continued. 'I came to Nice because I think you were right: Lee Jones will be here.'

'Will be. I think he *is*. But why do you think so?'

'Because he *said* he would be here. He wanted to worry you by telling you, but he couldn't leave it at that. He must follow through on his declared intentions – I think because of his basic inadequacy. He's created a world in which he's the star performer, the instigator of action.'

'So you now think he's the Winker?'

'It's possible; maybe even likely.'

'I think he tried to kill me today – me and somebody else.'

230

Howard related everything that had happened in Nice in connection with Emma.

'And do you think he *was* the one in the Cave?'

'Maybe not, but I'm certain he was the one who tried to run me off the road. So we should go to the police.'

'They wouldn't believe us. And anyway, where exactly is he?'

'I thought,' said Howard, 'that if we hung around on the Prom for long enough, he'd come to *us*.'

'Yes,' said Underhill. 'But he doesn't know what I look like.'

'Are you sure?'

'Pretty confident.'

'He was Pat Price's boyfriend, wasn't he?'

'Yes.'

'Was he your boyfriend?'

'I've just told you, Howard, that he doesn't know what I look like.'

'But I don't necessarily believe you.'

'That's reasonable enough.'

Howard told Underhill about the phone call from the plummy man – about Lee Jones having stolen the documents off Pat Price. Underhill seemed to listen with satisfaction. Why was he *smiling*, for Christ's sake? Because he had anticipated the news? Because it had somehow stimulated him?

Howard said, 'It's very hard for me not to go to the police at this point.'

'I think we can find him and confirm our suspicions.'

'Not before he's killed us.'

'Oh come on. That's not the real you . . . You strike me as pretty brave, Howard.'

Manipulation, thought Howard. But it had worked: he wouldn't be scurrying off to the cops just yet.

Charles Underhill said, 'Let's take one more day – tomorrow – to find him and confront him. I think we'll be safe 'til then. He doesn't know where your friend Emma lives, does he?'

'I don't think so.'

'And what about you?'

Howard shook his head '. . . Although I think he tried to find out.' Howard told that story as well.

When he'd finished Underhill said, 'I like the sound of your dad.'

Patronising, thought Howard.

'Look,' said Underhill. 'Tomorrow, you do what *you* said. Sit in the middle of the Prom – making your notes if you like. Everyone in town is on the Prom at some point every day. You'll be looking for him and I think he'll be looking for you. Try to get some sort of contact for him. I'm going to enquire in the best hotels. There's only about a dozen really good ones.'

No need to ask why I'm not fitted for that role, thought Howard. He said, 'What do we do at the end of tomorrow when we haven't found him?'

'Liaise.'

'How?'

'Well, you know where *I* am, and I have your phone number.'

As he walked back to the flat, Howard was asking himself the perennial question about Charles Underhill: why didn't he want Howard to go to the police? Because he would lack credibility; Emma had said the same. It was reasonable enough, he supposed. But he couldn't shake the idea that Lee Jones had damaging information on Underhill, and if they went to the police, that would come to light.

Howard was now in the Old Town – a matter of darkness and vivid colour, the latter in the small illuminated signs of the bars and restaurants and the stalls vending luminous ice creams, offered for sale as an antidote to the heat and the night. Then he was in the street of the Cave, walking along it until he came to the semi-circular window that looked down into the bar. His feet – the trainers selected by Emma – would now be among those visible from the bar. It would be undignified to crouch down and peer inside but he did it anyway. There was the important, low table with the usual artistic conference going on. He saw the back of Emma's head. The French cunt was alongside. Howard hadn't been invited.

He walked on, avoiding his flat, aiming for the small, bright *tabac* and trinket shop on the Prom where he could pick up a half bottle of rosé. He was checked on his way there by the sight of a late swimmer in the sea: a contented fat man doing backstroke like a clockwork machine. It seemed to Howard that he was swimming purposefully towards tomorrow.

Monday.

Nice

Lee – in hotel bathrobe loosely fastened – was at the window of his suite, looking down at early evening on the Promenade. So many of the men walking along the Promenade des Anglais were ridiculous in their gigolo regalia: medallions hanging around the necks, or cravats retained by a gold ring. He had more time for the women. There was an innocence about their summer frocks, and it was all right for a woman to wear sunglasses on her head, whereas among men, only beautiful ones with a lot of hair – Lee himself for instance – could get away with it, and he had brought the Vuarnets with him to Nice, because it seemed to him that this was where they belonged.

The little red and gold alarm clock by the bed started to trill. Lee turned and watched it do so. It always seemed to him that alarm clocks and telephones were trying, and failing, to make him jump. He'd forgotten he'd set the alarm. He'd been having a long afternoon nap. Well, his life had been such a whirlwind of late. To think that, only on Wednesday morning, he'd been trademarking in east London! Then lunch with Howard Miller, followed by Zanzibar in the evening . . .

Even if he hadn't met Miller, he might have gone abroad on the Thursday, to escape the intensification of the police search that would inevitably follow the latest and most momentous phase of the programme. (Its climax, possibly?) At ten on Thursday morning, he was all packed and ready to go when the phone had rung. He was so sure it would be Geoff that he'd nearly ignored it. But it had been a woman with a really sexy voice saying, 'Mr Jones? I have Mr Ormond on the line for you.' To be calling so quickly after their meeting . . . it could only be that he'd loved the tape, and so it proved. He wanted to arrange a lunch but was going away himself to Los Angeles (which was very much the sort of place a musician wanted his prospective manager to be going!), so could they pencil in a date one month hence? Reaching into his pocket for his pen, Lee had initially put his hand on the folder, which had been quite appropriate in a way, since it was the folder that had brought all this about. And of course he had brought it with him to Nice.

Lee had loved being on the car ferry: the best-looking man with the most stylish car (it amazed Lee that people would seek to underline the dowdiness of, say, a Morris Minor or an Austin A40 by going for a grey model). He had a recording contract in his pocket – as good as – and all his pink, lumpen fellow passengers were reading about him in the papers.

He had driven all day and some of the night on Thursday, and he was just past Paris when he'd heard on the car radio that Maureen's body had been found. And so the programme – his programme – had reached fruition amid the blanket news coverage he had predicted. But there was still the question of Howard Miller, who probably knew that Lee had sent the post-cards to Underhill, and also suspected him of being the Winker. Presumably Underhill knew, and suspected, the same things? That was an interesting one.

On the Friday morning Lee had gone into a call box on the Promenade and dialled the farm in Yorkshire, encountering a very ferocious Yorkshireman. It wasn't that this character had seen through Lee's pretence of being Miller's publisher. That wasn't the reason he'd been uncooperative. He'd been uncooperative because he was an uncooperative person. Lee had got the phone number out of him, but he didn't really want to have to call Miller, since that would scare him off. He'd known he might have to do it eventually though. Meanwhile he'd devoted the rest of Friday and Saturday to enjoying the town, keeping an eye out for the boy, and reading about himself in the papers. He was all over them – the French ones as well, but he couldn't read those.

On Sunday, he'd got up early for that day's papers knowing they'd be full of himself. But he'd forgotten that the British Sundays didn't arrive in Nice until Sunday evening or even Monday. He'd thought of going back to bed, but then decided on a drive. In the lobby of the Negresco he'd asked the valet to retrieve the Citroën from whatever unknown car park he'd taken it to when Lee checked in. The valet said he'd park the car on the Prom (which was only possible on a Sunday) and bring the keys up to

Lee's room. When the keys arrived, Lee had been standing at the window, looking down with amazement at Howard Miller and a girl engaging in a slanging match with some bin men of the town.

Where Howard Miller and the girl had been able to get hold of that cute little MG, he couldn't imagine. Miller was an unexpectedly good driver, and it had been very frustrating not to be able to force him to crash.

He switched off the alarm and sat down on the bed. He had the Cerruti white suit laid out there, ready for occupation. He took off the dressing gown – literally 'disrobed' – and walked over to the long mirror. This being the Negresco Hotel, the mirror was an antique, as beautiful in its way as naked Lee, and it seemed to make his own beauty timeless, almost ghostly.

'You get on very well with that mirror, don't you?'

Abi was in the room.

'Yes, I seem to hit it off with most mirrors.'

'You're being talked about a lot.'

'Yes dear, I know that, and I don't mind what people say as long as it's not accurate.'

'A Mick Jagger line, I believe.'

'Now I don't like to swear, but do fuck off, darling. Is it possible you're becoming jealous because you won't have me to yourself any longer?'

There was no answer from Abi, who had been banished by the ringing of the phone.

'There is a gentleman wishes to see you in reception.'

'Name?'

'Monsieur Charles Underhill.'

'I'll be right down,' said Lee, and he was smiling as he spoke, because this he had not expected.

Charles Underhill had apparently been a very handsome tearaway back in the early Fifties, and Lee could imagine what Price had seen in him. Today, he appeared to be an elegant, cultured older gent of the kind Lee could work on, or even with. He would play the willing pupil, as perhaps Underhill himself had done in his dealings with Price.

'Thanks for coming down,' said Charles as they shook hands.

'Pleasure,' said Lee.

Underhill said, 'I'm the man who wanted to find out about Pat Price. Howard Miller – who I think you know – said you were coming down to Nice. I was in town anyway, and . . . here I am.'

Lee said, 'How did you know I was at the Negresco? Perhaps Howard Miller saw me here?'

'Howard has not seen you in Nice,' said Charles.

Now that, thought Lee, giving Charles one of his really good smiles, *is a lie and he doesn't seem to mind if I know it.*

'I assumed you'd be in one of the better hotels,' Charles was saying, 'and there are only three with five stars. I came here after trying the Ruhl, just along the road.'

They were both taking in the hotel lobby, which reminded Lee of a white ballroom. It was . . . colonnaded, Lee believed was the word: white and gold columns in a circle, giving way at one point to the reception desk. Above them was a glass dome, displaying the pure blue Mediterranean sky. At intervals stood clusters of white velvet antique chairs, on which antique people tended to sit. Lee's white suit and shirt co-ordinated nicely, he thought. Charles said something to that effect, and Lee said, 'I feel a bit like the Snow Queen,' which very nearly made Charles blush.

'I like your shirt,' said Lee, and that did bring the blush. The shirt was blue linen, expensive but somewhat crumpled because Charles was confident enough to dress down. He wore a bit of red silk on his thin wrist, a hippy-ish touch to offset a manner that was otherwise . . . Foreign Office.

'May I buy you dinner?' said Charles.

'That would be very nice, but do you mind if I change?'

Lee returned to his room, where he took off the white suit in favour of his own dressed-down look: the Levis and a pink collarless shirt in Nepalese style, and then his own linen jacket. He didn't want to look too conspicuous this evening, because it might end in a variety of ways. Lee vaguely thought he might be needing his car keys, so he put them in the left-hand jacket pocket. Then he lowered the folder into the right-hand pocket and slid the Vuarnets into the top pocket. That all took a minute. He spent two minutes in front of the mirror confirming the rightness of his decisions before returning to the lobby.

As he and Charles were saluted out of the Negresco by a concierge, Lee said, 'I fear you may not get your money's worth if you intend asking about Pat. I told the boy everything I know, more or less.'

'I hope he didn't give you the third degree.'

They were walking through the heavy, perfumed air of the town.

'I'm afraid the boy had a rather poor opinion of me,' said Lee. 'I think he regarded me with the utmost suspicion, if I'm perfectly honest.'

'He has a vivid imagination, I believe. He's the author of a novel.'

Charles had not denied the boy's suspicions. But there were promising signs that he might not be completely on the boy's side. They found themselves on the Cours Saleya, that agglomeration of restaurant terraces, bounded by pastel-coloured mansions, with the Castle Rock soaring above in green and mauve illumination. The service was amusingly fast. Charles hardly had time to finish his cigarette before the food arrived. And the portions (Charles had fish, Lee a pizza) were amusingly big; the olive oil came in a kind of petrol can, the wine in a rustic jug, and the pepper mill proffered by the waiter was outrageous. Charles was fonder of the wine than Lee, who wondered whether his companion had been drinking beforehand as well. But he was very controlled, setting the tone of a gentlemanly conversation that Lee found himself quite enjoying.

They talked about Pat Price for a while, both lamenting his death. Lee said, 'I think I led him astray somewhat in Sixties Soho.'

'Oh, I'm sure that's exactly what he wanted. I hate to sound egotistical, but did my name ever come up?'

'Not that I remember,' Lee lied. 'His talk, even when he was in his cups, was . . . abstract, you know? He would talk about music, aspects of philosophy. He was very interesting on the subject of some French . . . Well, I can't recall exactly. But if people were puzzled by our friendship, wondering what was in it for me – because he was a good deal older than me, and I certainly wasn't after his money – then that was the answer: his conversation. I'd like to have gone to Oxford myself, if I'd been clever enough. I like the clothes they wear when they do exams!'

Charles now outdid him in modesty: 'I'm sure you could have gone to Oxford if you'd tried. In my day, brains hardly came into it. It was simply a matter of which school you went to.'

Lee began trying to give the impression that Charles might take over from Pat Price as his intellectual mentor. He solicited Charles's opinions about the economic emergency back home, then he began asking about the history of Nice. 'It was a winter resort at first,' Charles explained, 'and the English who came here were known as the *hivernants*. They came here for their health.'

'Whereas today it's the opposite,' Lee chipped in, waving his hand at all the drinking and smoking going on around them.

'In practice,' said Charles, 'the *hivernants* came here to die. Do you know the hymn "Abide With Me"?'

'Yes. They sing it at football games.'

'It was written in about 1850 by an Anglican clergyman called Henry Francis Lyte. It contains the line *Change and decay in all around I see*. He wrote that here in Nice.'

'Did he really? I know those lines. I always assumed they'd been written by some dour northerner in some dour northern town. All dark satanic mills, you know – whereas before there'd been green fields.'

Lee began asking Charles about his mother, which tended to be a safe bet in these circumstances. Charles told how she paraded her little snobberies on the Riviera. It seemed that to her many things were '*mal vu*', meaning off colour. For example, it was all right to play chemin de fer in the Monaco casino but not roulette.

After a while, Lee reached out and touched Charles's hand, saying: 'But hold on a moment. This is all very past tense. The lady is still with us, I hope?'

'Oh, she is very much with us. With *me*, especially.'

And when they'd finished laughing at that, Lee said, 'I'd very much like to meet her.'

This remark didn't have quite the effect Lee had been aiming for. Charles said, 'I think she'd enjoy that,' but not very convincingly, and he added, 'She can be very judgemental. She might be sitting in a restaurant, and she'll suddenly point at some complete stranger saying, "*Une crapule!*"'

'I'm sorry,' said Lee, 'I'm afraid I don't . . .'

240

'A criminal.'

Lee sat back, smiling. This meant that Charles knew something he wasn't saying. The remark had definitely been loaded. At last they were getting down to it! He would now attempt to verify whether Charles knew he was the sender of the cards. 'Tell me,' he said, 'do you keep in touch with the people from Oxford?' But Charles just shook his head whilst lighting a cigarette, so Lee was forced to say, 'You don't . . . get letters from them?'

'The occasional card,' said Charles. 'Do you want a pudding?'

The darkness had deepened. An open-air string quartet began playing somewhere out of sight, as if a charming but slightly rusty music box had been opened. They ordered ice creams for dessert and another jug of wine – which Charles set about smartly. He began asking about Lee's music, and Lee said, 'Oh you know. A fusion of folk rock, psychedelic rock and baroque pop. Ever heard of a group called Love?'

'I'm afraid not.'

'We were a bit like them. I'm currently on the comeback trail. Well, I hope so. About to sign a new deal.'

'Congratulations.'

But Lee could not progress to that future – not with Charles and Howard Miller and the girl (whoever she was) in the way. He had enjoyed the fencing over dinner, but he was becoming impatient. It was time to open negotiations.

'You've seen my hotel,' he said, when the bill came. 'May I see yours?'

Ten minutes later.

Nice

Howard was in – or at least *on* – the bed when the phone rang, and possibly asleep. He was tired, and probably very red. (He hadn't dared consult the mirror.) He'd spent most of the day walking up and down the Prom, trying – and failing – to be recognised, like that character who worked for a newspaper in the beginning of *Brighton Rock*. He'd been too tired even to light a cigarette. The clock had been nowhere near eleven when he'd last looked; now it said quarter to, and he believed he had been dreaming about Emma. He had been driving towards her through the crowded streets of Nice. She had not been in the dream, but she was always about to be in it.

He picked up the phone.

'Howard?' said a quiet voice. 'It's Emma.'

So it was as if he really had been approaching her.

That she had called him, Howard considered a personal triumph. It didn't matter why she had called him. But then it very quickly did matter, because she hadn't called him Man With Car, and she sounded worried.

She said, 'It *was* Lee Jones yesterday, wasn't it? On the Corniche?'

'Yes.' She had changed her mind – something he'd thought her incapable of.

'Have you been to the police?'

'Not yet, because I think you were right: there's nothing we can actually tell them. I want to see if Charles – the man who sent me to Oxford – has made contact with him. I don't think I've told you but he's here in Nice as well. I spoke to him in Paris, and he sort of followed me. I'm sure he knows something about Lee Jones – and I'm sure it's the important thing.'

She said, 'Can I come round to see you?'

'Yes,' he said, a bit too keenly. 'When?'

'Now.'

*

They did the double kiss at twenty past eleven. It went well, and Howard thought he must be in line to gravitate the inch or so towards her mouth. She wore her usual gypsyish ensemble, but with a thin cardigan on top that was improved, if anything, by a hole in the sleeve. She carried her skimpy bag.

'It's a nice place,' she said, stepping into the flat. 'And much bigger than mine.'

Surely she meant 'ours', the place she shared with her boyfriend. Howard was unable to resist asking, 'Where's Fabien?' (The question was excusable, he thought: Fabien might be expected to accompany her with such an important discussion in the offing.) She shrugged — so they'd obviously had a row, and Howard wondered if this was the real reason she was here. From his limited experience with women, he'd learnt that things could suddenly accelerate. It was all a matter of what the woman had decided to do, and they always decided things privately beforehand.

They sat down at the kitchen table. He offered her a drink, and she said, 'Do you have tea?' which seemed an assertion of their shared nationality; another snub to the thought — or memory — of Fabien. Tea was about the one thing he did have — and some Black Cats, which they smoked as he reviewed for her the situation with Charles. It was possible, said Howard, that Charles had suspected the trail of Price would lead to Jones, and that maybe Jones had something 'on' Charles.

Emma said, 'Do you know where Charles is staying?'

'Yes.'

'So we go to see him.'

There was no need to ask when.

About the same time.

Nice

Charles bought more Gauloises on the way back to the hotel. He lit one in the street as they were approaching the railway station. As they walked, Lee kept noticing something wrong with the hang of Charles's linen jacket. It was lopsided.

'You smoke too much,' said Lee.

'Oh, I don't smoke half as much when Syl's around,' said Charles. 'Sorry, Syl's my mother.'

'And you probably don't stay in this part of town when she's around either.'

In these streets, night held sway. Most of the buildings were shuttered and dark. Cats kept flitting away from them.

'When it's the two of us we do a little better than this,' said Charles, as they entered the garden of a dilapidated hotel. 'But we like to be off the beaten track. We try to avoid a certain kind of English person.'

The lobby was shadowy and deserted. Lee thought Charles would be sufficiently confident to reach over the reception desk and take his own key from the dark wooden board on which it dangled ... Which was just what he did, while calling out in

French. There was an answering shout from behind a door that stood ajar opposite the reception desk. The milky blue light of a TV seeped from this room. Nobody had seen Lee come in.

They creaked upwards in the lift, which couldn't possibly keep defying gravity for many more years. 'It's a family business,' said Charles. 'They're very friendly.'

Lee had adopted a louche stance, hands in pockets, in the corner of the lift. He had one hand on the folder, but its days were about done. Charles looked at him, and Lee smiled back. A lascivious one this time. They stepped out on the third floor, and Lee was walking a little way behind Charles, in a corridor barely illuminated by a couple of dangling bulbs in orange shades. The electricity flickered, so this might just as well have been have been candlelight. 'I think I have the whole floor to myself,' said Charles.

Lee put his hand on Charles's right shoulder and swivelled him around. They kissed, and Lee put his hand into Charles's jacket pocket, removing the gun. Charles broke off from the kiss at that point, but not with any great speed. 'I don't want to use this,' said Lee. 'But I don't want you to use it either.' He dropped the gun into his own pocket, where it lay with the folder.

The room was not surprising in light of the hotel – and it was stifling. Charles walked over to the window and lifted it, admitting no cool air but some monstrous industrial noises from the railway sidings. He seemed to have taken the loss of the gun in his stride. He was now peeing loudly with the bathroom door open. Nothing wrong with his prostate! Again, it was the upper-class confidence; or perhaps a flirtatious gambit. They kissed again when he came out of the bathroom, and this time it was hard to say who had taken the lead. The question in Lee's mind was whether they would now be going to the bed or sitting down on the greasy-looking easy chairs on opposite sides of the coffee table.

It seemed to be the latter, since Charles was bringing red wine and glasses to the table.

'Sorry again about this place,' said Charles.

Lee said, 'It's very atmospheric.'

They sat down. Charles lit a cigarette as Lee said, 'Something bad happened. In Oxford.' He'd made it a statement not a question.

'It did.'

'And we have a problem here as well.'

'Oh yes?'

'The boy.'

'I think he's rather more your problem than mine,' said Charles, blowing smoke.

Lee took a sip of wine. It was good – but then it would be. 'Well now,' he said. 'I thought we were friends – and that's not a very friendly remark.'

'He thinks you're the Winker. *Are* you?'

They exchanged smiles – excellent ones, Lee thought. 'If I'm the Winker,' he said, 'who was my inspiration?'

'Is that really the right word?'

'Inspiration,' said Lee with a shrug. 'Or realisation.'

'I'm not really following you,' said Charles, sitting back, apparently relaxed. He did seem to be equal to the situation, and Lee admired him for it.

'Are you familiar with the works of Guy Debord? Do you know how to disrupt the Spectacle? Do you know what a Situation is? A Situation with a capital "S", I mean?'

'Well,' said Charles. 'I would say we were in one.'

'I'm trying to find the address of the boy. I have his phone number, but I can't really ring him up and say, "What's your address?"'

'I don't know it.'

246

'Are you sure about that? You must have his phone number at least. You could lead me to him.'

'But why should I?'

'We go back to the events in Oxford. A document has come into my possession. It begins, "My actions this night . . ."'

'You have it here in Nice?'

'Let's just say that I have it, and you could have it back. I'd very much *like* you to have it back.'

'You might have photostatted it.'

'That is an unworthy remark, Charles. I don't want to harm you.'

'Then why send the cards?'

A long pause. Then Lee said, 'What's that word, bragga . . . something.'

'Braggadocio?'

'Yes. A power trip, I admit. I wanted to affect you, reach out to you. And I'm so glad I did because now we're both here together. You know . . . I want to go back to music now. You wouldn't understand the music, but you'd like me if I was doing it. I'd be a different person.'

'Nothing can be proved after all this time.'

'Well, I don't know about that. What about the brick in the tree, and the blood-stained handkerchief? There's every chance they're still there. I think I located the tree; I'm sure it still holds its secrets. A good lawyer might get you off – a *very* good one. Or we could resolve things much more agreeably, and to our mutual benefit. Incidentally,' Lee added, 'I do hope you're not going to wink at me.'

'I might say the very same thing to you.'

'I'm going to try very hard not to,' said Lee, and he took his best sunglasses from his top pocket and put them on.

'Because one can't un-wink,' said Charles.

'Absolutely not,' said Lee.

A few minutes later.

Nice

Howard and Emma had entered the territory of the railway station. Its clock said twenty to twelve. In the sky above it, stars were rapidly accumulating. After veering left, they were at the gate of the hotel. The garden was seething with broken pots and unseen life.

'What are we going to say to him?' said Howard.

'We say we're going to the police, and we ask him to tell us everything he knows, because we are going to tell *them* everything *we* know. So he can be on our side in going to the police, or he can be against us.'

'Sounds a good plan,' said Howard. 'Well, it sounds a *simple* plan at any rate.'

She stopped him on the garden path as though she were arresting him. She kissed him quickly on the lips and said, 'You're very amusing, Man With Car.'

It seemed to Howard that it was just his luck that he was making erotic progress at the same time as heading into serious bother. They stepped into the lobby. There was no one about.

'Do you know his room?' said Emma.

'Yes.'

'Then let's go there.'

About the same time.

Nice

There was silence between Charles and Lee Jones, punctuated by occasional sardonic smiles on both sides. From time to time, Charles would take a sip of wine or light another cigarette. He was enjoying himself, even though – or perhaps because – he didn't know what he was going to do. But he was going to do something, because everything was in the balance, and the release when he did decide would be tremendous.

Lee Jones must have stolen the confession off Pat Price. Price would not have given it to him. The boy Howard knew this, having been told by the plummy caller from Oxford. Charles had no idea whether the plummy caller or Howard knew the contents of the document. In conjunction with the evidence in the tree, it would probably do for Charles, but he wasn't going to end up in prison.

It occurred to Charles that, if it were necessary to kill the boy, he would rather do it himself. Because the beauty of this phase in which he found himself – for the second time in his life – was the possibility it held of the most dynamic action.

With every minute that passed, Lee Jones seemed to become more familiar to Charles, and it was as if they'd known each other for years. Jones, like Charles, was a psychopath. What else had Charles concluded? Lee was small, good at kissing (and probably very good at fucking), frustrated about his artistic failure, socially insecure, uneducated but intelligent. He had certainly outfoxed Charles in the matter of the Model C, although Charles was wondering whether he'd subconsciously let him get hold of the gun, so as to complicate matters in an interesting way. And Charles was no shootist. The simple and strange fact was that firing a gun was an insufficiently violent act.

Lee was leaning forward. He lowered his sunglasses and smiled. He did have the most amazing eyes. He said, 'Shall we go to bed?'

There came a knock on the door.

'Who's that?' said Jones, who had put his sunglasses back in place.

'It could be the boy,' said Charles. 'He's about the only person who knows I'm here.'

Jones moved rapidly to the door. He had not opened the door, but his hand was on the handle when Charles – from behind – drove the ashtray into the side of his head with a great ecstatic discus sweep of the arm. Lee Jones went down, and Charles pounded the small head until it was a mush with the broken sunglasses mixed in. He took from Lee's pockets keys, a knife, a wallet and the Model C.

Silence from beyond the door. Then the knocking came again. 'Go away, for God's sake,' said Charles, and even he was slightly surprised at the note of laughter in his voice. There was now some muttering from beyond the door, so there were two of them: the boy and the girl. Apparently the girl, the braver of the two, wanted to open the door. She did so.

Thirty seconds later.

Nice

Lee, not quite dead on the floor, felt that the night had been inserted into his head; or at any rate a great dark rectangle had been wedged in there, with small flickering lights in the blackness.

Like the way a large bonfire dies down . . . and there seemed something of the same smell; but it was only the boy, Howard, lighting a cigarette high above him. No, not the boy, he was elsewhere in the room: it was Charles, his killer. It was said you could easily be killed by smoking, but Lee had been killed – or nearly – by an ashtray. It was already back on the table, although with part of his brain now on it.

His memory had to go somewhere in its last moments, and it went to the French House pub in Soho. It was shortly after he'd first met Price. Nineteen sixty-six or so, because *Revolver* by the Beatles – an unbeatably great record – was in the air, although not in the French pub, in which music was never played. It must have been summer. Lee recalled Price talking too intelligently – attracting hostile looks from the more working-class types in that crowded bar, the smoke haze of which was pierced by three brave shafts of light coming through the windows. Price was drunk, and Lee – a bit disgusted – was eyeing the pretty barman. Price was fighting to keep Lee's attention, and in an uncharacteristic moment of weakness, he said, 'Did I ever tell you what became of the Little Byron?' Lee, hoping it was something very bad, turned back towards Price.

Price said, 'Do you remember I told you there'd been a murder at Oxford?'

Lee did, vaguely. The implication – now made for the first time – was that the Little Byron had done it. But it remained only an implication because Pat Price – perhaps disgusted in his turn by Lee's obvious keenness for grim news – clammed up at that point and went away. To be sick possibly, because Soho life back then was punctuated by vomiting.

Lee's curiosity had been piqued. Some questions asked in the pubs of Oxford had thrown up a likely name for the Little Byron: Charles Underhill. He'd found the confession in one of Price's older music manuscript cases, about a year after that. He'd had more sense than to remove it at that point.

Lee's memory was leaving Soho behind, and Lee was seeing those streets as if from the rear window of a speeding car. A pity. He'd liked the place in those days, before all the plastic sex. Another thought was rammed rather violently into his broken mind: it was a shame he would never hear what Ormond thought of his music. But he would no doubt have been let down gently over the lunch. Ormond bought lunches for a lot more people than he signed up as artists. Lee tried to get a tune going in his head, but the music box was broken.

Some new message came lopsidedly into his head: the boy was as far away as possible from dying Lee. He looked incredibly white. The girl, on the other hand, was much closer, looking down at Lee's smashed head. She was not seeing him at his best, to say the least. For instance, one ought not to wear one's sunglasses inside one's head.

'No, we can help you,' she said; but she did not mean Lee, who was beyond help. She meant Charles. 'We can get rid of the body,' she was saying. Well, of all the cheek! But none of this really mattered. What did matter was that realisation would come to the world, and Lee would get the credit.

'He's only little,' the girl was saying. 'Even I could lift him.'

She deserved a good trademarking, this one, and she was peering into what used to be his eyes. But Lee knew he couldn't do anything about it because both his eyelids (if that was the word for what remained) were now coming down simultaneously.

The next evening.

Nice

In the ticket hall of Nice Côte d'Azur airport, Howard was looking along the line of palm trees planted in white wooden boxes.
The line was about a hundred and fifty yards long (the ticket hall
being a very horizontal building) and he thought he saw Charles
Underhill smoking by the farthermost one. It was certainly a man
who resembled Charles, and this person was now putting out his
cigarette on a free-standing ashtray (there was one by each palm
tree pot). He picked up what was known in airport circles as 'a
small item of hand luggage' and headed for the departure gate. It
was 6.15 p.m. or, as the departure boards had it, 1815. At seven,
an Air France flight would be leaving for Heathrow, and Howard
had reason to think Underhill would be on it. Or he might be
on Howard's own British Airways flight to Heathrow, but that
wasn't leaving for three hours, and it wasn't like Charles – Howard
thought – to be early for anything.

It was very like Howard though, particularly in the present
circumstances. He had a very powerful force impelling him out
of Nice. He had realised the morning after the killing of Lee
Jones that he couldn't keep the window of the flat open, because
he kept hearing police cars, and the flat was far too hot with the
window closed. He had decided then to leave, and he had taken
all the bedclothes – which were his editor's bedclothes – to a
launderette near the *tabac* where he bought his Black Cats. As
they churned in the machine, he had walked to a travel agency
off the Prom and booked his flight. Back in the launderette – the
bedclothes were now drying – he'd written a letter to his editor
thanking him for use of the flat, and apologising for leaving early,

but saying the novel was going well, and he needed to do some research in London. In fact, the novel was not going at all, and Howard hadn't thought twice about checking in his typewriter just then. He didn't care if it ended up in Kuala Lumpur or somewhere. He didn't think he'd ever write another crime story. He'd just spend the rest of his life replaying in his mind the one he'd lived through.

The flight was three times the cost of the night train, but he wanted to leave Nice at speed. And he sought distraction – any experience that would jolt his thoughts away from the events of last night. Howard had never flown before, but his nerves about the flight were nothing to his nervousness about being arrested and charged with murder. The departure lounge, for example, was full of armed police. He tried to tell himself – for the hundredth time – that the offence would be the lesser one of disposing of a body. And might it be a mitigating factor that the body had been that of a murderer?

He was looking at a poster advising him to take out flight insurance. It showed a doomed-looking plane flying through a dark night. The memory was inflicting itself on him again like a wave of nausea. He sat down on a baggage trolley and lit a Black Cat.

He pictured Charles smiling in the gloomy, hot, brown room with the body on the floor. Apparently, Charles was admiring the energy of Emma, who was saying, 'We can help you. We have an Englishman with a car.' Then she'd thrown the keys – they had sailed over the body – to Howard, saying: 'You know where it is.'

'For Christ's sake,' Howard had said. It was all he was able to say. Charles was going through the dead man's pockets. Emma was at the other end wrapping the head in a towel. They made a good team, like a posh father and daughter. 'You know where it is,' Emma said again to Howard. Obviously, she was becoming cross at his immobility. 'You can be back outside the front of the hotel in half an hour's time. Park, then come up. There's no night porter.'

'You'll need this as well,' said Charles, and he gave Howard the key to the front door of the hotel. He had some other keys in his hand as well. Howard walked and ran to the subterranean car park. His mind was filled with images of French prisons drawn from paperback thrillers – Maigrets mainly.

He saw few people as he approached the middle of town but in the street of the car park itself stood a police car. The two policemen inside – both sallow – represented to Howard hard-core Frenchness. They ignored him as he passed.

His footsteps echoed in the grey silence of the car park. But when he arrived at the MG, other footsteps continued. A man was walking down the ramp. All Frenchmen were types, and this one was a *bon viveur*, horribly cheerful in sports coat and cravat. Howard, sitting in the MG with the hood down, was exposed to the *bon viveur*, who said something in French. Howard nodded and pulled away fast, trying to whisk the MG's registration plate out of the Frenchman's eyeline.

He parked the car outside the hotel gate, walked into the hotel and up the stairs to the room. He was more or less immediately invited by Emma to pick up the body. He knew he must comply otherwise she would do it herself, which he couldn't allow. With the assistance of Charles, Howard got Lee Jones over his shoulder in a fireman's lift. He was soaked in sweat even before he began descending the stairs. Emma was going on ahead, making sure the coast was clear, like a female Native American scout, which she did somewhat resemble. Howard had not realised until now that the stairs were lit by a timer switch. The fucking thing would keep going off. Every time it came back on, Emma would be revealed, always beautiful and always mad.

When they reached the car, Howard didn't know where they were going to put the body. The other two did – in the boot.

'Now we go down to the Prom,' Emma said.

'Why, for Christ's sake?' said Howard.

'Collect stones!' Charles said cheerfully, because he was in on the plan.

Howard had parked opposite the crumbling Palais. The pink neon sign reading NEGRESCO projected beyond the dome of the hotel, so that SCO seemed suspended in mid-air. There was nobody about; a good deal of rubbish lay under the benches along the Prom. Emma was running back from the beach, now looking peasant-like, with rocks held in a gathered-up blanket.

Then they were heading for the Corniche. Charles was like a man who'd done a good night's work, and he kept saying things like, 'On the whole we've been remarkably lucky,' whereas Emma would say more urgent things like, 'Hurry up, Man With Car. We want to be finished before dawn.'

The sky was a very dark, velvety green. There were many stars but absolutely no moon.

Howard parked in exactly the same place he had done for the film, and he was sure they must be being filmed again – this time by some special hidden unit of the police.

Howard had carried Lee over the sand. Emma already had the dinghy on the water. Howard went in up to his knees and lowered the body onto the boat. The sea was not cold. Emma pulled the choke cord, and the sound was appallingly loud, but it seemed to lessen as they began bombing over the small waves. Howard looked at Emma; she winked at him and he was glad that he had it in him to laugh. He still loved her, even though she was mad.

Charles was at the front of the boat, smoothing back his slightly receding hair. When the shore became hard to discern, they began wrapping the body in the blanket and a dressing gown that had come from somewhere, and putting in the stones. The rolling over the side of Lee Jones was a joint effort.

Then Emma turned the boat in an arc whose gracefulness matched her own.

*

Howard put out his cigarette as a crowd of holidaymakers walked past – *package* holidaymakers, all with Laker Airways labels on their luggage, and here was another thing they had in common: they were all non-murderers. Some glass doors gave on to an outdoor balcony, a viewing platform. Howard walked through the doors, joining half a dozen plane spotters in the hot, fuzzy night air. Down below to one side were the runways and a few planes, all lit up like a fairground. There was a central tower, also illuminated, and Howard felt that this was about to perform some trick, such as revolving. The planes were moving around in a thoughtful sort of way, and some were being meekly towed by incredibly small vehicles. Only one, the show-off of the group, was taking off in the distance, a task it accomplished successfully. Howard read the name on the side: Dan Air, which had a science fiction sound, like Dan Dare.

If you turned the other way, you could see the bay of Nice stretching away and glittering in the dark – a Christmassy array. Howard could hardly bear to look.

But he was back in Nice anyway, in his mind. On the outskirts of the town anyway, in a petrol station at dawn.

They had pulled up to it on their way back from dumping Lee Jones, because the needle on the MG had been showing empty for a while. The petrol station had actually been more than just a petrol station. It had been like a sort of conspiracy to get the day started.

There was a café, and as Emma paid a man for the petrol, a woman brought in a tray of hot croissants and fresh coffee. So they had breakfast. A radio was playing French pop music; a lorry driver was making a phone call, using a wall-mounted phone that was inside a glass cabinet. The door did not close properly, and they could hear him. When he came out, Emma went into the cabinet. Howard stopped eating his croissant, and he wished he could turn off the radio because he wanted to hear what she was saying. There wasn't much doubt about who she was calling, and a lot of emotion appeared to be involved.

'Is she talking about what we've been doing?' Howard had asked Charles, who shook his head. After a couple more minutes, Howard was unable to stop himself from asking, 'What is she saying?'

'You don't want to know,' said Charles.

'But I *do*.'

'She's making up with her boyfriend. She said she's been worrying about him all night.'

'Worrying about *him*?'

'I'm afraid so, Howard.'

Emma had finished the call on what was obviously a happy note. Then she came over for a slurp of coffee. 'Everybody OK?' she'd said, before heading – positively bounding – towards the ladies'.

Howard had asked Charles, 'What happened in Oxford in the Fifties?'

'I killed a man, or a boy.'

('Really?' Howard had said, absurdly.)

'Have you ever heard of a party game called Wink Murder? You wink at someone and they pretend to die. I'd been playing that game immediately beforehand. I mean, I ended up killing a person I'd winked at in the game. Lee Jones found out about all this through Pat Price, and he began sending me anonymous postcards, letting me know that he knew.'

'Why would he do that?'

'To torment me; make himself feel important.'

'So that's where the whole winking thing came from?'

'Quite possibly. But Jones seemed to have a predilection for winking anyway.'

'Why did you kill the person in Oxford?'

'Because I wanted to.'

'There must have been provocation.'

'Some objectionable remarks. But the main reason was that I knew I'd enjoy doing it; and I *did* enjoy doing it.'

'But there was provocation with Lee Jones.'

'Well, yes. Let's face it, the man was an absolute little shit, wasn't he? He wanted you dead because he thought you knew he was the Winker. And he said it would be in my interests too, since you were on to me as well. So he wanted me to help in getting rid of you, starting with telling him where you lived. But, you see, that was all a sort of . . . what do the crime writers say? A red herring. As with the previous time, I killed him because I knew I would enjoy it. It seems that when a certain context is created around me, Howard – a context of excitement – it's only going to have one outcome. Someone's going to die. It doesn't really matter who.'

'But you wouldn't have killed me? Or Emma?'

'Don't flatter yourself. If you'd blundered straight in, instead of knocking, there *would* have been a certain logic in getting rid of you.'

'There might still be, in view of what I know.'

Charles had smiled at that – and Howard saw that it was a murderer's smile.

'So you're going back to Paris?' Howard had said.

'I'm going to London actually, for a couple of days. Then I must get back to my mother.'

'What are you going to do in London?'

'I'm not going to tell you, Howard.'

*

Howard was down to his last Black Cat. He would need some more for the plane. He realised he had no idea how long the flight would take. Should he go through to Departures and try to find the man who might have been Charles? He was thinking about what Charles might do to him in London. On the other hand, he didn't much give a fuck. You could only be so worried about everything.

Two days later.

Paris

Syl had the jug of wine and the plate of nuts laid out on the balcony table when Charles walked in. He carried his suitcase, because he was just back from the airport, and since his taxi had passed Bertrand's newspaper kiosk at about the right time (7 p.m.)

he'd got out there and picked up his two copies of *The Times*; then he'd dropped in at the Tabac au Bon Vin for the four Gauloises and a quick read of his paper as he drank the one small glass of wine. There'd been nothing much to interest him. On the front page was a map of Britain with annotated arrows coming in from the west and the south, as though the paper were trying hard to puzzle out the strangeness of the weather – and indeed the terrible heat had been briefly interrupted by a couple of thunderstorms when he was there. But the British weather was not his problem; nothing to do with Britain was any longer his problem.

After their kiss hello, they went on to the balcony. Syl had made a real effort: a pretty new bowl for the nuts, and the wine was better than usual.

'White burgundy,' she said.

Normally it was Muscadet. Unfortunately, the weather wasn't playing along here in Paris either, and an insolent, greyish wind was disturbing the trees in the park (and the doily under the nuts).

'So it was mission accomplished?' she said.

She wasn't referring to his actions in Nice, which she already knew all about. She was referring to his actions in London: the latest instalment of her very own private thriller, with her dashing – if psychopathic – son in the lead role.

'I think so,' he said.

'How did you get in?'

His mother had an unlit cigarette in her mouth, which made her look like an elderly prostitute. Charles lit it for her, and lit one of his own.

'The building has no concierge,' he said, blowing smoke. 'I waited until someone came out, and they held the door for me, and said "Good afternoon" as I went in.'

'People are so innocent, aren't they? Compared to you. But you're talking about the front door of the block. I meant how did you get into the actual room?'

'Well, I had his keys. I told you that on the phone. I took them from him in Nice.'

'When he was dead?'

'Yes. Or dying. I took some ID from him as well: his Musician's Union card, which is how I got the address.'

Syl sipped wine. 'I wonder if you can steal from the dead? Legally speaking, I mean.'

'You can steal whatever isn't yours,' he said, 'which reminds me.'

He went back into the living room and took a Bush cassette player and a couple of cassettes out of his suitcase. He put them on the balcony table.

'These were Jones's as well?' she said.

'They were.'

'Well, why on earth have you brought them here?' She leant across the table and touched his shoulder. 'Cal,' she said, 'did you get the document?'

He took it from his inside jacket pocket and handed it over. She read, *My actions this night . . .* in the unmistakable, if faded, handwriting of her son. She put it on the table, with the wine jug as paperweight.

'Where was it?' she asked.

'Just in a drawer with a pile of bills and bank statements.'

Charles had been rather disappointed about that. He would have thought the document deserved a bit more reverence.

'Did he leave a will?'

'Not that I saw, and I went through the whole place. I'm not sure he really had anyone to leave anything *to*.'

'It's sad, in a way.'

'No it isn't.'

'If you had found a will,' his mother said, beginning to laugh, 'you could have altered it in your favour! By the way, I do hope you dusted the place for fingerprints?'

'I'm sorry?'

'You know very well what I mean. Did you clean off your own prints?'

'I didn't leave any. I bought a nice pair of silk gloves beforehand.'

'Where from?'

'Harrod's – burglary department.'

She poured out the second glasses of wine. He knew he wouldn't be needing another one: he had reaffirmed his status in the world, at least for now.

'But why *did* you bring this horrible thing?' Syl said, indicating the recorder again.

Charles stood up, and put a tape in. A guitar was being strummed, then came some talk. Lee, speaking in a voice slightly higher than usual, said, 'How many people have to die before the programme is complete, Lee?' Lee then answered his own question in his normal voice, and while playing in a slightly fancier way on the guitar.

'It's not a question of how many people have to die, Abi my dear. It's not about numbers. That would be like asking how many people have to look at a painting before it can be declared great.' A tune was emerging from what had seemed fairly abstract guitar playing, and Lee Jones began to sing:

If I go drifting, on the seas of fantasy
Will you come along and rescue me?

I think you probably would
I think you probably would now . . .

'It's a rather pretty tune,' said Syl, but she had no more interest in listening to the rest of it than Charles. 'What else was there?' she asked.

'A lot of newspaper reports about the killings, all cut out and laid neatly on the bed.'

'And you took those?'

'Naturally. I also removed a jacket that had stains on the sleeve – might have been blood.'

'So he will never go down in history as the Winker?'

'Not if I can help it.'

'. . . After all the effort he put in,' she said, almost with a sigh. She was now standing up with the document in her hand.

'What are you going to do with that?' he said.

'The fire's all made up. Pass me the matches, will you?'